BAD MEDICINE

A shot pinged into a tree to the right of where Mitch Bushyhead stood.

He ran his tongue over the parched roof of his mouth. "Keep still," Mitch said urgently. He'd left his gun in the trunk of his car. A rank rookie would have known better than that. They were defenseless against an armed man, and if they tried to get away through the woods, they'd never make it to the car. Oh, God almighty...

"Mitch, I think we've stumbled into something here we shouldn't have. Do you know what it is?"

"What?"

"This is where the Nighthawks meet. Has to be. A hidden clearing deep in the woods, a light for night meetings. We better get the hell out of here while we can still navigate."

Mitch hesitated. It would be a waste of effort to go after the sniper. He wouldn't find him. The Nighthawks knew these woods. Mitch didn't.

THE GRANDFATHER MEDICINE
WINNER OF THE 1990 OKLAHOMA TEPEE AWARD
PRESENTED BY THE OKLAHOMA WRITERS FEDERATION

———————— ★ ————————

"An intriguing plot, colorful characters and a likeable lawman." —*Kirkus Reviews*

"An excellent police procedural and a first-rate mystery." —*Library Journal*

A Forthcoming Worldwide Mystery by
JEAN HAGER

NIGHTWALKER

THE GRANDFATHER MEDICINE

JEAN HAGER

WORLDWIDE.

TORONTO · NEW YORK · LONDON · PARIS
AMSTERDAM · STOCKHOLM · HAMBURG
ATHENS · MILAN · TOKYO · SYDNEY

For Al Zuckerman
with appreciation and gratitude

THE GRANDFATHER MEDICINE

A Worldwide Mystery/November 1990

First published by St. Martin's Press Incorporated.

ISBN 0-373-26059-8

Grateful acknowledgment is made for permission to include copyrighted English translations of Cherokee incantations from *Run Toward the Nightland: Magic of the Oklahoma Cherokees,* by Jack Frederick Kilpatrick and Anna Gritts Kilpatrick. Published by Southern Methodist University Press. Copyright © 1967. The author found this book and *Friends of Thunder: Folktales of the Oklahoma Cherokee,* also written by the Kilpatricks, invaluable in the background research for *The Grandfather Medicine*.

Permission to include the above material is granted by Jack Frederick Kilpatrick, Jr., in memory of Jack F. and Anna G. Kilpatrick, who held an uncommon love and concern for the recognition and preservation of the culture of their people. They authored *Friends of Thunder* and *Run Toward the Nightland* as well as other books.

PROLOGUE

CRYING WOLF remade the tobacco at daybreak.

He stood on the creek band, facing east, as first light pearled the sky above the dark trees. Cupping the tobacco in his left palm, he kneaded it with the gnarled fingers of his right hand. He spoke two names and chanted the incantation, blowing his breath on the tobacco at intervals.

> "Now! Someone has just come to frighten
>   and separate their souls.
> Somewhere upon a lonely road in a valley
>   in the wilderness your two lonely souls
>   are to be broken!"

Meticulously he formed each Cherokee word in his mind before he wrapped it in sound. Performing the *idi:gawe:sdi* was a fearful responsibility because the discord thus created could not be rigidly limited. The tobacco could become infected with evil and cause great harm if the incantation was faulty in any detail.

As he performed the ritual, he could feel the spirits pressing closer, just outside the far edges of his perception like wild beasts beyond the light of a campfire. His consciousness of their presence heightened all his senses. The whippoorwill's song shrilled uncomfortably and the sweetly pungent smell of vegetation was intense.

After repeating the ritual four times, he took a cigarette paper from his shirt pocket and shaped the tobacco into a thin cylinder, returning it to his pocket reverently. Then he stood quietly, head bowed, and waited for the feeling of serenity that told him the line between the natural and supernatural worlds had reestablished itself.

Bird songs receded and his heartbeat slowed. His intense concentration on the ceremony had left him feeling drained and a little lightheaded. Dawn filtered through dense leaves in ghostly gray patches. There was no sound except for his own quiet breathing. Slowly the lightheadedness left him, and once more the woods were familiar, normal.

Yet a vague apprehension remained, brushing his skin, making him shiver. He reviewed the ceremony he had performed and found nothing amiss. Then he thought of the mission that had brought him through the dark woods to the creek and felt a second tremor of unease.

A yellow leaf settled on the scuffed toe of his boot. He stared at the ground in front of him. In early September few leaves had fallen, but twigs and stones were strewn over the creek bank. He inhaled the rich earth smell, which was merely pleasant now rather than overpowering. He was a part of these woods, this earth. Each tree and rock was as known to him as his own hand. The familiarity steadied him.

Silent steps carried him away from the creek down a twisting trail, and trees closed around him. He touched his shirt pocket, felt the shape of the cigarette, and was reassured.

Twenty minutes later he came out of the woods on the west edge of Buckskin. He halted to survey the square clapboard house a hundred yards ahead. It squatted, dark and silent, beneath giant oaks. Limp, ragged curtains hung partially outside screenless windows. He crept closer, alert for the sudden appearance of a dog. The family's aged collie had died weeks ago, but it was possible they had a new one. He didn't want to be surprised once he was engaged in the medicine ceremony.

Convinced there was no dog, he walked closer to the house. When he reached the northeast corner, he took out the cigarette and struck a match on the sole of his boot. The flame flickered as he drew smoke into his lungs and then exhaled slowly, blowing it toward the house. He circled the house until he had blown the smoke toward each of its four corners.

The battered Ford pickup truck that usually sat in the drive was gone. He crept closer to the front door, which was sheltered by a small porch. He was startled to see it standing ajar. He glanced over his shoulder, right, then left; no one was there.

Cautiously he climbed the two steps to the porch and peered inside. The interior was blurred in shadow until his eyes adjusted, and it was a moment before he could see anything but varying shades of gray.

He sucked in his breath. Extending from behind a couch in the shadows was a hand. The fingers that some had called magic fingers were long and blunt-nailed. He knew, without seeing any more, that there was no life in them. Atavistic revulsion raised the hairs on the back of his neck and a sour gorge clogged his throat. Swallowing forced a guttural sound from his mouth.

He wanted to bolt to the familiar protection of the woods, but a horrible compulsion to know more held him there. After looking over his shoulder again, he stepped into the house.

The dead man was on his stomach, legs and right arm extended. He wore ankle-high leather boots, jeans, and a plaid shirt.

He was about thirty years old, a Cherokee. His eyes stared unseeing toward his angled left arm. His cheek rested in a congealed pool of blood. The blood had spilled from a punctured wound on the left side of his neck. His left hand—what remained of it—lay in another dark puddle. His ring finger and little finger had been severed from the hand. Joseph Pigeon's fingers would work their magic no more.

Nausea churned in Crying Wolf's stomach; he clamped a hand over his mouth and closed his eyes, fighting sickness. The room was hot and close with the fetid smell of congealed blood. Equally strong was a primitive terror that shrieked at him to flee. Several moments passed before he could order his thoughts.

When he had gained control of himself, he opened his eyes and looked down at Joseph Pigeon, remembering the medicine ceremony he had performed. He had scrupulously observed the exact wording and proper number of repetitions of the *idi:gawe:sdi*, the ritual for sowing discord between individuals. He had not fasted the previous day, but he had not thought it necessary. He had used Cotton Bowl Twist rather than *tso:lagayv:li* because his supply of the Ancient One was too minute and precious to be used in any but the most urgent circumstances. But the situation as explained to him by King-fisher Pigeon had not seemed difficult enough to require the Grandfather Medicine.

After he had taken all of this into account, the presence of death remained incomprehensible. He remembered how King-fisher Pigeon had repeatedly wiped the palms of his big hands down his jeans to dry them. He remembered Kingfisher's nervous pacing, and felt a tingling at the base of his skull.

Minutes earlier on the creek bank, the dead man's name had taken shape in his mind four times. He fought his growing horror with the thought that he had done everything humanly possible to limit the forces he was invoking. Even so, it was not possible to have absolute control over the working of the tobacco after it had been infused with magical power. His skin prickling with alarm, Crying Wolf gazed at the dead man and wondered how his medicine could have gone so terribly awry.

As he pondered the frightening ramifications of the question, he remembered Joseph Pigeon's wife. Perhaps his medicine hadn't done this, after all. Perhaps the white woman had done it, and then had run away in the pickup. If that was the case, it was white man's business. He wanted nothing to do with the white man's law.

All at once the atmosphere in the house felt so thick with violence that his flesh sprang into goose bumps and he couldn't breathe. He left the house and hurried back toward the woods, fleeing the bad medicine that emanated from the corpse.

ONE

CHIEF MITCHELL BUSHYHEAD leaned back in his creaking swivel chair and gazed through the front window of the police station at Buckskin's main street. Sequoyah, it was called, after the man who'd invented the Cherokee syllabary and made the tribe literate almost overnight.

This block was lined with the oldest buildings in town. Most of them were two-storied, made of huge, tan hand-hewn blocks of native stone quarried from the surrounding hills when the town was established in the 1890s. There had been no rain since July and on this sun-blanched September Monday, Buckskin lay in a lethargy of drought and enervating heat. Brown dust puffed from beneath the wheels of passing cars. The strip of grass in front of the corner post office was dead, and the American flag drooped limply against its tall pole.

Since the tire factory west of town had laid off half its eleven hundred workers a year before, a few businesses had gone under. Directly across the street from the police station, there had once been a shoe store. Now the building was vacant, its blank windows gazing back at Mitch. At eight-fifteen in the morning, Buckskin's business district resembled a ghost town. It looked exactly the way Mitch felt—deserted and dead. The street, though, would stir to life at nine A.M. when the stores opened; Mitch, on the other hand, was not finding it so easy to recover from his wife's death six months ago.

"Mitch," Helen Hendricks, the dispatcher, called from the next room. "Your daughter's on the line."

Mitch picked up the phone. In his present mood, any interruption was welcome. "Hi, honey. I thought you had to be at school early today for some meeting."

"Pom-pom practice, Daddy. I just got here," Emily said breathlessly. She had come home Friday afternoon, radiant over being elected to the pom-pom squad. Mitch wasn't sure what that entailed, but if it made Emily happy he was in favor of it. At dinnertime her eyes were still aglow with the thrill of being chosen. She had tossed back her long, straight hair, its layer of sun-bleached gold over the brown already fading, and cocked her head to one side in the way that always reminded him of Ellen. When had his daughter become so grown-up? Emily was a high school sophomore now. This year pimply-faced youths would start hanging around the house. He wasn't sure he was ready for that. "I forgot to tell you," Emily was saying. "You have to come to a meeting today at five-thirty in Mrs. Macpherson's room."

Mitch thought he knew all the teachers at the high school, but this was a new name to him. "Macpherson?"

"She's the new English teacher and she sponsors the pom-pom squad."

"I'll try, Emily, but if I get tied up—"

"You have to, Daddy!" Her alarmed tone made it clear that this was a matter of vital importance. "It's about our uni-forms."

Uniforms? His memory stirred, sending up a picture of young girls in skimpy skirts waving pom-poms, jumping around, showing their butts.

"You have to be there in person or I'll be cut from the squad. Mrs. Macpherson said."

"She sounds pretty intractable." Ellen had always handled these things. She had seemed to be able to put herself in her daughter's place and understand Emily's feelings. Mitch was doing his best to be both mother and father to Emily, but he worried that his daughter was getting short-changed. They hadn't had pom-pom girls when he was in school; he didn't see why they had to have them now. But then what did he know?

"She's not so bad, but she means what she says. Daddy, I'll die if I get kicked off the squad!"

Emily hadn't been this excited about anything since Ellen's death. He was glad that school was again in session. He'd hated leaving the girl alone in the house all summer, even though she'd repeatedly assured him she didn't mind. Seemingly she'd handled it pretty well, although her normal buoyancy and cheerfulness were missing—until this pom-pom thing.

Whatever might come up at the station could probably be put off. "Okay, I'll be there."

"Promise?"

"Promise."

"Thanks, Daddy. I have to go now. The secretary's making motions for me to get off the phone."

The instant he replaced the receiver, the telephone rang again. One ring and then silence. Helen had picked it up. He turned back to the window.

"Mitch!" Helen yelled. "You better take this. It's Callie Roach. She's all shook up about something, but I can't make sense of it."

Mitch swiveled around. He wondered what could have gotten Callie worked up so early on a Monday morning. Callie Roach had been a Bushyhead, a cousin of his on the Cherokee side of the family. She wasn't the hysterical type. He felt a faint ripple in the sluggish depression that had characterized his waking state the past six months. It was an instant before he recognized it as curiosity. He reached across the desk and grabbed the phone.

"Callie, it's Mitch." He kept his tone neutral, telling himself that a speaker for Callie's ladies' club had probably canceled at the last minute, and she wanted him to fill in.

"Mitch? . . . Mitch!"

"That's right, Callie."

"Oh, Mitch . . ."

"Callie, take a deep breath and tell me what's wrong."

"It's—oh, God—at the Pigeon place."

It sounded like police, not ladies' club, business. His curiosity increased. "Which Pigeon?" There were at least five branches of the Pigeon family in and around Buckskin.

"Joe—Joe Pigeon . . . over by Going Snake Mountain. You know where I mean?"

"Yes. What's going on there?"

"Barry says he's dead!" Callie's voice wasn't as shrill now. She seemed to be gaining control of herself.

"Joseph Pigeon?"

"Barry isn't sure. He didn't see his face."

Mitch said quietly, "Now, calm down, Callie, and start at the beginning."

"Well...uh, Barry was delivering the morning paper. And the Pigeons' front door was standing open. Barry wouldn't have looked in if it hadn't been."

"I don't care about that. What happened?"

"When nobody came out, Barry went up on the porch and...Mitch, Barry says a man's laying on the floor and—" She paused to take a shaky breath. "There's blood everywhere."

"All right, Cal. I'll get right out there. You tell Barry to keep his mouth shut about this at school. You, too, hear?"

"Okay, Mitch, okay. Only I want to know what you find. If you don't call me pretty soon, I'll go crazy wondering."

He swallowed his irritation. Lately he irritated easily; even the simplest things seemed to require too much effort. She was only asking for a phone call, for God's sake.

"I'll take care of it. Remember, tell nobody. Make Barry swear to keep quiet about it." All he needed was half the town over at the Pigeon place before he had a chance to find out what had happened.

"I will."

Mitch hung up and headed for the door. "Helen, send an ambulance to Joseph Pigeon's house on Caddo Street. Then see if you can raise Roo and Duck on the radio and tell them to meet me there." He would have preferred his most experienced officer, Virgil Rabbit, but Virgil worked the four to midnight shift and was probably still asleep. Virgil and Trudy Rabbit had been his and Ellen's closest friends. Mitch wasn't sure how he would have gotten through Ellen's illness and the months following her death without them.

He felt a rush of adrenaline as he ran to his squad car, parked behind the station. Deciding against using the siren, he peeled out of the lot, turned north on Sequoyah and west on Caddo.

The asphalt, residential streets through which he passed were shaded by big elm and cottonwood trees and suspended in the early morning stillness. Two-story frame and newer, ranch-style brick houses were set back from the street behind deep front lawns.

To his relief, Mitch saw no one about as he approached the Pigeon place. It was the last house on the west end of Caddo Street, separated from its nearest neighbor by a half-block. It was a plain, square five-room box with weathered wood siding and a sagging front porch. Neglected and sullen, as though it dared you to pity it.

Rising immediately northwest of the Pigeon house was a rocky, jagged hill, known in this rural area of eastern Oklahoma as Going Snake Mountain. Beyond it rippled more hills, their surfaces so thick with trees and underbrush that they were virtually impenetrable in places.

As Mitch pulled up, a second squad car wheeled in and Harold Duckworth got out and lumbered toward him. Duck's excess weight made his head look too small. His crew-cut hair and close-set eyes, one brown, the other hazel, added to the impression that somebody had assembled him hastily from parts of several bodies. Sweat stains from his armpits made dark circles on his khaki shirt. For at least the hundredth time, Mitch thought about instituting weight and fitness requirements for the members of the force.

"What's up?" Duckworth panted.

"Callie Roach's boy, Barry, came out here to deliver the paper. Says he saw a dead man inside." Mitch looked around but saw no newspaper. Barry must have panicked and forgotten to leave it. The Pigeons' Ford pickup wasn't around, either. The front door was standing half-open, and the two men stepped onto the porch. The silence was oppressive. Then, suddenly, it was shattered by the wail of an approaching siren.

Duckworth jumped. "What the hell . . ?"

"Gotta scatter all that traffic," Mitch grumbled.

Duckworth snorted. "Yeah, get all the dogs howling and the babies crying. Make sure everybody in town knows where they're going so the good citizens can hightail it over here."

"Any spectators show up, keep them off the Pigeon property." Mitch pushed the door back and entered the house. Duckworth reached for his gun, then followed Mitch inside.

"You won't need that, Duck." Mitch looked down at the dead man and thought how close death was to everybody. At least, Pigeon had not known he was going to die for months before it happened; he had probably known it only seconds. That didn't make him any less dead, though, and a sharp pang of pity made Mitch's chest feel tight. What had Pigeon done to deserve this? The numbness with which Mitch had protected himself for six months was cracking. He had a murder case to investigate; it would keep him occupied until he tracked down the killer.

Joseph Pigeon had been a bronze, ruggedly handsome man. Mitch had seen him often around town, spoken to him on the street; but he hadn't known him well. He had always thought of him as a lazy full-blood who lived off welfare, as did many of the full-bloods whose shacks were scattered over the surrounding, wooded hills.

Joe had painted pictures of Indians. Mitch, like everybody else, hadn't taken that seriously until the Gilcrease Museum in Tulsa had exhibited Joe's work. Recently Joe's paintings had been selling for respectable prices and Joe had strutted around town, bragging about the money and the recognition. His moment in the sun had finally come. But Joe wouldn't be strutting now, or bragging, or painting any more pictures. An image of the Buckskin cemetery flashed up in Mitch's mind. It was a sunless place where Joe was going.

"Gawd Almighty," Duckworth said, "why'd they cut his fingers off?"

Mitch shook his head, scanning the room. He stepped around the corpse and bent over for a closer look at the neck wound. "Must have taken the fingers with 'em."

Duckworth looked pale. "Sicko."

"You gonna faint?"

"No." Duckworth concentrated on holstering his gun. The ambulance arrived. Duckworth waddled to the front door and yelled, "Shut off that damned si-reen!" He came back into the room, grumbling, "It's enough to deefen the whole town." He dropped his head and swiped a hand across his mouth. "Jeez, ole Joe Pigeon never hurt nobody. Once in a while when he was drunk and rowdy, he'd get into a fistfight, but he wasn't a mean sort. Who'd want to kill him?" The wail of the siren stopped abruptly, and the silence screamed. Then a dog howled down the block, and another took it up.

Mitch shrugged. "A thief, maybe." He jerked his head toward the open wallet on the couch. Duckworth reached for it and Mitch stopped him. "Don't touch anything. Go and get the camera and my notepad out of the car."

Duckworth left, and Mitch heard him importantly telling the ambulance attendants to wait on the porch until he finished taking pictures of the murder victim and the scene of the crime.

After noting down physical details of the living room, Mitch went outside.

A few minutes later, they carried the Cherokee artist out on a stretcher, under a green plastic sheet. As the ambulance attendants crossed the threshold, Joseph Pigeon's left arm slipped from beneath the sheet and his mutilated hand dangled over the side. The dogs had stopped howling and slunk back into the shade. Now the only sound was the humming of the locusts. He took a cursory look around, then returned to the house.

Back in the living room, Mitch examined the wallet, touching it only at one corner in case the killer had left his prints on it. Pigeon's social security card and driver's license were still in it, but there was no money. In one of the bedrooms, all the dresser drawers were pulled out, their contents strewn about the room. It looked at first glance like a robbery. The severed fingers—the little finger and ring finger—weren't in the house. Mitch made a mental note to ask Joe's wife, Mary, if Joe had worn a wedding ring. There was still no sign of Mary or the pickup. The big question: Had she left before Joe was killed, or after?

Mitch was alone in the house now. Since the Pigeons had no telephone, Duckworth was calling Helen on the police radio, telling her to find Dr. Sullivan and tell him the chief would be by the hospital, where the ambulance was taking the body, to see him later. Buckskin had no morgue; the medical examiner would come over from Tahlequah, the county seat, to examine the body.

Sitting on the threadbare couch, Mitch looked around the room. Poverty was everywhere. The few pieces of furniture were cheap and shabby. There were no curtains, except in the bedroom where the Pigeons slept, and no other decorations. The only thing on the paint-peeled gray walls was a large set of

deer antlers mounted on a thick pine board over the couch.
Mitch stared at the dark congealed blood on the floor. Some of
it had seeped into the cracks in the wood. The pool of blood
was roughly in the shape of a tree with thornlike spikes where
the floor cracks were. Joe Pigeon's final, obscene work of art.

There was no sign in the house that it was the home of a
painter. None of Joe's paintings were on display. Joe Pigeon
had worked in a large shed behind the house. It was pad-
locked, but in his look around Mitch had seen through a window tubes of paint and brushes lined up on a shelf along the
wall. Six canvases were leaning against another wall. Three of
the paintings seemed to Mitch to be finished; the other three
were in varying stages of completion. An easel and a wired-
together straight-back chair were placed where they would receive the morning light from the window. A rolled-up sleeping
bag stood on end in the corner. About a dozen deer antlers—
none as large as the pair mounted over the couch—hung from
nails around the shed. Like many Indians in Cherokee County,
Joe Pigeon had evidently supplied much of the meat for his
family by hunting.

Duckworth loomed in the doorway, cutting off the sunlight.
"You want me to see if I can find Mary Pigeon? Somebody's
gotta tell her."

"Maybe she already knows."

"Huh? Hey—you mean, you think she might've done this?"

Mitch got to his feet. "I don't think anything yet. If you spot
the Pigeons' pickup, let me know. Don't approach Mary. I'll
talk to her."

Duckworth, who was clearly insulted by the inference that he
lacked the tact to break the news to Joe Pigeon's wife, slouched
resentfully out of the house. Mitch heard him drive away and
felt the atmosphere of death close around him. He went outside and shut the front door behind him. He walked slowly
around the house once more, scanning the ground. He didn't
expect to find a clue in the yard, but proper police procedure
required him to make sure he hadn't missed anything. He went
through the motions, deliberately cultivating the curiosity and
interest that had been reborn in him with Callie Roach's phone
call.

Near the northeast corner of the house he saw a half-burned kitchen match lying cradled between two blades of grass. He picked it up. The unburned end looked clean, as though it had just come out of the box. The match couldn't have been there long or dew would have soaked it and the wood would have darkened. It was probably nothing, but he pulled out his handkerchief, wrapped it around the match, and tucked it in his shirt pocket.

A few minutes later he spied a cigarette stub down in the grass to the left of the front steps. Upon closer examination, it appeared to be the remains of a homemade smoke. It hadn't been soaked, either. He put the stub in his handkerchief with the match and made a mental reminder to ask Mary Pigeon if she or Joe rolled their own cigarettes.

About a dozen people had gathered in a front yard in the next block. They looked toward the Pigeon house, one woman doing most of the talking, the others frowning and shaking their heads. As Mitch walked toward his car, a man detached himself from the group and approached him. The police chief waved. "Hi, Bill," he said, and picked up his pace to avoid the man's questions.

When he got to the car, Duckworth was trying to reach him on the radio.

"BPD-One, this is BPD-Three. Do you read me?"

Mitch started the engine and reached for the speaker as he drove away. The curious neighbor stopped at the corner of the Pigeon yard and stared after the squad car.

"Duck, this is Mitch. Go ahead."

"Geraldine saw that vehicle you told me to watch for, about an hour ago." Duckworth was breathless, from excitement, not exertion, this time. It wasn't often that the BPD investigated a murder case. There hadn't been a murder in Buckskin since Harney Flight came home from his traveling job a day early and caught his wife in bed with his brother, Len. While Len was trying to get his pants on, Harney grabbed a shotgun and blasted him. That was six years ago, and Harney would be up for parole next year. "It was parked at the Starlight Motel," Duckworth was saying. "I talked to the manager. She says the subject has stayed at the motel for the past two nights."

"Mary Pigeon, you mean?"

"Heck, yes. She's the subject ain't she? Nobody knows where she is right now, but she could be back any minute. Maybe I better stay on stakeout in the Three Squares for a while." He would also be stuffing his face with whatever he could sneak from the kitchen, Mitch thought. Duckworth's wife, Geraldine, worked as a waitress in the cafe across the street from the motel.

"That won't be necessary, Duck. I want you and Roo to drive every street on the east side of town, looking for the Pigeons' pickup. I'll take this side. Tell Geraldine to call the station if Mary returns to the motel before we find her. And tell the manager not to talk to Mary before we can."

"Helen says Roo hasn't checked in yet."

"He can catch up with you later. Get going."

"Ten-four. This is BPD-Three. Over and out."

Mitch hung the speaker on its hook and pressed harder on the gas pedal. Word of the murder would be all over Buckskin before noon. News of anything out of the ordinary traveled fast in a small town. A homicide was guaranteed to overload the phone lines.

TWO

CRYING WOLF sat cross-legged on his porch floor. The two-room cabin was in a small clearing surrounded by woods, the scrubby grass of the clearing long since dead from drought. It was so still that no leaf or blade of grass moved, and the temperature gauge on the porch post hovered at ninety degrees. But about noon, clouds had begun to gather to the west; they had spread eastward until now the sun was only a pale haze. If the clouds kept building, there could be rain before night. It was too late to save Crying Wolf's garden; the bean and squash vines had dried up in the relentless heat weeks ago. But a good rain would cool the cabin a little, and he would be able to sleep tonight.

He had had nothing to eat that day, preferring to meditate on Joseph Pigeon's murder; but no revelation had occurred to him. The only thing he was sure of was that he would not leave the cabin until the next dawn, when he would once more go to the creek bank to perform the ritual for cleansing the talisman that protected his house. The ritual would restore the power that had been defiled because he had been in the vicinity of a corpse.

Hunger gnawed his stomach and, sighing, he got to his feet a little unsteadily. Crying Wolf was seventy-five years old, and lately he had felt himself weakening under the years. There had been a time when he could walk for miles without tiring. Now, a half hour stroll made him short of breath. There had been a time when a twenty-four-hour fast did not sap his energy. Now he trembled from weakness after missing only two meals. He was not tempted to break his fast, however; he wanted the cleansing medicine he would make at dawn to be very powerful. Cool water from the well behind the cabin should refresh him.

As he turned to enter the house, a voice called to him. "Grandfather!" It was a term of respect used by the Cherokee for any elderly male in the tribe.

Crying Wolf turned and saw Kingfisher Pigeon walking out of the woods toward the cabin. There was nothing wrong with Crying Wolf's ears and, as he watched the other man silently, he wondered why he had not heard Kingfisher's approach.

Kingfisher Pigeon was both tall and broad. His features were blunted, not fine-drawn like his handsome brother's. When Kingfisher stepped up on the porch, Crying Wolf saw that he carried something in his hand wrapped in brown paper.

"I brought you some fresh catfish," Kingfisher said. "There's fry bread, too, from my mother."

Crying Wolf accepted the parcel and gestured for Kingfisher to precede him into the house. Burlap curtains covered the windows, and the interior was dim. "Joe's dead," Kingfisher said. Crying Wolf gazed sharply at him, but he couldn't see the man's eyes well enough to guess what he was thinking.

"I was at my folks' house when Bushyhead called to tell them about Joe," Kingfisher added. "Somebody stabbed him. The folks took it hard, 'specially my mother. Bushyhead was supposed to come out and talk to them, but I left before he got there."

"I will visit them tomorrow. I cannot go anywhere today."

"Are you sick?"

"No, but I must cleanse myself first. I knew that Joe was dead—murdered—before you told me. I saw him, after I'd performed the medicine ceremony."

"Then you did the ceremony. I was wondering..."

"I did it right," Crying Wolf said sharply. "I do not think my medicine caused your brother's death. I was careful not to make a mistake that could taint the medicine. Besides, I think Joe had been dead for some time when I got there." Kingfisher seemed to be avoiding his eyes. Crying Wolf walked past him. "I must put the fish in the wellhouse. It will make a good dinner tomorrow."

After taking a cool drink from the tin dipper beside the well, Crying Wolf came back into the cabin. Kingfisher was still standing near the front door. He shuffled his feet restlessly. "I came to ask you…" Kingfisher began, then paused to clear his throat uneasily. "Did anyone see you at Joe's house?"

"No. It was very early. The neighbors were still sleeping."

Kingfisher expelled a long breath. "Good. Can I count on you to tell no one that I asked you to make medicine?"

Crying Wolf studied the big man in silence. He knew that Kingfisher and his brother had been estranged for some time. He didn't know what had driven such a deep wedge between the two men. Family ties were important to the Cherokee, so it must have been something extremely serious. Knowing of the estrangement, he had been surprised when Kingfisher came to him on Saturday and asked him to make medicine to separate Joe and the woman. Finally Crying Wolf said, "I will tell no one unless it becomes necessary to prevent a greater evil. That is all I can promise."

Kingfisher stared at him for a moment before he nodded. It was obvious he was not satisfied with Crying Wolf's words; but he knew the medicine man would take orders from no one.

"Now I have a question for you, Kingfisher," Crying Wolf said with great earnestness. "Did you ask another medicine man to make medicine also?"

Kingfisher frowned. "No. You're the only medicine man I ever use."

"I will not use my medicine for evil. There are others who might." This thought had begun to take shape when Kingfisher stepped into the clearing. Kingfisher could have enlisted a second medicine man to perform the dark ritual to lower his brother's soul to the Nightland.

"No, Grandfather. I had nothing to do with my brother's death," Kingfisher said, looking sorely troubled. But he had hesitated, and he seemed uneasy under Crying Wolf's scrutiny.

Crying Wolf could not be sure whether Kingfisher told the truth or not. Kingfisher was said to be seized by violence when he was under the influence of whiskey. He was said to be like a baited bear at such times, spoiling for a fight. And he was said to have been responsible for a burnout of a Cherokee man who had talked for a television camera about the Nighthawk Keetoowahs, the secret society of the Cherokee dedicated to the preservation of the old ways.

"If you have touched a dead person in the last four days," Crying Wolf persisted, "you have contaminated your house and mine." Although being in the close vicinity of a dead person, as Crying Wolf had been, was defiling, touching the corpse caused even worse contamination.

Kingfisher's nostrils flared and his black eyes narrowed. "I have touched no dead person, old man." His tone held a warning that he would tolerate no further questions. Angrily, he spun around to leave.

"Thank you for the catfish," Crying Wolf said as Kingfisher shoved open the creaking screen door. "Give my thanks to your mother for the bread."

Kingfisher hesitated in the doorway, as though he wanted to say something else. Then he decided against it, strode abruptly across the porch and the clearing, stepped into the woods, and disappeared.

With his leaving, the air in the cabin seemed even closer than before. In spite of the heat, Crying Wolf felt a chill. Kingfisher hated his brother. Had he gone to Joseph Pigeon's house drunk last night? Had the brothers argued? Crying Wolf very much feared that Kingfisher was capable of killing a man under those circumstances. The warning in Kingfisher's tone suddenly took on a more ominous meaning. A man who had killed once would find it easier to kill the second time, especially if he felt threatened with exposure.

Crying Wolf did not return to the porch. Somebody with a shotgun could kill him before he knew anyone was there. He fastened the latch on the screen door and pulled a chair near it where he could feel the breeze that passed and detect signs of anyone approaching the cabin.

It would be a long afternoon and a longer night.

THREE

MITCH AND VIRGIL RABBIT sat at Virgil's kitchen table, sharing carry-out fried chicken that Mitch had brought with him. The round oak table was large enough to accommodate Virgil, Trudy, and their six kids. The kitchen was large, too. Virgil had added fifteen feet at the back of the house, which included the kitchen, when the fifth baby was born. He and Trudy had ordered pine cabinets from the Sears catalog and had assembled and installed them themselves, as well as the blue and yellow square tiles on the floor. It was a warm, sunny room where family and guests tended to congregate.

The last of the Rabbit brood had started school this year, freeing Trudy for things like attending her sewing club's meetings regularly. Today she had gone to the club's monthly luncheon.

"Not much to go on yet," Mitch said in answer to Virgil's question about the investigation. "I went out to Joe's parents' house to talk to them, but they weren't any help. I'll send Duck and Roo this afternoon to question Joe Pigeon's neighbors, see if anybody saw someone coming or going at Joe's house in the last twenty-four hours. Then I'll see if Doc Sullivan can hurry the medical examiner along. I can't talk to Doc until two. He's been in surgery all morning."

"Still no idea where Mary Pigeon is?"

"We haven't found anybody who knows. She hasn't returned to the motel."

Virgil nodded and chose another drumstick from the box between them. A wiry man of medium height, his lean body tough as shoe leather, Virgil was a full-blood, his skin two or three shades darker than Mitch's. "That starting to worry you?"

Mitch shrugged. "She left her clothes at the motel. I had the manager check."

"That could be to throw you off."

"Yeah. I got the tag number of the pickup. I'll put it on the wire if she doesn't turn up soon. Thing is, I'd like to question her when she's not expecting it." He wiped his fingers on a paper napkin and took a drink of cold milk. "You and Trudy know her very well?"

Virgil shook his head. "She and Joe pretty much kept to themselves."

"The old man said they hadn't seen Joe in a while."

"Joe split with the family."

"When did that happen?"

"Last spring when he came back from Tahlequah."

Mitch remembered that Joe had won a scholarship to study art at the university in the county seat. He'd lived there for nine months, leaving his wife in Buckskin. "What caused the rift, do you know?"

"Joe took some damn course in Cherokee culture while he was at Northeastern State. When he got back, he quit the Nighthawks. Told his dad Redbird Smith let some Oneida Indian, back in the early nineteen hundreds, pull the wool over his eyes. Apparently, Cornelius—that was the Oneida's name— claimed to know the ancient Cherokee ways and taught Smith all the old ceremonies, but Joe said it was all a crock. The old man and Kingfisher took it as a personal insult."

After his father's death when Mitch was eight, he had been raised in Oklahoma City by his white mother. He had known nothing about his Cherokee heritage when he came to Buckskin ten years ago, but over the years he'd picked up bits and pieces of it from Virgil in casual conversation. He remembered Virgil telling him once that Redbird Smith was revered as having purified the Nighthawk Keetoowahs, a secret society made up of conservative members of the tribe, by restoring ancient Cherokee beliefs and ceremonies. Virgil had told Mitch early on that he was a Nighthawk, but he had never talked about what they did at their meetings and Mitch hadn't asked, knowing instinctively that it wasn't something outsiders were supposed to ask about.

"You believe what Joe said?"

Virgil munched on his chicken leg before answering. "I don't know. I read up on this Cornelius when Joe quit the society. Some of the Nighthawks mortgaged their farms in nineteen-seventeen and made some investments recommended by Cornelius. They lost everything."

"You think Cornelius conned them?"

"Maybe. He was a lawyer. If he'd had the society incorporated and made the investments in the names of the corporation, nobody could have touched their home farms. But he didn't. Some of them deeded their property directly to Cornelius and he foreclosed on them. He probably claimed he had to, to pay off what he'd lost in the venture himself. It's possible, I guess, that he just didn't know the law that well. Almost anybody could call himself a lawyer in those days." Virgil spread a napkin on the table and made a pile of chicken bones. "I always figured it wasn't that important whether Redbird got it all exactly right or not. It's the feeling of tradition and respect for our ancestors that counts." Virgil grinned. "I wouldn't say that in front of another Nighthawk. Some of them would agree with me, others would bust a gut."

Mitch finished off the last piece of chicken. "Like the Pigeons?" The Pigeon family was said to be prominent in the society. What Virgil had told him about the reason for Joe's split with his family seemed to confirm that Kingfisher Pigeon, Joe's older brother, was rumored to be the keeper of the ceremonial fire on Going Snake Mountain.

"Right."

Virgil got up to dispose of their leavings. The phone on the kitchen wall, next to the refrigerator, rang and he put down the carry-out box to answer it. "Sure, Duck. He's right here." He offered the phone to Mitch, who came around the table to take it.

"Yeah, Duck?"

"That vehicle's back at the motel," Duckworth said, his words falling over each other. "The subject just drove up. I'm calling from the Three Squares. I'd just ordered lunch when I saw her. She's in Unit Ten right now." He carefully avoided mentioning Mary Pigeon's name. Duck had watched too many TV cop shows. Periodically he searched the station for listening devices. He'd never found any, but he continued to search. At the moment he evidently feared being overheard by the cafe's kitchen help.

"Sit tight. I'll be there."

"Want me to apprehend her if she leaves again?"

"No. Just follow her and let me know where she goes."

"Aw—okay," Duckworth said dejectedly.

Mitch hung up. "Mary Pigeon's back at the motel."

"Should I come with you?"

Mitch paused at the kitchen door. "Two of us might spook her. If I go alone, as though I'm only there to inform her of Joe's death, in case she doesn't know, she might talk to me. I'll fill you in when you get to the station at four."

THIN CURTAINS were drawn over the window at Unit Ten of the Starlight Motel.

Mitch knocked on the door.

"Who is it?" a woman's voice asked.

"Mitch Bushyhead, Mary."

He waited. After several moments, the door opened a crack, held by a night chain. Mary Pigeon was a tall woman in her early thirties. Her face was pale and thin, like the rest of her. Her blond hair was pulled back and secured at the nape of her neck.

"He told me I could have it," she said resignedly. "Now I guess he's changed his mind."

Mitch frowned. "Pardon?"

She jerked her head toward the old Ford truck parked a few feet from the door. "The pickup."

Her expression was disgusted. Mitch could detect no wariness or fear. Either she didn't know what had happened to Joe or she was a better actress than he'd given her credit for. "This has nothing to do with the pickup."

"Oh," she said. She did not remove the night chain. "Well, what do you want then?"

"Mary..." He hesitated. He'd had to tell perhaps a dozen people that someone close to them was dead, but he didn't know any gentler way of doing it than he had the first time. Even when you were expecting it, you were never ready for it, and there was no way to soften the news. "Joe's dead," he said finally.

She stared at him for a long moment in silence. "Are you sure? What..."

"I'd like to come in, Mary, if you wouldn't mind."

"Oh, yes. Of course."

She closed the door and he heard the chain being removed. The door opened wide. In the shaft of daylight admitted by the open door, he saw that she was wearing a cotton housedress, green with white dots, leather loafers, and little makeup. The room beyond was small, its only furniture a bed, a dresser, and a tattered wicker chair that looked as if rats had been gnawing on it.

Mary Pigeon was staring at him as though she suspected some trick. She blinked and asked, "Would you like to sit down?" She indicated the beat-up wicker chair, then lowered herself to the side of the bed.

Mitch sat and decided he might as well get it all said. "Joe was murdered."

She seemed petrified for an instant, and then she shook her head adamantly. "There must be some mistake. It must have been a heart attack or an accident..." An instant before she'd been denying Joe's death, now she clung to the idea of death from natural causes to avoid accepting the far worse alternative of murder. Mitch had seen it before.

"No mistake. He was stabbed."

"When? Where?"

"He was at home. We won't know the time of death until we get the medical examiner's report, but it must've happened within the past twenty-four hours."

She dropped her head and stared at her hands clasped in her lap. "It doesn't make sense," she said in a low voice, her denial weakening now. "I don't understand. Was he drunk?"

"We don't know that, either, but we'll find out when we get the report. I can't tell you much at this point. Whoever did it..." He faltered, wanting to spare her, but he had to tell her about Joe's fingers. If he didn't, she'd get another shock when she saw the body. "They cut two fingers off his left hand, Mary."

She winced and continued to stare at her hands. Finally she swallowed and looked up at him. "His fingers?"

He nodded. "Did Joe wear a wedding ring?"

She blanched visibly, but she didn't appear to be about to cry. Maybe her mind's accepted it, Mitch thought, but not her emotions.

"Yes." She cleared her throat. "A gold band with a diamond in it. I worked and paid for it before we got married."

"Was the ring difficult to pull off?"

Mary swallowed again, harder this time. "Sometimes the stuff he used to clean his brushes made his fingers swell, and he couldn't get it off without soaping his fingers good."

Mitch marveled at a robber determined enough to cut off two of a man's fingers to get his wedding ring. "Did he carry much money in his wallet?"

Holding herself rigidly straight, she pressed her thin lips together. "Lately, since he'd been selling his paintings, he had two or three hundred dollars on him most of the time. I tried to tell him it was risky but he wouldn't put it in the bank."

If Joe had wanted to protect his welfare check, he'd have dealt in cash and he wouldn't have used a bank.

"Was there any money in his wallet when you found him?"

Mitch shook his head. "It was open on the couch, but there was no money." He pondered for a moment. "Later I'll want you to look around the place, see if you notice anything else missing." She nodded and he went on. "Was Joe still active in the Nighthawks?" Thanks to Virgil, he already knew the answer, but he wanted to gauge her honesty, see how much she would tell him.

Her eyes widened; his question had obviously surprised her. "Not for months. His family blamed me for it. They never wanted Joe to marry a white woman. But I didn't have anything to do with it."

"Did Joe say why he quit?"

"He learned about the history of the Nighthawks when he was at the university. When he came home, he said he didn't believe that way anymore."

"Did Joe argue with his family over it?"

She searched his face before she replied. "I can't say for sure. They didn't come to the house much, called it Joe's white woman's house. And Joe and me—well, we haven't had a lot to say to each other lately."

"Is that why you're staying here at the Starlight? Did you and Joe split up?"

She lifted her bony shoulders in the cotton dress. "Yes. I moved in here Saturday. I went to Muskogee this morning to look for a job. I used to work as a nurse's aide at the hospital before I got married. But they don't have any openings and none of the nursing homes did, either."

"What will you do then?"

"Herschel over at the cafe told me I could work there as a waitress, that I could start Saturday. I was hoping to find something that would pay more, but I guess I'll have to settle for that for now." Briefly she looked abstracted. "I reckon I can move back to the house now. Would that be all right?"

It was beginning to bother him that she hadn't cried. She'd had time to absorb what he'd told her, but her eyes remained dry. "You can go back tomorrow afternoon. I want to take another look around first and get somebody over there to check for fingerprints. Why did you leave him, Mary?"

She darted a sharp look at him, then looked away quickly, almost furtively. "He didn't care about me anymore. He'd go for days without talking to me unless I asked him a question. That was when he was home. It got so the past few months I never knew when or if he'd be there. He took to sleeping in the shed, and some nights I never knew if he'd been home or not. I used to try to make allowances for him—artists have strange ways—but I finally got my craw full." She never looked at Mitch as she talked, and he had a strong feeling she was hiding something.

"Did you tell him you were leaving for good?"

She nodded. "Saturday morning. He yelled at me, told me to go ahead and get out, he didn't care. So I left." She examined a chipped nail and added almost defiantly, "Just my luck. The first time in his life Joe was ever making any money, and I wasn't going to share in it." She heaved a sigh. "At least he said I could have the pickup. He'd saved enough to buy himself a good used Mustang.'' She fell momentarily silent. ''That doesn't matter now, does it? There won't be any more money.'' She looked up. ''You think the Nighthawks killed Joe?''

''I'm only trying to turn up some leads, Mary. Did you go home yesterday?''

She gazed at him with her light, watery blue eyes, and he could see her trying to figure out where he was headed. ''I haven't been back since I left Saturday. What are you getting at?''

''I have to think of all the possibilities, Mary. You and Joe might have argued. Maybe you went back to the house for something and he tried to make you stay. Maybe you came to physical blows. Maybe in the heat of anger you grabbed a knife and took a swipe at Joe, accidentally punctured the big artery in his neck. If something like that happened, it wouldn't be murder. It would be manslaughter. You might even get off with probation.''

''It wasn't like that. I told you, I haven't seen Joe since day before yesterday.''

Mitch held her gaze for a minute, but she didn't waver. ''Did Joe smoke?''

She looked bewildered, as though she found Mitch's sudden changes of subject confusing. ''He chewed sometimes.''

''But he didn't ever smoke cigarettes?''

''Not that I know of.''

''What about you?''

''I never took up the habit. We couldn't afford it.''

''Did Joe have any enemies?''

''Maybe. I don't know what he might have got himself into lately.''

''Can you think of anything that's happened in the last few weeks, anything at all that might have made somebody mad enough to kill Joe?''

''No, nothing.''

''All right, Mary.'' Feeling frustrated, Mitch wondered if she'd tell him, even if she knew something. Some of the full-bloods felt no obligation to cooperate with the police. Joe Pigeon had probably been one of those, and maybe Mary had come to think like her husband. Or maybe she simply didn't want to get involved. Mitch pushed himself out of the chair. "By the way, the body will be at the hospital until the medical examiner looks at it. We'll let you know when you can make the funeral arrangements." He paused at the door. "Is there anybody you'd like me to call for you—a friend or relative?"

"I don't have any close relatives, and there's nobody else I want to see right now."

"All right. Oh, Mary—I wouldn't want you to leave town without telling me."

She had followed him to the door. "Don't worry." There was an edge of resentment to the words. "I got no other place to go."

She closed the door behind Mitch, and he heard the night chain sliding into place. He stood on the sidewalk, frowning.

So Mary and Joe had been having marital problems for months. Love had probably died somewhere back down the line, but you didn't live with a man for years without a strong attachment. You didn't break those emotional ties easily.

He recalled his feeling that Mary was holding something back. He had an uneasy sense of having been very close to finding out something important in that motel room. Mary had definitely not told him the whole truth, and she hadn't cried, yet he would have sworn she didn't know about Joe's death until he told her.

On the other hand, maybe she was a better actress than he'd thought.

FOUR

THE STARLIGHT MOTEL fronted on Highway Ten, which intersected Buckskin's main street, Sequoyah, four blocks to the east. Most of the town's business establishments were either on Sequoyah north of the highway or strung out for eight or nine blocks along Highway Ten. The glare of the afternoon sun was softened by cloud cover, but it still felt more like August than September.

Directly east of the motel was a lumberyard and a farmer's produce and feed store. West of the motel was a small strip shopping center housing a doughnut shop, a flower shop, and the Sears catalog store. Farther west a trailer park and a few scattered houses marked the western outskirts of the town.

An industrial park a half mile beyond the strip center on the highway contained the struggling tire factory, a plant that produced small electric motors, and the new Stelco plant, which employed almost a hundred people in the manufacture of steel shopping carts. A few of those laid off at the tire factory last year had been able to get on at Stelco and there was talk that the company planned to expand the plant. If that happened, Buckskin's currently depressed economy should improve.

Mitch examined the sky for a moment, hoping to see that the clouds were darker than before, but he couldn't tell. Leaving the Starlight, he checked for traffic, then crossed the two-lane highway to the Three Squares Cafe, still pondering his interview with Mary Pigeon. It appeared that she would be better off now that Joe was dead. She'd have the house. It wasn't much, but better than paying rent at the motel. He should find out if the house was paid for.

Duckworth was sitting in a booth eating apple pie with vanilla ice cream. Duckworth's wife, Geraldine, sat across from him. The other booths were unoccupied. The lunch crowd had come and gone.

"Herschel in back?" Mitch asked.

"Yeah," Geraldine said. Duckworth didn't say anything. His mouth was full.

Mitch pushed through a swinging door and found Herschel Lee, owner of the Three Squares, with flour up to his elbows. He had a bibbed apron tied around his protruding stomach and was kneading dough. The pleasant aroma of yeast hung in the air. Herschel, who was short and bald and had drooping eye-lids, always reminded Mitch of a sorrowful kewpie doll.

"What happened to your cook?" Mitch asked.

Herschel pummeled the dough. "The one looked like a professional wrestler?"

"That's the one."

"Hadn't been here a month when she was demanding a raise. You believe it? People don't take any pride in their work any-more. Money, money, that's all they care about."

"It's a sorry world we live in, Herschel."

"I heard that." Herschel frowned, shook his head. "Too bad about Joe Pigeon."

By now, everybody in town would have heard about the murder.

"Crying shame," Herschel was saying. "You know his wife is coming to work for me?"

"So she told me. I wanted to talk to you about that. When did she speak to you about a job?"

"Yesterday morning. Came in after the breakfast crowd had thinned out. Eight-thirty, nine, something like that."

"Did she tell you she'd left Joe?"

"No, but I saw that brown Ford pickup parked in front of the motel Saturday and it was still there yesterday when I opened up. Then Mary shows up and asks if I could use an-other waitress—I kind of figured they'd split the sheet." He shrugged. "I said, sure. I can always use a good waitress."

"How did she seem? Upset? Angry?"

Herschel began squeezing off walnut-sized balls of dough and arranging them, three to a cup, in greased muffin tins. "No, can't say she did. Seemed pretty calm and collected for a woman who'd just left her husband. Like she'd settled everything in her mind. But then Mary's not the excitable type. Not the kind to blab her problems all over town, either.''

Settled everything in her mind. How? Mitch wondered. By deciding to kill her husband? "How well do you know her?"

"We ain't bosom buddies, but she comes in here once or twice a week for a cup of coffee, maybe a sandwich. Joe used to shut himself up in that shed and paint for hours." Mitch noticed that Herschel was already speaking of Joe in the past tense. "Mary's lonely," Herschel went on. "We say hello, talk about the weather, like that. Feel sorry for her. A man shouldn't treat a woman like Joe treated her."

"How'd he treat her?"

"From all I hear, he mostly ignored her. Can't remember seeing the two of them together in a long time. He came and went as he pleased, no questions asked. She could like it or lump it."

That squared with what Mary had told Mitch. "Was Mary's pickup parked at the motel all day yesterday?"

"Can't say. I was back here most of the time."

"What time did you leave the cafe last night?"

"'Bout ten-thirty."

"Did you happen to notice Mary's truck at the motel then?"

"I think so. I was tired and looking forward to going home and getting a hot bath, watching the fights on TV. Wasn't paying much attention."

"You couldn't swear it was there when you closed, then?"

"Swear? If you mean make an official statement and sign my name to it, no." Herschel added another ball of dough to the last muffin tin and wiped his hands on his apron. He looked as though he might burst into tears at any moment, but that was the way Herschel always looked. "You don't seriously think Mary had anything to do with Joe's death, do you?"

"I don't know yet, Herschel. But I have to check her out. I take the town's money, I have to do the job they pay me to do." Mary Pigeon's reaction to her husband's murder still bothered Mitch, even taking into account that they'd decided to separate. Maybe she wasn't the excitable type, as Herschel said, but most women in Mary's place would have registered some emotion. Unless they were focusing so intently on concealing something that there was no room for emotion.

"Yeah, I guess you do. You might ask Geraldine if she noticed the pickup leave the motel any time yesterday. I gotta cut up some chickens."

Geraldine and Duckworth were still sitting in the booth when Mitch returned to the front of the cafe. Charles Stephens—known as Roo—the youngest of the three police officers under Mitch, had joined them.

As Mitch slid into the booth next to Roo, Duckworth said, "Is that a chigger bite on your neck, Roo?" He grinned at Mitch. "Why, no, I believe it's a hickey. Roo's got a hickey, Chief." Duckworth slapped the table and cackled.

"Now, you stop that, Duck." Geraldine was trying not to laugh. She was short and chunky. Her dark hair was pulled back in a bun that was covered by a hairnet.

Roo's Adam's apple bobbed and his freckled face flamed. Lately he'd been keeping company with a plain, shy girl who worked at the city library, Laura Tucker. As far as Mitch knew, Laura was the first girlfriend the bashful Roo had ever had. Duckworth wouldn't let him forget it.

"Where were you about eight-thirty this morning, Roo? Helen tried to reach you on the radio to tell you to come out to Joe Pigeon's house."

Roo's embarrassment receded as disappointment took over. "I left my squad car for a few minutes to have breakfast."

"Must've been more than a few minutes, Roo."

"I'm sorry, Chief. I wasn't watching the clock, and I forgot to turn my pager on."

Mitch let it drop. He knew his reprimand wouldn't hurt Roo nearly as much as having missed his first chance to be at a murder scene.

"He was with Laura," Duckworth put in, drawing out the first syllable of the name and winking at Mitch. "What'd you have for breakfast, Roo, a little shaky puddin'?"

Roo reddened again. "None of your damn business! Doesn't your mind ever rise above your belt?"

Duckworth kept on cackling. "Oh, he don't mean nothing, Roo," Geraldine said. "Don't pay no attention to him." If Roo

could take that advice, Mitch thought, and quit firing up every
time Duckworth started razzing him, Duckworth would soon
tire of the game.

Roo glared at the laughing Duckworth, then turned to Mitch.
"It won't happen again, Chief. Shoot, I wish I'd been with you
this morning. You need me to go to the Pigeon house now?"

"Why don't both of you go over there? Take the fingerprint
kit and see if you can lift any prints. Also, ask around the
neighborhood, find out if anybody saw the Pigeons' pickup or
any other vehicle at the house yesterday or last night. I'm going
to the hospital if anybody needs me."

"You bet, Chief," said Roo, excited now. "Come on,
Duck."

The two left, Roo loping behind. He moved with the awkward lankiness of a kangaroo, from which he'd earned his
nickname while playing high school basketball. As the two officers went out the door, Mitch heard Duckworth say, "You
sure you were at Laura's house just for breakfast, Roo? You
sure you weren't there all night?"

Geraldine giggled. "That Duck. He's always kidding somebody."

Especially those incapable of giving as good as they got,
Mitch thought. "I hear Mary Pigeon's going to be working with
you."

She sobered. "Isn't it awful about Joe? You know who did
it yet?"

"I'm still gathering evidence. How well do you know
Mary?"

Geraldine scowled uncertainly. "Just to speak to, when she
comes into the cafe. Sometimes, if I don't have any customers,
I'll sit down and have a cup of coffee with her."

"What do you talk about?"

"Nothing special. Whatever's going on around town. You
know."

"She ever talk to you about Joe?"

"Not much. She'd say he was painting, or something like
that."

"She never criticized him?"

"Not to me. Once last winter, she came in here with her face and hands all red and chapped. Said she'd been cutting wood all morning. They heated with wood, and from what she said, Joe wouldn't keep the woodbox full. She said he didn't have time because he was going to school and only came home on weekends. When he was home, he was painting. But you know he didn't paint all weekend. I saw him in town on Saturday several times, usually going into a bar. She was just making excuses for him. I don't see how she could keep from resenting the way he treated her. I guess he thought he was too good to get a job. Might hurt his precious hands." She faltered and looked pained. "I wasn't thinking when I said that. Why on earth would anybody cut off Joe's fingers?" She didn't wait for Mitch to answer. "Anyway, what I'm getting at is that Mary had plenty of reason to criticize Joe, but she never said a word against him to me."

Mitch had a fleeting image of Mary Pigeon wielding an axe at the base of a tree. He'd seen an axe propped against the wall in a broom closet in the Pigeon house. It could have been an axe that cut off Joseph Pigeon's fingers. Mitch felt a prickle of excitement and castigated himself for not having thought of checking the axe sooner. It could make a woman feel sorely used, working to buy a man a diamond ring, only to have him kick her out when his financial prospects improved. Mad enough to take the ring back, even if it meant chopping off a couple of fingers to get it? He held his sudden urgency in check and continued to question Geraldine.

"Did you know she'd left Joe?"

"Not till yesterday when she was in here talking to Herschel about a job. She told me then."

"Did she say why?"

Geraldine shook her head. "No, but like I said, she had good reason. I know I shouldn't speak ill of the dead, Chief, but if a man won't work, in my opinion he's about as much use to the world as the teats on a boar."

"Maybe Joe looked on painting as his work." Odd that he had an impulse to defend Joe now, when he'd held about the same opinion as Geraldine when the man was alive. For the first time, it occurred to him that an artist might find Buckskin an

unaccommodating place in which to live. The town's population consisted largely of conservative Cherokees and rednecks
to whom manliness was defined in terms of physical prowess.
Work that required brute strength was respected; painting pictures not a bit.

"Hmmmph," was Geraldine's comment.

"How late did you work yesterday?"

"Until four."

"Did you notice if Mary Pigeon's pickup left the motel while
you were here?"

"Maybe," she said reluctantly. "She might have gone to the
store for a little while in the afternoon."

"How do you know that's where she went?"

"When she came back she was carrying a grocery sack. She
probably bought some snacks. Mary can't afford to eat in cafes
regularly, that's for sure."

"Who worked last night?"

"Dicey and Sue. They won't be here till three, though." As
they talked, four men had come in and occupied a booth across
the room. "Mitch, I got to go to work now or Herschel will
have my hide."

"Thanks, Geraldine." Mitch had a cup of coffee before he
left the cafe, dawdling while he tried to put the little he'd
learned about the Pigeons so far into perspective.

When he got to his car, he called Duckworth on the radio.
Roo answered, "This is BPD-Four. Duck'll be back in a minute, Chief."

"Find anybody who saw a car?"

"Not yet. We've talked to the close neighbors already, and
now we're going to move on to the next block."

"Before you do, Roo, I want you to get the axe out of the
Pigeons' broom closet. Bring it to the station when you come
back. Wrap a handkerchief around your hand before you handle it. Try not to touch either end." He didn't hold out much
hope of picking up any fingerprints on the porous wood handle; it was the blade he was interested in. If the axe had been
used to cut off Joe Pigeon's fingers, there might still be traces
of blood on the blade.

"You got it, Chief! Golly, you think somebody used that axe—"

Mitch cut him off. "We'll talk about it later, Roo. I'm on my way to the hospital now."

FIVE

THE ROUTE to the hospital took Mitch down Pawnee Street past his own house, a white, two-story Victorian that he and Ellen had bought ten years ago when they'd moved to Buckskin with their five-year-old daughter. They'd bought it cheap, because it was in a dismal state, and fixed it up as they had the time and money. The place reflected Ellen's tastes, from the needle-point cushions on the dining room chairs to the blue-and-white wallpaper in the entrance hall.

For weeks after her death, it had been difficult for Mitch merely to open the front door and step inside. If it hadn't been for Emily, Mitch would have sold it, quit his job, and left Buckskin. He knew that flight was not an uncommon reaction to grief and that the desire, if not acted on, would pass. But he would have gone, anyway, if he hadn't known that uprooting Emily, after the loss of her mother, would be unwise.

He was making progress, though. Last week he'd managed to pack all of Ellen's clothes and give them to the Salvation Army. He told himself to give it time, as he'd done every day for six months. Time would heal the wounds. It would leave scars, but scars didn't feel pain.

As he neared the hospital, he noticed that darker clouds were banking in the west. It looked as though they'd get some desperately needed rain, after all.

He pulled into the hospital parking lot and got out. The hospital was a one-story, buff brick building, a fifty-bed facility owned by the city.

When Mitch entered, he saw Dr. Sullivan, in a white jacket, coming down the hall toward him, a metal-covered patient chart in his hand. Mitch went to meet him. "You're hard at it, Doc."

"'Afternoon, Mitch. I've been hard at it since before six A.M. Mimi Griesel's new son decided to get himself born this morning. Then I had two tonsillectomies and a hernia repair. I haven't even had a chance to grab a bite to eat yet. Let's go to the kitchen." He laid the chart on the desk at the nurses' station.

A young nurse hurried down the hall and caught the doctor before he could leave. "Dr. Sullivan, Mrs. Griesel is upset because her baby won't nurse. Could you talk to her?"

"Bother," growled Sullivan. "Let him get hungry enough, and he'll eat."

"I told her that, but she insists on talking to you."

"First-time mothers are a royal pain, Chief. If the baby doesn't act exactly the way some book says it should, they're sure it's got something terrible wrong with it. They relax a little with the second one, and after that they shell them out like peas and want to go home the next day. Tell her I'll be in to see her in a few minutes. Right now I'm going to take a break. And you don't need to mention that to Mrs. Griesel."

"You think I want a furious woman on my hands, Doctor?" asked the nurse, pretty and starched in her white uniform, young-looking enough to have just finished nursing school but already taking the head of the medical staff's crustiness in stride.

"She'll do," Sullivan said to Mitch as they walked toward the kitchen. "Most of the new ones are scared of their shadows for the first few months. Cower when I come around as though I might bite 'em if they misplace a chart."

Knowing of Sullivan's reputation as a stern taskmaster, Mitch smiled. "Where would they get a notion like that?"

"I've no idea," Sullivan said. They entered the small dining area of the hospital kitchen, where the staff ate their meals. "Help yourself to coffee, Mitch, while I find something to eat."

"Thanks, but I just had some."

"Then pour a cup for me."

Sullivan rummaged in the refrigerator, found the remains of a meatloaf, and cut himself a couple of thick slabs. He slapped the meat between two slices of whole wheat bread with a healthy slathering of mayonnaise and brought his sandwich to the table where Mitch was sitting. He took a bite of the sandwich and studied Mitch. "You doing all right?" He was Mitch's family doctor. Sullivan had diagnosed Ellen's cancer and sent her to an oncologist in Tulsa.

Mitch nodded. "I'm sleeping better."

"Good. How is Emily?"

"She seems fine now that school has started." Mitch hadn't come there to talk about his personal problems. He changed the subject. "Have you had a chance to examine Joe Pigeon's body, Doc?"

Sullivan stirred cream into his coffee. A gaunt, raw-boned man in his early sixties, he'd settled in Buckskin thirty years ago. Of the town's four doctors, he was the busiest and most respected, in spite of his gruff manner. Some people didn't trust the breezy, joking younger doctors who played tennis at the country club in Muskogee on their afternoons off; evidently it was felt that dealing with the sick and dying was too serious an undertaking to leave room for levity or recreation.

"I looked at him, but the postmortem is the medical examiner's job. He'll be here later this afternoon."

"Any ideas about the time of death?"

"No. The cause is obvious, though. His carotid artery was cut. It would have taken only a few minutes for him to bleed to death."

"Would you say it was done with a knife?"

Sullivan ate more of his sandwich and sipped his coffee. "If I had to guess, I'd say no. The wound isn't clean and even, as it would be if a knife had been used. I ordered blood samples taken. We'll have the results in an hour or two if you need them in your investigation. You'll have to wait for the M.E.'s report for the rest."

Sullivan's response was about what Mitch had expected, but he couldn't help being disappointed. "Would you call me as soon as he's finished? It'll be Thursday or Friday before I get the report in the mail. I'll want to send somebody out here to get Joe's fingerprints, too. Duck and Roo are dusting for prints at the Pigeon house now."

Sullivan agreed and Mitch went back to the station. Roo and Duckworth brought the axe in later. There was no blood on it visible to the naked eye, but Mitch wrapped the axe carefully and shipped it to Oklahoma City for analysis.

Questioning the Pigeons' neighbors had turned up one possible lead. Bill Lancaster, recently retired from the postal service, had seen a '78 or '79 gray or blue Chevy at the Pigeon house Sunday. Nobody could remember seeing the Ford pickup there the previous day or night, but most of those questioned couldn't swear they hadn't seen the truck, either. When you're used to seeing a vehicle in the same place every day, you stop noticing it.

Midafternoon Mitch had to spend a half hour with Floyd Harrington, editor of the *Buckskin Banner*, the local newspaper. It took that long for Harrington to be convinced that whatever the Chief knew about Joe Pigeon's murder, he wasn't going to talk about it.

At four, Mitch briefed Virgil. At four-thirty, Dr. Sullivan called the station. "Mitch, Dr. Newhouse, the medical examiner, is here. You'll be getting a full report later, but I thought you might like to know that he confirmed my first impression. The wound in Pigeon's neck was made by something blunter than a knife. Something like a sharp rock, Newhouse said."

"What's his thought on the time of death?"

"He won't venture a guess until he sees the results of all the tests. Mitch, there's something else."

"What's that?"

"Joe Pigeon has a hematoma as big as an egg on the back of his head. Made with a blunt instrument, Newhouse says, blunter than whatever tore open his carotid. I didn't notice it earlier because we didn't turn him over until Newhouse arrived. Pigeon was already unconscious when his carotid was punctured. He didn't have a chance to try to get help in those first few minutes. He just lay there and bled to death."

That explained why there hadn't been a trail of blood or other evidence that Pigeon had tried to get up or crawl outside. With Joe's thick, longish black hair, Mitch hadn't noticed the head injury, either. "Thanks, Doc. That answers one of my questions."

"Officer Duckworth just took Joe's fingerprints. We're ready to send the body over to the funeral home. You can tell Mary they'll be calling her about the arrangements."

When Mitch left the station, the clouds in the west were even darker than before. He swung by the Three Squares Cafe to question the late-shift waitresses. Neither of them had noticed whether the Ford pickup had left the motel Sunday evening. They'd been busy, they said, and had barely had time to look up.

Leaving the cafe, Mitch noticed the pickup still parked in front of Number Ten. He wondered what she was doing in there. How was she feeling—regretful? depressed? anxious?

Because of the dark clouds, an eerie early dusk made it seem later than it was, but it was late enough and he was tired. He also had a vague feeling that he'd forgotten something. He wanted to have another look around the Pigeon house, but that wasn't it. He frowned and glanced at his watch. Five forty-five. Emily would have been home for two hours. Emily...oh, hell, the meeting at the high school. He'd promised, and he was already fifteen minutes late.

He jumped into his squad car and sped toward the school.

SIX

MITCH PUSHED through the high school's double glass entry doors. He thrust his head into the secretary's office. No one was there, nor in the principal's office beyond. He turned into the first tiled hallway he reached, reading teachers' names above the doors as he passed.

It was six by the time he located Mrs. Macpherson's room. Ten girls and nine mothers occupied seats in the first three rows of student desks. His eyes searched out Emily, who was sitting in the front row, her head bent in an attitude of dejection, her hair half-covering her face. Little Orphan Annie.

The woman in charge was leaning back against the big oak desk at the front of the room. She appeared to be in her late twenties and wore a long-sleeved red silk shirt and a navy-and-red plaid skirt. Her hands were thrust deep into the skirt's big pockets. The outfit displayed her breasts and narrow waist charmingly. She was wearing navy shoes with two-inch heels. Her gold hair was loose against the red collar of her shirt. This had to be the strict but fair Mrs. Macpherson. Lucky man, Mr. Macpherson.

Nobody noticed Mitch at first. Then the teacher glanced toward the door. "Come in. You must be Emily's father."

Nineteen female heads turned in his direction. If Mitch wasn't mistaken, there was censure for his tardiness on a couple of them. He felt like a Saint Bernard at a poodle show. He wished he'd left his gun in the car.

A girl in the second row snickered. Emily straightened and gave the snickerer a hard look. The cloudburst in her eyes was beginning to clear as she glanced at the teacher, then at Mitch, and smiled. He didn't care about the others as long as he'd redeemed himself in Emily's eyes.

Mitch slid into the nearest empty desk. "Sorry to be late." The gun on his right hip dug into his back. He adjusted it.

"No harm done," said Mrs. Macpherson. "We're discussing the girls' uniforms. We're agreed that the least they can get by with is two sweaters, two blouses, two skirts, and a reversible vest. They'll also need a pair of red canvas topsiders and saddle oxfords for colder weather."

He nodded sagely. What in tarnation were red canvas topsiders? He noticed a column of five numbers on the chalkboard. Their total came to two hundred and forty-five.

"We'll order the sweaters and shoes," Mrs. Macpherson was saying. "Connors in Tahlequah has the fabric for the skirts, vests, and blouses. In all, it comes to about two-forty-five."

Two hundred and forty-five dollars? On top of that, he'd have to hire a seamstress. Round off the sewing charges to a hundred. That came to roughly three hundred and fifty dollars. Total idiocy. What did girls from welfare families do? They probably made up 20 percent of the school population; Buckskin had a relatively high per capita welfare rate. Maybe poor girls didn't get elected to the pom-pom squad. Or maybe the school had some kind of charity fund. He glanced at Mrs. Macpherson, who was looking back at him. Her eyes were somewhere between blue and gray, he noted.

He looked at the column of figures again. Now he knew why the parents' attendance at this meeting was mandatory. If the dough was going to be a problem for anybody, they wanted to know up front.

"Do you have any questions, Mr. Bushyhead?"

Yeah, he had a question. Why weren't these mothers rebelling? "No," he said.

"Anybody else?"

"Will the uniforms have to be finished for the first football game?" a mother asked. "That only gives us three days."

Mrs. Macpherson shook her head. The movement made her glistening gold hair bounce. "It's probably not going to be possible for all of you to buy the fabric and have an outfit made by then. The girls can wear jeans and white shirts Friday. The second game's out of town. Uniforms won't be required until the third game—that's the twenty-seventh."

A murmur of relief ran through the mothers. Mitch sat there and tried to look unruffled. Another day, another three hundred and fifty smackers. So what else was new? He didn't even know any seamstresses. Ellen had made all her's and Emily's clothes. He'd ask Macpherson after the meeting.

"The mothers are going to take turns helping me chaperone the girls at out-of-town games, Mr. Bushyhead. Since we'll have to leave before five o'clock, we'll exclude you from that chore."

Ellen would have been the first to volunteer. "I appreciate that."

A little flutter of laughter.

"Well, is there anything else we need to discuss?"

Nobody could think of anything.

"That about does it then," Mrs. Macpherson said. "Thank you all for coming, and I'll be seeing you at the ballgames."

Mitch dawdled until everybody else was drifting toward the door. He went up to the desk where a nameplate sat on a stack of papers. Her name was Lisa, Lisa Macpherson. He said, "I'll have to hire a seamstress to make Emily's uniforms. I don't think I'm going to have time to get out the old Singer."

Her smile exposed even white teeth, transforming her face from merely arresting to truly beautiful. "Pity. I'll bet you're a mean man with a needle, too."

He grinned. "Yeah, but I've got a new thimble and I can't do a thing with it. So I was wondering if you know of any seamstresses in town."

She stood about three inches shorter than his six-feet-one. Allowing for her high heels, that made her about five-eight. She held herself very straight, as though she was proud of her height. She turned and picked up the name plaque, set it aside, lifted the stack of papers, put it back down. Then she shuffled through a box filled with pencils, paper clips, and thumb tacks. "Here it is." She waved a scrap of paper. "One of the mothers gave me two names." She got a pen and piece of paper and copied down the names and phone numbers for him. "You should be able to get one of them to do it."

"Thank you."

When she looked at you, she gave you her full attention. He guessed her age at twenty-eight or twenty-nine. Nice age for a woman. Fleetingly he wondered where she'd lived before coming to Buckskin, what her husband planned to do there.

"May I make a suggestion?"

He lifted a brow. "Please do. You may not have noticed, but I'm sort of out of my element here. I need all the help I can get."

Again, she flashed that sunrise of a smile. "Call today and get the fabric to the seamstress tomorrow, or Emily will be last in line. Incidentally, you have a fine daughter."

"You are obviously a woman of astute judgment."

"Spread that around, will you? I'm on probation here my first year."

"You got it." He stuffed the paper with the seamstresses' names on it into his shirt pocket and went to find Emily. She was pulling books from her locker. "You mad at me?"

She straightened. "I was, but I'm not now."

"I'm new at this stuff. You'll have to bear with me."

"It's okay, Daddy."

He put his arm around her. "Let's go home. We need to make a phone call." They walked down the hall.

"It's your turn to cook," Emily said. When school started, they'd agreed to alternate making the evening meal. Since neither of them was any great shakes in the kitchen, dinner was usually simple. Lately Mitch had been thinking it was time for him to branch out, try some recipes from Ellen's collection of cookbooks on the weekends when he had more time. He'd probably never be a gourmet cook, though. He didn't enjoy it that much.

"I was hoping you'd forgotten."

"Hah!"

In the car, Mitch said, "I guess we'd better go to Tahlequah tomorrow after school and get that fabric for your uniforms."

"I can go with Temple Roberts and her mother, if you're going to be busy with the murder investigation."

"You know about that, huh?"

"It was all over school today."

"Of course."

"Do you know who killed Joseph Pigeon?"

"Not yet. Well, are you sure you don't mind going with Mrs. Roberts?"

"No. Temple invited me. I imagine Mrs. Roberts knows how much material to buy and all that."

"You insinuating I don't?"

"Yes."

"Smart mouth."

She giggled, then turned to watch the members of the football team working out in the big field south of the school building.

"When we get home," Mitch said, "you can line up a seamstress. Mrs. Macpherson gave me some names. While you do that, I'll whip up another of my culinary delights."

Emily groaned and turned away from the window with some reluctance, it seemed to Mitch. Did she have her eye on one of the football boys? "Not peanut butter and bacon sandwiches again."

"Nope. Omelets oozing with cheese and ham and green onions. And I bought a cherry pie at the bakery. How does that grab you?"

"Better than peanut butter, but do you realize we've had omelets four times in the past two weeks? Aren't too many eggs bad for you? They're full of cholesterol or something."

"Good point. Tomorrow we start getting serious about what we put into our bodies. You can get some bean sprouts and soybean burger. How about seaweed salad and yogurt for dessert?" He smacked his lip. "Yum yum."

She rolled her brown eyes. "Let's not overdo it, Daddy."

When they opened the front door, the telephone was ringing. "I'll get it!" Emily cried and dashed to answer. "Hi. Oh, hi, Callie. Yes, he's here." Callie Roach. He'd forgotten to return her call. Emily was clearly disappointed as she laid the receiver down. "It's for you."

"You expecting a call?"

"Not really. Kevin Hartsbarger said he might call me about helping with the pom-pom squad's float for the homecoming parade, but he's probably still working out with the team."

Kevin Hartsbarger, eh? Kevin's dad owned the local Mercury-Ford agency. Kevin seemed like a nice enough kid. Last year he'd been one of two sophomore offensive starters on the football team. Mitch felt a frisson of worry as he remembered that Kevin was a junior now, sixteen, and had his own wheels. He caught himself before he could ask Emily more questions. He was going to have to watch himself, or he'd be overprotective. Three years and Emily would be off to college or a job. He'd better start letting go a little at a time so it wouldn't hurt so much all at once.

Life was just one relinquishment after another, he reflected as he went to the telephone.

SEVEN

THE STORM BURST upon Buckskin an hour before dawn. Lightning flashed brilliant bolts across the sky, and thunder cracked and shook the house. Mitch jerked awake and was briefly disoriented. He was tangled in the sheet and wet with sweat. He freed himself and lay listening to the storm.

Slashing rain beat against the windows beside his bed. Water hammering on the roof had a hollow sound. The smells of wet leaves and damp earth permeated the room. When the downpour slacked off, he opened a window and lay exposed to the cool draft. He was wide awake.

He'd told Dr. Sullivan that he was sleeping better, but he still had too many restless nights. Those first couple of weeks when he'd awakened, he had instinctively reached for Ellen and his arm closed on emptiness and reality came rushing back on a wave of desolation. Now his sleeping, as well as his waking, self had accepted that she was gone. He didn't come awake expecting to find her beside him, but he still roused frequently and couldn't get back to sleep. After a few minutes, he knew that this was going to be one of those nights. At least tonight he had something constructive to think about.

Mentally he lined up suspects. It was a thin lineup. An unidentified and possibly nonexistent burglar. What self-respecting thief would hit a place like the Pigeon house? There were whole blocks in town where the pickings in any of the houses would be more profitable. Still, Joe Pigeon's money was gone and the bedroom had been ransacked, Joe's fingers cut off, his wedding ring taken.

So maybe he was looking for a crazy burglar. A druggie? Even Buckskin, population 3,648 at last count, hidden as it was in the hilly remoteness of Cherokee County near an arm of Lake Tenkiller, hadn't escaped illicit drugs. Three high school seniors had been suspended last spring for marijuana in their lockers. College kids brought pot and hash—sometimes even speed and cocaine—back with them when they came home on vacation.

There were a few dealers in town, and where there were dealers there were customers. The upright citizens of Buckskin, probably including Mitch, would be shocked if they knew the identity of every one of those customers. But Mitch didn't think there was anything big going on; all known dealers were small-time hustlers like Jeeter Rheeves, who'd dropped out of OU after a year because the stuff got hold of him and he couldn't leave it alone.

Now Jeeter dealt to keep himself supplied. Mitch had arrested him a couple of times but they had never been able to stick him with anything but possession. Jeeter's father had obtained the services of Jack Derring, probably the wiliest criminal lawyer in northeast Oklahoma, and Jeeter had been back on the street in twenty-four hours. The police kept an eye on Jeeter and the other suspected dealers, hoping they'd lead them to their source eventually. Somebody like Jeeter, zonked out on dope, might decide to commit burglary and blunder into the next house that appeared in his foggy line of vision. Possible. Anything was possible.

What about Mary Pigeon? She leaves her husband on Saturday, after being ignored for months and finally told to get out. Mitch had checked with the county clerk and learned there were no liens on the Pigeon house. Mary must have brooded over how she would manage rent on a waitress's wages. Then sometime Sunday evening, Joe was murdered in a manner that pointed, not to careful premeditation on the part of the killer, but sudden rage. Surely it would take a pretty frenzied state of mind to grab an axe and chop off a man's fingers, then walk off with the fingers and Joe's ring.

Come to think of it, that was a puzzle. Once he'd severed the fingers, why didn't the killer take the ring and leave the fingers? Maybe he'd been so gripped by panic, he still couldn't get the ring off? Or maybe he couldn't get it off because the two fingers were still connected? Mitch pictured the murderer—whose face he couldn't even imagine—running from the Pigeon house clutching Joe's bloody fingers.

The scene made him feel a little sick. It was straight out of one of those teenage horror movies.

It was difficult to picture Mary Pigeon berserk with rage, but it was often the quiet ones who finally exploded. Like that University of Texas sniper a few years back. Such a nice boy, everybody said. Mary's manner yesterday made Mitch sure she was hiding something.

Who else did he have in his lineup? The Nighthawks? Joe's father or brother? Pretty flimsy. If the Nighthawks wanted to visit retribution on one of their own for deserting the society, why had they waited so long? That didn't wash, anyway, because most Cherokees, including the conservative Night-hawks, abhorred murder. There were strong taboos connected with death, whatever the cause. If the killer was a member of the society and had ignored the taboos, he'd acted alone, without the sanction of the group. If he was a member of Joe's family, there must be something more involved than Joe's break with the old ways. Another thing, Mitch couldn't think of any reason why a Nighthawk, Joe's relative or not, would want his wedding ring.

Nothing straightforward about this case. It was going to take a lot of digging. He was accomplishing nothing, but he couldn't stop thinking about the case, and thinking about it made him feel more alive than he had since last winter.

He pulled on a pair of jeans and went to make coffee.

THE CLOUDS HAD begun to disperse as Crying Wolf reached the creek bank. A good omen. Carefully he removed the Venus's-flytrap root, known to the Cherokee as *yu:gwila'*, from its small deerskin bag. The precious inch-long section of root had been in his possession for years, brought back from Qualla, North Carolina, by one of his daughters.

When Crying Wolf had returned to his cabin yesterday, the power of the talisman had been broken by *ul(i)sdu:dhanv:hi*, a Door Closer, because he had been in the vicinity of a corpse. Now he must cleanse the root so that its power would return.

He faced the direction of the rising sun. His empty stomach grumbled, but he kept his mind off food and concentrated on the cleansing ceremony. Nobody had come to his cabin yesterday after Kingfisher Pigeon's visit, but Crying Wolf had kept watch, his mind blank as though his power of thought were suspended. He didn't remember going to bed but he'd awakened there. A sense of lightness and relief had spread through him, like thick sorghum molasses, as he walked to the creek through the rain-cooled early morning, because he was about to dispel the evil that had contaminated his talisman. Once the rain had stopped, the clouds dispersed quickly.

The first faint pink tinge of light rimmed the short line of horizon that he could see through the trees, and he held the *yu:gwila'* in his right hand and chanted in Cherokee:

"Long Man, You have been designated Protector.
You were designated to be cleaning it of the Blue who, bent
     down, is burrowing in and out.
You who were informed, very quickly you have just come
     over here to clean us.
You have just come to put my soul Over There!"

After the recitation, he dipped the talisman into the stream, then blew his breath upon it. He repeated the ritual four times.

The serenity that had left him when he stepped inside Joseph Pigeon's house returned as he walked back to his cabin. He had done all he could to protect himself. Today he would pay a visit to Joseph Pigeon's parents.

THE PIGEON HOUSE had the metallic smell of dried blood. The windows were closed and Mitch left them. He didn't want the atmosphere disturbed by cars passing in the street.

He sat on the worn couch, letting his eyes adjust to the early morning gloom. He had wanted to come back to the house alone before Mary Pigeon returned, in the vague hope that it might give up something. A nuance of feeling, a secret.

He imagined the house cloaked in night, a knock at the door, Joseph Pigeon admitting someone. The visitor was insubstantial, a shadow. He carried something in his hand—a rock or blunt metal object; and when Joe turned his back, the visitor brought the object down on the back of his head. Stunned, Joe fell, and the visitor thrust something at his neck.

Wait. There was something wrong with that scenario. What did the visitor stab Joe with? Was he carrying two weapons? Or did he use the same object he'd used to knock Joe unconscious?

Maybe he dropped the object when he hit Joe, and Joe fell on it. Mitch could think of no object that was sharp enough to slit an artery, yet blunt enough not to break the skin when it hit the back of Joe's head with enough impact to knock him unconscious.

Mitch sighed and rethought the scenario. It might have happened that way, but it could as easily have happened some other way. There were no signs of forced entry. Either the door had been left unlocked or Joe admitted the caller, which probably meant he knew him well. That pointed to a relative or friend, rather than a burglar who'd picked the house at random.

Mitch stood and began slowly and methodically to look through the house. In the bedroom, he picked up the clothes thrown from the dresser, one piece at a time, and returned them to the drawers. There was a bureau in the room, too, but it hadn't been ransacked. Why? Perhaps the killer had run out of time—or he'd found what he was looking for.

He searched the bureau, lifting the contents out one by one and replacing them in the same order. Feminine underwear and a nightgown in one drawer; Mary hadn't taken everything. Or had she known she'd be coming back to stay?

In the bathroom he went through the medicine cabinet. Nothing there but toothpaste, deodorant, aspirin, shaving cream, a razor. And the dirty clothes hamper. Underwear, a few shirts, a cotton dress.

What was it like for you here, Mary Pigeon? Why does it feel as though nobody has lived here for a long time?

He moved on to the kitchen, opened the cabinets, pulled out the drawers. Looked in the refrigerator—a few cans of beer— half gallon of milk, package of cheese slices. Not even enough food for batching. Joe must have been eating out, spending some of that sudden cash. Mitch opened the broom closet door—broom, mop, plastic bucket. And a chain hanging from a nail in the corner with a key on it. He'd noticed the key yesterday, but now he took it down and went out through the back door to the shed. The key fit the padlock. The hinges squawked as he opened the door.

The shed smelled of paint and turpentine. Mitch studied the paintings lined up against the wall. He didn't know much about art, but he liked Joe's paintings. The three completed ones might be worth quite a bit now that the artist was dead. Joe had left his wife a legacy, after all.

Mitch walked to the sleeping bag propped in a corner. He untied it and rolled it out. It was a good one, plenty of padding and double-sized. It smelled musty. When he unzipped it and laid the top layer back, he caught a whiff of something else, too, a floral scent. Perfume.

Mitch closed his eyes to better see Mary Pigeon as he'd seen her yesterday, sitting rigidly straight on the side of the bed in Unit Ten at the Starlight Motel. *Joe and me . . . we haven't had a lot to say to each other lately.* She'd hesitated before she said that, as though choosing her words with care. *He took to sleeping in the shed, and some nights I never knew if he'd been home or not.* Joe had even bought a new sleeping bag and kept it in the shed. Somebody else had been in the sleeping bag, too, a woman, and recently. The scent of perfume still clung to it. From what Mary had said, Mitch didn't think she was the woman who had left the scent there.

He zipped the sleeping bag closed, rerolled and retied it. He locked the shed, returned to the house, left the key where he'd found it, and exited by the front door. He'd been right about Mary withholding information, and now he knew what she was hiding. He wouldn't like confronting her with it or poking around in what little pride and dignity she had left, but he had to do it. Except for that Chevy that Bill Lancaster thought he'd seen, this was the only lead Mitch had. The fact that Mary had concealed it might mean it was too humiliating for her to talk about. Or it might mean she realized the police could look upon it as a motive for murder. Mitch started his car and headed for the station, feeling geared up and energized by what he'd discovered at the Pigeon house. His investigation finally had a direction.

EIGHT

WHEN MITCH REACHED the station at eight-forty-five, a delegation awaited him: Bob Devay, the mayor, and two other members of the city council—George Turnbull, president of the First National Bank, and Jack Derring, the aggressive young criminal lawyer who was making a name for himself in the county. Mitch didn't care for Devay or Derring, but Turnbull was a friend and fishing buddy.

"What's this?" Mitch asked. "Don't you fellows know we can't have a council meeting without a quorum?"

"This is an unofficial call," Turnbull said. He was fifty-one, a tall man with a narrow fringe of hair bordering a shiny, bald pate and gold-rimmed spectacles that Mitch thought gave him a scholarly look. Turnbull's gray eyes behind the spectacles often looked melancholy, and no wonder. The man's wife and daughter had given him plenty of reason to be unhappy. Right now, Turnbull looked merely embarrassed about being in Mitch's office.

Devay grinned. Derring showed no response at all; he had on his courtroom demeanor. The three followed Mitch into his office and Turnbull closed the door behind them. Mitch sat down at his desk and let the three fend for themselves. There were only two other chairs in the office. Devay settled things by hitching his fat rump on the corner of Mitch's desk.

Derring got right to the point. "What do you have on the murder, Chief?" Jack Derring was engaged to Turnbull's daughter, Valerie. For months, Valerie Turnbull had dated both Devay, the mayor, and Derring, the lawyer; but a few months ago she'd accepted a two-carat diamond engagement ring from Derring. Shrewd girl, Valerie. She had hitched her wagon to a rising star. Jack Derring was clever and ambitious enough to end up in the state's attorney general post someday, or even higher.

Mitch leaned back with his hands clasped behind his head. It was a studied attempt to appear at ease, but Derring's question irritated him. He'd known the department would be under pressure to solve the murder fast, but he hadn't expected it to start so soon. "We're following up on a few leads. Nothing concrete yet."

Devay shifted to a more comfortable position on the corner of the desk. As Valerie Turnbull's discarded suitor, he seemed to be bearing up well. Maybe he'd known all along that he was no match for the banker's daughter who, if rumor could be credited, had run mighty wild at Northeastern State.

Devay said heartily, "We were talking at breakfast, and we decided it would be prudent for you to supply the city council with your reports on the investigation, as they're added to the file."

Mitch felt his face heat with sudden anger. So the meeting had started before they got here, he thought. Was it planned or accidental? He sat upright, picked up a ballpoint pen, looked at it for an instant to give himself time to hide his ire, and put it down. "Whose idea was this?" He looked at Turnbull.

The banker didn't answer, but his expression was apologetic. Poor George. Between his wife and his daughter, he hadn't had an easy life. Turnbull hadn't wanted to come there, Mitch was sure. He'd probably been talked into it by Derring, who would soon be a member of Turnbull's family. Turnbull would have wanted to placate Derring, who was doing Turnbull a favor by taking Valerie off his hands.

Derring said, "We all agreed that it's a good idea."

"That's right," Devay put in.

Mitch studied Devay more closely. He was a blond man of about thirty-two, a former OU football player who'd spent one season with a Canadian pro team after college graduation. He'd sustained a knee injury and had come home to recuperate. He'd never returned to pro ball, and Mitch suspected they'd dumped him. The knee injury was a face-saving excuse. Devay had the flab problem common to many ex-athletes—a roll of fat around his middle and a double chin in the making. "You want to run this investigation, Bob? The insurance business a little slow these days?"

Devay laughed. "Don't get your bowels in an uproar, Mitch. Nobody wants to take over your investigation."

"We merely want to be kept up-to-date," Derring added. "After all, the operation of the police department is our responsibility."

Mitch's temper rose another notch. "I was under the impression that's what you hired me for."

Derring glanced at Turnbull. "If you could give us a few encouraging tidbits," Turnbull said placatingly. "We're already getting calls from worried citizens."

Mitch slapped his hands on the arms of his chair. The loud noise startled Devay and he jumped off the desk. "At the moment, I don't have anything to tell you, encouraging or otherwise." Mitch stared at each of them in turn. "I haven't even seen the medical examiner's report yet. Hell, George, you guys get phone calls all the time. I've heard you gripe about it at council meetings."

"This is different," Devay snapped. He was mad at Mitch for making him jump off the desk.

"How?"

"There's been a murder," Derring said. "People are frightened."

"I see." Forcing himself to relax, Mitch leaned back in his chair again and eyed the rangy, red-haired attorney. He took a long look to give himself time to hide how much he resented what they were asking him to do. "It just occurred to me that a lawyer who could get Joe Pigeon's murderer off might merit a lot of publicity. I imagine that's occurred to you, too, hasn't it, Jack?"

Derring's expression didn't change, except for the quick flare of anger in his eyes. "I won't even dignify that remark with a reply. It's just possible, Mitch, that the council might be able to help if we're kept informed."

"If you're worried about leaks..." Devay began. He'd recovered himself and gave Mitch another friendly insurance salesman grin. "We'll make sure the council members understand the reports are confidential."

Mitch stared at Devay, realizing he was perfectly serious. "With seven men on the council? You've got to be kidding.

Somebody'll tell his wife, and the next thing I know the women at the beauty parlor will know more about the case than I do. No way, gentlemen. The council can either trust me to handle the investigation or fire me."

Turnbull glanced at the others uncertainly. "Nobody's doubting your competence, Mitch. I think we've been a bit hasty..."

Derring frowned at Turnbull. Defection in the ranks.

Without giving them time to regroup, Mitch got to his feet. "We have the investigation well in hand. If that should change, I won't hesitate to inform the council."

"That sounds reasonable," the banker said. He rose abruptly and strode to the door. The other two followed him. At the door, Devay paused to say, "I know a bunch about a lot of people. It's the nature of my business. If you need anything—background information or something like that—I'll be glad to cooperate."

Turnbull gave Devay such an icy look that Devay's plastic grin slipped. At the last minute, Turnbull dropped back and said in a low voice, "Sorry, Mitch. This wasn't my idea."

"I know it wasn't, George." Mitch clapped a hand on his shoulder to show there were no hard feelings. "How's Valerie?"

"Oh, she's fine. She went to Tulsa this morning. She's going to stay a few days to shop for her wedding gown and trousseau. They've decided to put off the ceremony until November so Opal can be there." Turnbull's wife, Opal, was in an alcoholic treatment center in Houston. It was the third time for Opal. For George's sake, Mitch hoped the program took this time. "Let's go fishing soon, Mitch," Turnbull suggested.

"Sounds good. Call me."

Turnbull caught up with his companions. Mitch stood at his office door and watched them leave the station. Devay and Derring really rubbed him the wrong way, especially Derring, who didn't seem to care if an accused criminal was guilty or not. All he cared about was a flashy defense and getting the defendant off—on a technicality, if necessary. Mitch conceded that criminals had rights, but he didn't think their fate should be decided on the basis of whether or not they had a hotshot lawyer to defend them.

MITCH CALLED A MEETING in his office that afternoon of all members of the Buckskin Police Department, to review the Pigeon case and bring everybody up-to-date on what everybody else was doing. Virgil had only been on duty half an hour.

Mitch spread the Polaroid shots of the crime scene on his desk and paced while the three officers studied them.

"You told me how you found Joe, Mitch," Virgil said, "but it didn't seem real until now."

"What bothers me," Roo said, "is those missing fingers."

When Roo didn't go on, Mitch gave him an encouraging look.

"I mean, it doesn't seem likely that somebody would do that just for a man's wedding ring. It know it looks like a burglary, but how valuable could Joe's ring be? If the murderer takes it to a pawnshop, he'll get a few dollars and run a big risk of getting caught."

"Maybe the ring had nothing to do with it," Virgil suggested.

Mitch waited. When the silence lengthened he became impatient and started pacing again. "Let's think about that for a minute. I'm having trouble making this a burglary. Except for the money Joe had in his wallet, the house contained nothing of value. And the killer searched only the dresser."

"He could have been looking for something in particular and found it," Roo said.

"Or he might have been trying to make it look like a burglary," Mitch added, "but he didn't have time to do it right."

"If the killer didn't want the ring," Duckworth said, "why'd he cut off Joe's fingers?"

"They could have struggled," Roo suggested. "Joe could have scratched the killer, got blood and skin under his fingernails. He would've known he could be identified by fingernail scrapings."

"Joe scratched the killer with only his ring finger and little finger?" Duckworth snorted. "How could the killer be sure it was only two fingers? Naw, that won't wash."

Roo sank down in his chair and offered nothing more.

Virgil had been listening quietly and now he said, "Joe was a painter. His fingers were the instruments of his trade, like a boxer's fists."

"Yeah," Mitch muttered. "What else?"

"I—uh, it's probably nothing, but . . ."

"Come on, Virgil, what are you thinking?"

"This is farfetched, but what if somebody was envious of the attention Joe'd been getting? Cutting off Joe's fingers is like getting even or something. Like 'I defy you to paint pictures now.'"

"He was already dying from the neck wound," Mitch pointed out. "He wasn't going to paint again, anyway."

"That wouldn't have mattered to the killer if he wanted to make some kind of crazy statement," Virgil said. "He probably wasn't rational."

Mitch nodded.

"That's for sure," Duckworth responded. "I think we've got us a nut case on our hands here. Wonder where Jeeter Rheeves was when Joe was killed?"

Mitch shot Duckworth a sharp look. "Funny you should mention Jeeter. I was thinking about him last night when I couldn't sleep. Maybe we ought to check him out. You want to do it, Duck?"

"Sure."

"Anybody know if Joe had something going on the side?"

Duckworth came to attention. "Another woman?"

"You hear anything?" Mitch asked, knowing that the waitresses at the Three Squares were usually up on the latest gossip. He wasn't ready yet to tell them about the discovery he'd made in Joe's shed. He wanted to talk to Mary first.

"No. If he had something going, he was being mighty discreet about it. It's pretty hard for a married man to get away with that in Buckskin without word getting out."

"Nothing says he couldn't have had a woman someplace else," Virgil observed.

"Want me to ask around?" Roo asked eagerly.

"Okay," Mitch said, "but be careful how you go about it. I don't want any irate citizens in here saying we're accusing them of engaging in extracurricular activities." He turned to Duck-worth. "You get Mary Pigeon's fingerprints?"

Duckworth nodded.

"Virgil," Mitch said, "you call all the pawnshops around here. Tell them to be on the lookout for Joe's ring. Gold band with a diamond in it." He scanned the faces of his officers. "Anybody else got any theories?"

Nobody spoke.

"Okay. Meeting's adjourned. Virgil, would you stay for a minute." When Duckworth and Roo had gone, Mitch closed the office door and took a small tissue-wrapped package from a desk drawer. He opened it and revealed the cigarette stub and burned match he'd picked up in the Pigeons' yard. "Does this mean anything to you?"

Virgil glanced at Mitch, his black eyes perplexed. He bent over for a closer look. "Appears to be an ordinary kitchen match and a homemade cigarette."

"I found them in the Pigeon yard, but Mary doesn't smoke and she says Joe didn't either."

Virgil shrugged. "So they had a visitor who did."

"Yeah, and whoever it was was there late Sunday night or early Monday morning because this stub hasn't been soaked with dew. That means this person could have been there when Joe was killed. It could even mean the cigarette belonged to the killer. You sure nothing came to your mind when you saw that stub?"

"Like what?"

"Medicine."

Virgil's black eyes widened with sudden understanding. "No, that didn't enter my mind, but now that you mention it..." He examined the stub again. "You know I'm not really an au-thority on Cherokee medicine, don't you?"

For an instant, Mitch wondered if Virgil would feel obliged to lie about it, if he were an authority. Any other Nighthawk he questioned would, he felt sure. Mitch was still considered an outsider by many of the full-bloods in Cherokee County. It wasn't his half-breed status that had put a wall between him and them; he'd encountered little racial prejudice among Chero-kees. He was distrusted because he hadn't been raised in the

Cherokee way and therefore couldn't be expected to understand anything having to do with their Indianness. But Virgil
was a friend, and he'd always shot straight with Mitch. "I'm
not trying to get you to break a solemn vow or anything, Virgil. I was just wondering if you think that cigarette was used in
a medicine ceremony."

Virgil stuffed his hands into the pockets of his khaki trousers and considered the question. "Almost anything is possible."

Mitch persisted. "Do you know what kind of ceremony
would be done outside a man's house?"

"Before the tobacco has any power, it has to be remade,"
Virgil said hesitantly.

"That requires a ritual, doesn't it?"

Virgil nodded. "It's usually done at dawn. After it's remade, the tobacco has supernatural powers."

"Go on."

"After it's remade, it's customarily used in one of three ways.
It can be smoked close enough to the person who is its target
that the smoke touches the person. It can be blown toward the
person from a distance. It doesn't even have to be smoked. It
can be placed where the person it's intended for comes into
contact with it. As for why, remade tobacco is used in dozens
of ceremonies. To ensure success with a member of the opposite sex, for protection from bodily harm, to bring peace to a
marriage—"

"Or trouble?"

Virgil paused, then nodded. "I guess so. As I said, I don't
know all the rituals."

Mitch scratched his head. "If you wanted a medicine ceremony performed, who would you go to?"

Virgil's look narrowed. "There are several medicine men
around Buckskin, but I'm sure none of them would be a party
to murder."

"Isn't it possible, though, that one of them has information
that might lead us to the killer? I don't want to put you on the
spot, Virgil, but this is a murder investigation."

"I know—" Virgil sighed "—and I haven't forgotten that I'm an officer sworn to uphold the white man's law. I can't give you a name right now, Mitch, but I'll talk to some people."

Mitch decided Virgil probably wanted to conduct a private investigation of his own among the Nighthawks. If he came up with anything, he'd pass it along to Mitch and Mitch would get a name. "Okay. I'm going over to the Pigeon house in a little while. Mary was supposed to move back in today. She and Joe were separated before Joe died. Did you know that?"

"Yeah, somebody told Trudy."

"By the way, are you and Trudy going to the funeral tomorrow?"

"Yes. Joe's parents are friends of ours."

"I'll see you there then."

Virgil studied him. "I didn't know you were that well acquainted with the Pigeons."

"I'm not. I want to see if anybody arrives in a late seventies model dark-colored Chevrolet."

"Like the one seen at Joe's house Sunday?" A report on the sighting of the Chevy was in the case file, which Virgil had been going through before the briefing session.

"Does it bother you, me trying to conduct police business at the funeral?"

"No. It's probably a good idea to look for the car there. I know the statistics as well as you. Odds are the killer was a relative or close acquaintance of Joe's. The statistics don't change because I happen to know the people involved." Or because the murderer might have been a Nighthawk, Virgil might have added but didn't. "We have to proceed on the assumption that Joe knew his murderer. You want to ride to the church with Trudy and me?"

"No, thanks. I probably won't go on to the graveyard."

"Well, look, why don't you and Emily come over for Sunday dinner?"

Mitch hesitated. "I'd better not make any plans for Emily without consulting her. She might have already made plans. She and Temple Roberts are getting pretty thick. They're both involved with that pom-pom thing. And I think she's infatuated with the Hartsbarger boy."

Virgil laughed at Mitch's expression. "It was bound to happen, Mitch. You're lucky she didn't go crazy over some kid before this."

Mitch smiled crookedly. "I guess."

"She could've gone for somebody a lot worse than Kevin Hartsbarger. Count your blessings, buddy. It won't last, anyway. It never does at that age."

"I need you to keep talking to me like that," Mitch admitted. "Emily has to grow up, and I have to let her."

Virgil nodded agreement. "It gets easier. Well, I'll go make those phone calls," he said as he left Mitch's office.

NINE

MARY PIGEON WAS wearing jeans and an oversized denim shirt that must have belonged to her husband. She had been crying. With sudden insight, Mitch realized that a part of her hadn't really believed Joe was dead until she came back here where they'd lived together. He recalled that it had been the thick silence of his house and the almost suffocating emptiness that had finally forced him to face the reality of Ellen's death, and he pitied this woman.

"Hello, Mary."

Glancing past her, he saw that she'd scrubbed the floor. Only a faint discoloration remained where the blood had been, and there was a strong smell of bleach. It looked as though she'd washed the walls and windows, too. People did funny things after a death in the family, trying to keep reality at bay a little longer. Apparently Mary cleaned house.

"Come in," she said.

Looking into her puffy red eyes, Mitch decided he preferred the calm and stoic Mary he'd talked to at the Starlight Motel. It seemed indecent to pry into the Pigeons' private life now, but a police investigation was an indecent business when you got right down to it.

She turned to precede him into the living room, and he saw her face in profile, a fine straight nose and firm chin above a long, somehow elegant neck. For the first time, he realized that Mary Pigeon might have been called pretty ten years ago. She was still as slender as a girl. Makeup and the right clothes might do wonders yet, had she lived another sort of life. But poverty, hard work, and an indifferent husband had stooped her shoulders and dulled her hair, drawn her face and reduced her outlook to a stoic expectation of continuing bad luck. At one time she might have apologized for her present appearance. Now she didn't bother.

"I could get you something to drink," she offered tentatively. "Tea? Coffee?"

"No, thanks," Mitch said. "There are some more questions I'd like to ask about Joe."

"Well . . . sit down then."

He sat on the couch, she in a chrome kitchen chair that had been moved into the living room since Mitch was last there, perhaps to facilitate mopping the kitchen floor. They sat there in uncomfortable silence as Mitch tried to think of a courteous way to broach the subject of marital infidelity. It was something they would never have conversed about if her husband hadn't been murdered. In fact, they probably wouldn't have said a dozen words to each other in their lifetimes if the crime hadn't occurred. The silence grew oppressive, and they both spoke at once.

"Mary—"

"You told—"

"Sorry," Mitch said. "What were you about to say?"

"You told me to look for anything missing from the house."

"Yes?"

"I thought at first I'd just mislaid them, but I've looked everywhere I can think of and they aren't here."

"What's missing?"

"The hatchet and axe. We always kept them in the broom closet. I—we cut our own wood for heating."

"I sent the axe to Oklahoma City for analysis, but there was no hatchet here when we found Joe. Are you sure you didn't leave it outside somewhere, at the woodpile maybe?"

"No, I looked. It's not on the place."

If she was telling the truth, and Mitch's gut told him she was, the hatchet must have been used to remove Joe's fingers and then taken from the scene by the murderer. If Mary had killed Joe, would she volunteer the information about the missing hatchet? It seemed unlikely, but he wasn't ready to cross Mary off the suspect list yet. Who else did he have?

He sighed, thinking that the lab would probably find no blood traces on the axe. He wondered if Mary realized the significance of the missing hatchet.

"They'll have his hands at his sides," she said, "so the silk coverlet will hide them—at the funeral, you know."

The statement, seemingly unconnected with the subject at hand, made it plain she knew exactly why the hatchet had disappeared. He nodded and cleared his throat. "Mary, I'm sorry to have to ask you this right now, but it's important."

"Yes?" she said and looked past him, then down at her white, water-shriveled hands. Somehow she knew what he was going to say. The knowledge was plain on her face; it turned her eyes to red-rimmed wounds.

He despised himself for having to ask, as she would despise him for leaving her nothing, not even her wretched pride. He remembered the shocking questions people had asked when Ellen died. Did she lose all her hair? Was she in great pain? Had she known him at the end? Damned vultures, he'd thought then, and that was probably what Mary was thinking about him. He clamped down on an impulse to go and leave Mary Pigeon in peace. "Did Joe have another woman?" he asked.

She didn't reply immediately. She simply stared at her hands as though she might find the answer there. Then her chest heaved as she drew in a gulp of air and exhaled it. "Yes."

"Is that why you left him?"

"Yes," she whispered.

"Mary," he said gently, "I have to know who it is. You can see that, can't you?"

She looked up then, her nostrils flaring. "Whoever told you about her must have told you her name. Probably half the people in town know her name by now."

"I don't think so. Nobody told me Joe was fooling around. I figured it out for myself—from Joe's sleeping bag. It smells of perfume."

For an instant she looked as though she were in pain, and then a little spasm of relief lit her blue eyes, as though his words gave her back the hope that nobody else need know, after all. "You think the woman had something to do with Joe getting killed?"

"I don't know. It's possible. It's something I'll have to check out. So if you'll tell me who she is..."

"I can't do that."

"Mary—"

"I can't tell you because I don't know."

"But you said—"

"I said he had a woman. I didn't say I knew who she was."

"Then how do you know there was another woman?"

"How does any wife know? There are always little signs, I guess. I'd suspected for weeks before I finally brought it out in the open."

"What signs?"

"Lipstick on his shirt collar, the smell of perfume on his clothes. Joe getting all slicked up before he went out at night. He hadn't taken so much care in his appearance in years. Some nights he didn't come home at all. Besides, I heard them."

"When?"

"Friday night. They were in the shed. I heard Joe come home about eleven and go into the shed. The hinges are stiff, and they creak when you open or close the door. I didn't think too much of it then. He'd slept in the shed several times lately—even bought that new sleeping bag."

"You didn't go out or call to him?"

"No. I turned over and went to sleep, but after midnight the sound of the shed door woke me again. I thought Joe had decided to come inside. He didn't, though, and I wondered if he was restless, maybe walking around in the yard. This past year, I hardly knew him. We were like two strangers living in the same house. I didn't know what Joe was thinking or where he went when he left the house at night. I tried to tell myself he went to a bar. I knew things couldn't go on indefinitely like that, so I decided to go out and try to talk to him." She stopped, reluctant to finish.

"What happened then?"

She sighed. "When I stepped out the back door, I heard laughter coming from the shed—Joe's voice and a woman's. The sound I'd heard wasn't Joe coming out, it was *her* going in."

"Didn't you think about confronting them?"

She made a bitter sound, a laugh caused by hurt and tension, not amusement. "Oh, I thought about a lot of things. I wanted to throw the shed door open and pour water on them, or shine a flashlight in their faces. Then I was tempted to call the police station and say I'd heard somebody in my shed, so you or your officers would come and surprise Joe and his woman. But I didn't have the nerve, I guess, so I just went back to bed."

He could imagine her standing in the yard in her nightgown and hearing them laughing together. First there would have been shock, then denial, and finally anger and her mind going back over a dozen inexplicable little things she'd noticed in recent months, making them all fit. He would've liked to say something comforting, but he knew there was no comfort in situations like this. So he waited and at length she continued. "I lay there counting up the times Joe had slept in the shed lately and realized it probably wasn't the first time that woman had been in there with him. She left before daylight because I woke up about five-thirty and heard Joe in the kitchen, whistling and making coffee."

"You didn't see anything at all, or recognize her voice?"

"No. The shed was dark." She hesitated and finally added, "The truth is I didn't want to see her. I didn't want to know who she was. And I didn't hear them talking—just laughing, low like people do when . . . Well, you get the picture."

Mitch got the picture, all right. Joe Pigeon couldn't have made his contempt for his wife's feelings any plainer, getting it on with another woman not fifty feet from Mary's bedroom. "When you went outside Friday night, did you see a car?"

"No. I looked out the living room window before I went back to bed, but there wasn't any car. She could've parked it a ways from here, or she could've walked."

Almost any two points in Buckskin were within easy walking distance of each other. If the woman had wanted to keep her affair with Joe Pigeon a secret—from a husband, say—she wouldn't have risked leaving her car parked in the wrong place at night. Even if she was from out of town, she might have parked a block or two from the Pigeon house. "Saturday morning, did you tell Joe what you'd heard?"

"Yes. I had to know how he felt about her, and me. I was willing to try to work things out if he wanted to. He wasn't the first married man to stray from the straight and narrow. But he started hollering at me and I lost my temper. It ended with me packing my bag and him yelling at me to get out."

"Did he say anything, give you any hint, as to who she might be?"

"No." She looked directly into Mitch's eyes with a pathetic kind of defiance. "But he said he loved her, said what they had was more of a marriage than what he had with me. He said she was more of a wife to him than I ever was. Even said he'd never known what real love was before." Her defiance wavered, and she glanced away. "Maybe if Joe and me could've had children . . ."

From the way she said it, he knew her childlessness was painful for her, an old, old regret. She'd exposed her deepest sorrow to him, told him things she would never have told anyone if Joe hadn't been murdered. He felt ashamed. "I'm sorry, Mary."

She shrugged. "Not your fault," she said grudgingly. "These things happen. But if you're wondering, I'll tell you straight out. I might've been upset enough to wish him dead for a minute or two, but I didn't kill him. I didn't have anybody but Joe. If he was alive, at least there might be a chance we could get back together."

All at once, Mary Pigeon's stark, devastating loneliness was a presence in the room. She had no close family and the people who might have been expected to provide comfort—Joe's family—never had accepted her. Without Joe, she was alienated from life. Mitch was luckier. He still had Emily and his friends and his job. "One more thing. Did you and Joe lock your doors at night?"

"Yes, always."

So Joe had admitted his killer. Mitch said, "I'm going now. If you think of anything else later, will you call me?"

She might have nodded; he couldn't be sure. She remained seated as Mitch walked to the door. "If you find out who she is," she said, "I don't want to know, not unless I have to."

If she didn't know the woman's identity, Mitch thought, she couldn't picture them together. He got into his car, thinking that Mary Pigeon would probably never forgive him for making her talk about Joe's lover. He'd have a hard time forgiving himself. But seeing Mary again, listening to her, made him nearly certain she hadn't murdered her husband; and that left him with even less to go on than he'd had an hour ago.

TEN

WEDNESDAY AT NOON, Mitch stopped for lunch at a sandwich and ice cream shop on Sequoyah. All the tables were occupied, and he was debating whether to try elsewhere or order a sandwich to go when a woman at a corner table waved at him. It was Lisa Macpherson. He went over to her table.

"Hi. I thought you teachers ate at school."

She wrinkled her nose. "Usually, but they're having wieners and sauerkraut today and I couldn't face it. Would you like to sit down?"

"Yes, thanks." He pulled out a chair and rested his elbows on the table. She liked bright colors, he thought, remembering the red shirt she'd worn the first time he saw her. Today she had on a yellow dress with lime green beads and earrings. The waitress came and Mitch ordered a chicken salad sandwich and iced tea. Then he said, "Tell me something. How did you happen to end up in Buckskin?"

She put down her half-eaten grilled cheese sandwich and dabbed at her mouth with a paper napkin. "There was an ad in the Kansas City paper—that's where I was living before. I applied, was hired, and here I am."

He chuckled. "Just like that?"

"Exactly like that."

"Does your husband travel, or what?"

She cocked her head to one side. "I don't have a husband. I'm divorced."

That hadn't occurred to Mitch, and he felt like an idiot because it should have. "Sorry."

"No need to be." She ate a potato chip daintily. "I'm not."

"Lisa . . . is it okay if I call you Lisa?"

She nodded, smiling. "And you're Mitch." He must have looked startled because she laughed. "I was curious, so I asked one of the other teachers."

For some reason, Mitch felt pleased. Also faintly flustered because he couldn't think of how to respond.

"Did you find a seamstress?"

She didn't seem to expect any response to her previous remark; he was grateful. "Yes, Emily's all set."

"She'll look great in red. Her coloring's perfect for it, not like poor Temple Roberts, whose hair is going to clash with the uniforms." She studied him for an instant. "Emily's mother wasn't Indian, was she?"

The question wasn't prompted by morbid curiosity, and Mitch didn't mind it. "No."

"I didn't think so. Emily has that ivory complexion with just a hint of tawny undertone. Like some Italians have. It's lovely." She paused. "I don't mean to run on. Am I being too personal?"

"It's all right." Surprisingly, it was.

"Good. I like to know all I can about my students, especially the pom-pom girls, because we'll be spending a lot of time together."

"I understand."

She nodded and let it drop. "Emily says she's learning to cook."

Mitch laughed. "We both are. We had to. Carry-out food all starts to taste the same if you eat it every day."

"Like cardboard, I know. Very salty cardboard. I went through a period, right after my divorce, when it seemed pointless to cook just for myself. One day I was sitting in my kitchen about to eat a burger and fries I'd picked up on the way home, and all at once I couldn't do it. I couldn't swallow the stuff. So I tossed it in the trash and ate half a honeydew melon. Then I pulled out three or four cookbooks and made elaborate menu plans for a week and I went to the supermarket and bought everything I'd need. I stayed up past midnight, baking three kinds of bread. It felt good, like turning a corner and seeing a nice, new neighborhood after walking through a slum."

Mitch liked watching her, listening to her. She was so vibrant and real. He was glad she would be spending time with Emily. Before he could stop himself, he verbalized his next thought. "Your husband was some kind of fool to let you get away."

She flushed prettily. "That's a nice compliment. Thank you."

"You're welcome."

She glanced at her watch. "Oh, gosh, I have to go."

She bent to retrieve her purse from the floor, as the waitress set Mitch's order in front of him. "I'm glad we ran into each other," she said as she rose.

"So am I, Lisa."

She hitched the purse strap over her shoulder. "See you later." As she took a hurried, zigzagging path between tables, Mitch noticed the subtle movement of narrow hips beneath the swirling yellow dress. He looked away guiltily when he realized he was watching her as a man watches a woman who attracts him, and concentrated on his plans for the afternoon, starting with Joe Pigeon's funeral.

THE FUNERAL SERVICE was scheduled for two o'clock in the Indian Baptist Church, a little rural church reached by a long, twisting road—trail really—that wound around the base of Going Snake Mountain, then cut east through dense woods. The trail led past a few small frame houses with garden plots in back, and eventually forked, with the left branch ending a half mile farther along at the Indian church.

Mitch drummed his fingers on the steering wheel and whistled tunelessly between his teeth. He was driving his own car, a four-year-old, cream-colored Buick, and had on a rarely worn gray suit that he'd changed into after lunch. He wasn't looking forward to the next hour; he'd rather spend it almost anywhere else.

He parked in the graveled area beside the church, got out, and circled the cars already there, looking for a Chevrolet that could have been the one seen at the Pigeon house Sunday. There were a few Chevys, but none fit the description given by Bill Lancaster.

Disappointed, Mitch shrugged to settle the suit jacket more comfortably on his shoulders. Although the sun was bright, the intense summer heat seemed to have been broken by the recent rain. That was fortunate, since the church didn't appear to have air-conditioning; the windows were open.

He heard several voices harmonizing on "Rock of Ages," accompanied by a tinny piano. He walked reluctantly toward the church. Pink petunias in clay pots sat on either side of the steps, looking washed and refreshed by Monday night's rain. The building was a white, rectangular affair with a small bell tower, and in spite of the bright petunias he was conscious of an unwillingness to go in. He hadn't been inside a church since Ellen's funeral. Although this country chapel was nothing like the red brick Methodist edifice in town, the atmosphere of solemn gloom was the same. He stifled the impulse to retrace his steps. He was there in his best suit and starched white shirt, so he might as well go through with it.

The quartet was singing the last verse of the hymn as Mitch glanced over the mourners, whose backs were to him. Ceiling fans stirred air around, and the pews were full. Mitch saw a few white people, but most of the group were Indian. The preacher, a middle-aged, heavyset Cherokee, stepped to the pulpit and began to speak in a deep, resonant voice.

Mitch saw Virgil and Trudy seated near the front, behind the large Pigeon family. He saw Mary Pigeon on the front pew beside her mother-in-law. From the side, Mary's face looked pale and drawn, her eyes dry. In contrast, Joe's mother wept audibly. She was a small, retiring woman whose name often appeared in the church news section of the local newspaper. Joe's parents were regular churchgoers, apparently finding no conflict between the Baptist creed and the tenets of the Nighthawk Keetoowahs.

The hulking Kingfisher Pigeon sat in the second pew with his wife and four children. He turned his head to scan the pews behind him and, as his glance took in Mitch, his wife whispered something and he frowned and faced the front.

Mitch finally spotted an empty space in the back pew and slipped into it. Kingfisher shifted and squirmed throughout the minister's remarks, as though he were unaccustomed to being in church. Mitch wondered if the preacher's words about resurrection and eternal life in heavenly mansions aroused Kingfisher's resentment. Perhaps he'd been unable to fuse the old ways with the white man's religion, as so many of his parents' generation had done.

The preacher was long-winded and Mitch was as fidgety as Kingfisher by the time the last prayer was said and the casket opened. He escaped from the building as the last people who shared his pew rose to file past the casket for a last look at Joseph Pigeon. Standing on the front steps of the church, he removed his jacket and pulled out a handkerchief to swipe his sweaty brow. He drew the pure, woodsy-smelling air into lungs that felt deprived, admiring the petunias once more, then wandered back to his car where he could watch unobtrusively as the mourners left the church.

They appeared alone or by twos and threes, and Mitch studied faces. He knew most of them, by name at least. He watched until the family came out of the church, Joe Pigeon's sobbing mother supported on either side by Kingfisher and his father. Then came Kingfisher's wife and sisters and their families and, last of all, Mary Pigeon, still dry-eyed, but dazed-looking, gazing straight ahead with unfocused eyes. If Mitch had hoped to detect a guilty look on any of the faces or overhear an unguarded remark revealing knowledge only the killer could have, he was disappointed. The mourners stood around the churchyard, talking quietly before they dispersed, heading for their cars. Mitch started his Buick and drove away ahead of the others.

Having no desire to take part in the funeral procession to the cemetery in town, he returned to the fork in the road and followed the other branch. The woods on both sides of him became denser, the farther he went. In places, the road cleared between the trees was hardly wide enough for two cars to pass. Fortunately, Mitch didn't meet another car.

He went on because it had occurred to him that someone might have stayed at the elder Pigeons' house, perhaps to prepare a meal, while the family attended the funeral. Maybe if he found somebody there alone, they'd talk to him about Joe.

Occasionally he passed a clearing where a small, unprosperous farm had been established. Joe's parents' farm looked much like the others. A few cars were parked in the yard, but there was no sign of anybody about. The cars' owners must have traveled to the church with other family members.

He parked and scanned the cars, his gaze stopping on a dusty blue 1978 model Chevrolet that sat beside a blackjack tree at a back corner of the house. Mitch uttered a satisfied, "Ah ha," at having found a Chevy that matched the one Bill Lancaster had seen at Joe Pigeon's house Sunday. Chances were at least fifty-fifty it was the same car.

As he got out of the Buick, a dog started barking nearby. Having been badly bitten as a child, Mitch had a healthy respect for hostile dogs. He hesitated, torn between his eagerness to check out the Chevy and caution over the whereabouts of the barking dog. He waited beside his car for it to appear, and when it didn't, he walked far enough to see that the dog— a big, black Heinz 57—was tied by a rope to a tree and mad as hell about it. When he saw Mitch, he lunged in midair to the end of the rope, barking frenziedly until the rope checked his forward momentum and cut off his air. As the dog hacked and made choking sounds, Mitch retreated. Though the dog could no longer see Mitch, the barking resumed as soon as he got his breath back.

The house was closed and silent, but Mitch went up to the front door, anyway, and knocked. He wanted to know if anybody was there before rifling through the Chevy. Nobody came, and he retraced his steps and hurried around to the back.

The Chevy was unlocked, and he slid into the passenger seat and opened the glove compartment. It was jammed with Milky Way wrappers, a worn deck of playing cards, a can of Skoal, a flashlight, three pencil stubs, some melted-together gum drops, and, underneath everything else, the registration papers. The car belonged to Kingfisher Pigeon.

Mitch sat back, staring at the name, as his heart leaped once in recognition of the logic and tidiness of this new development. He no longer doubted that this was the car he sought. Well, well, he observed to himself. Kingfisher, who was supposed to be estranged from his brother, paid a call on Joe the very day he was killed. Mitch gazed through the dirty windshield, trying to keep his elation in check and not jump too quickly to the obvious conclusion. The fact that Kingfisher had been at Joe's house Sunday didn't prove he was the killer. You needed a damned strong motive for murder. Still, Kingfisher was known to have a black temper.

He had to question Kingfisher, but was today the best time? Maybe he should wait until evening when he could probably find Kingfisher at home, and it might be a good idea to take Virgil with him.

Mitch replaced the contents of the glove compartment and climbed out of the car. The dog had stopped barking, and the stillness seemed abnormally quiet by contrast. Mitch stood beside the car, thinking about Kingfisher Pigeon. He knew little about the man personally. Kingfisher farmed a few acres on the other side of Going Snake Mountain, even deeper in the woods than the elder Pigeons' place. Since he was a Nighthawk Keetoowah, Mitch assumed Kingfisher held to the old Cherokee ways, perhaps spoke Cherokee at home so his children would know their native language. Except for the farming he did, Kingfisher was unemployed.

It was possible, Mitch had learned since moving to Cherokee County, for a man to feed his family with only a few acres of anemic farmland. The wife would raise a big vegetable garden and can enough to last all year. They'd have a milk cow or a couple of goats and raise a butcher calf each year. Whatever crop was grown—wheat, corn, maize, soybeans—was sold for a bit of cash. It wasn't much of a living, but people survived all over the world with no more than that.

Mitch was jerked from his reverie by a noise somewhere beyond the house. It sounded like a dry twig snapping beneath a heavy foot. He froze and listened, but he didn't hear the sound again. It was probably nothing but a dead branch falling off a tree. That damned dog had him spooked.

He slammed the car door and stepped away just as the black dog flew around the corner of the house, dragging a two-foot length of rope. Mitch stiffened, paralyzed for an instant, as the dog came after him, teeth snapping. With the desperate thudding of his heart in his ears, a hot surge of fear galvanized Mitch's limbs. He fumbled behind him for the car door; but before he could open it, the dog had buried his teeth in Mitch's ankle and was snarling and trying to shake his head. The pain was excruciating.

Cursing, Mitch kicked with his free foot and landed the toe of his shoe in the dog's rib cage. At the same time, he jerked the car door open and half fell into the seat. But the dog wouldn't let go of his leg, and Mitch came close to fainting from the pain. The dog's low snarling faded as Mitch slipped to the edge of unconsciousness. He shook his head hard and the sound came back.

Cursing and yelling, he tried to pry the dog loose with his free foot, but the beast had a death grip. Flashlight, he thought, and banged the heel of his hand against the glove compartment, popping it open. Grabbing the flashlight, he brought it down on the dog's head with all his might. The dog howled in pain and let go. Mitch was ready. He jerked his injured leg inside and slammed the car door.

Clenching his jaws against the waves of pain, Mitch lifted his torn trouser leg. His sock was soaked with blood. He peeled the sock down and examined the wound. Blood continued to ooze from four punctures at the back of his leg above the ankle. Shaking, he tied his handkerchief around his leg to stanch the bleeding. He let his head fall back against the seat and wished fervently he had his gun so he could kill the dog.

The dog, who had been standing spread-legged, addled and slinging his head around, recovered enough to lunge at the car door. He rammed his nose up to the glass and barked, slinging saliva. Visions of Cujo danced in Mitch's head. He hoped to God the dog had been vaccinated. The rope dangling from his collar was hardly frayed. It would take a lot of force to break a rope that cleanly. That devil had really wanted at him.

More than an hour passed before anybody showed up to rescue Mitch. The dog had finally grown tired of lunging at the car and hoarse from barking. He stretched out beside the car with his head on his paws and watched Mitch.

Mitch tried to nap, but his cramped position and the pain in his leg kept waking him. His wounds stopped bleeding and he loosened the handkerchief and carefully pulled his blood-soaked sock up over it. He heard the cars coming before he saw them—five in all. They stopped in the front yard and numerous dark-clothed, drawn-faced Pigeons got out. Mitch rolled the car window down a couple of inches and hollered, "Hey, somebody get this crazy dog!"

Kingfisher Pigeon, who was a little ahead of the others, threw his head up. He turned to say something to his father, and walked toward the Chevrolet. Other members of the family cast curious glances in Mitch's direction as they straggled into the house.

"You ought to put up a sign to warn people," Mitch yelled as Kingfisher stopped in front of the car and whistled for the dog.

Kingfisher gave Mitch a stolid look and ordered the dog to come. The dog trotted obediently at Kingfisher's heels to an old barn a hundred yards back of the house. Mitch waited until Kingfisher put the dog in the barn, secured the door, and started back before he eased out of the car.

Kingfisher stared at him. It was definitely not a welcoming stare. "How long you been in there?"

"More'n an hour. That dog mangled my ankle. He had a rabies shot this year?"

Kingfisher had to think about it, or pretended he had to. He hunched his massive shoulders and screwed up his eyes. Mitch had a sneaking suspicion he was getting a kick out of his predicament. Finally, Kingfisher said, "Last April or May. Before the hot weather. Dad asked me to come get him and take him to the vet when I took my own dogs."

Thank God, Mitch thought. "That's a dangerous animal. Your father should keep him penned up."

"He wouldn't be much use as a watchdog penned up, would he?" Kingfisher studied Mitch. "He was protecting Dad's property. You're trespassing."

"I'm investigating your brother's murder."

Kingfisher bristled. "Did you expect to pick up clues at the funeral?"

"You never can tell."

"Did you come here when you left the church?"

"Yes."

"What for?" Kingfisher's tone was challenging.

"Just out for a drive. I saw your father's house and decided to see if anybody was here."

"You knew we were all at the graveyard."

Mitch shrugged.

"You think somebody was hiding in that car?"

Mitch ignored the sarcasm. "I have to talk to Joe's relatives sooner or later. I saw the dog tied up and thought it was safe to walk around. He broke loose and was on me before I knew it. If I hadn't managed to get in the car, he'd have killed me."

"You ought to be more careful where you go walking around."

Mitch had a sudden urge to punch Kingfisher's smug, ugly face. "He'll hurt a kid one day, and then your father will have a lawsuit on his hands. Tell him to put up a sign and get a stronger rope."

Kingfisher's upper lip curled contemptuously. He stuffed his big hands into the pockets of his navy polyester trousers. The pants were shiny at the knees. "I know you got no respect for my people." He wasn't referring to his family. Kingfisher meant the Cherokee. They were "my" people, not "ours." Mitch was still an outsider and always would be to a certain type of full-blood, like Kingfisher Pigeon. "But I can't believe even you mean to talk to my folks on the day of their son's funeral."

"Joe was *murdered*." Mitch realized he was repeating himself in an effort to break through Kingfisher's tough exterior, and having no luck.

"They don't know anything about that."

Mitch leaned his weight against the car, heedless of the dust that was being ground into his clean shirt. His trousers were probably beyond repair, anyway. Might as well finish off the shirt, too. Since he'd stepped out of the car, his left leg had started to throb with a rhythm roughly approximating the speed and intensity of a jungle drum. Shifting his weight off that leg helped a little. "Right now I'd rather talk to you, Kingfisher."

It was impossible to guess what the big man's reaction was. His eyes were black and impenetrable.

"I hear you and your brother didn't get along."

Kingfisher lifted his broad shoulders and scowled. "Ain't no secret about that."

"What caused the trouble between you?"

"Family disagreement."

"Over Joe leaving the Nighthawks?"

Kingfisher's look reminded Mitch that little more than a hundred years ago Kingfisher's forebears—and some of Mitch's, too—had been painted savages brandishing war clubs, with scalps dangling from their lances. He had a feeling that, with Kingfisher, the flimsiest veneer separated the man from his ancestors. Mitch wouldn't want to meet up with this one in the woods on a dark night. Kingfisher was silent for so long, Mitch thought he would refuse to answer.

Finally he mumbled, "Joe quit the Nighthawks, sure, but that wasn't all. It was his whole attitude. That year at college ruined him. Thought he was shit on a stick. Those teachers over there filled him so full of bull, he had delusions of grandeur. He really thought—" Kingfisher broke off as though suddenly realizing he was saying too much. "Hell," he continued, "I don't know why I was surprised. He ignored everybody's advice when he married that woman he found in a bar over in Muskogee. College just put the finishing touches on Joe. He came back a paleface, like some others I could mention."

MITCH RETURNED KINGFISHER'S glare. "Your car was seen at Joe's house Sunday evening."

"Don't mean I killed him." This was said in a tone that dared Mitch to prove otherwise.

He wasn't even going to try denying he was there, Mitch realized. That rather surprised him. "If you didn't kill him, you may have been the last person to see him alive except for the murderer. You have to admit it looks odd, Kingfisher. You and Joe haven't spoken for months, then the day of his death you go to see him. Why?"

"It grieved my mother, Joe not having anything to do with the rest of us. I went to talk to him, to see if we couldn't smooth over some of the hard feelings. For myself, I didn't give a damn, but Mom was always fretting about the family being divided. I thought maybe we could tolerate each other a couple times a year, for Mom's sake."

The words were too glib, as though they'd been rehearsed. He's lying through his teeth, Mitch thought. The role of concerned son and family mediator didn't suit him, in the first place. Kingfisher's attempt to mend his fences with his brother and Joe's being killed the same day was simply too much coincidence to swallow. "Did Joe agree with you?"

"Said he'd think about it." Kingfisher made a sound in his throat similar to the watchdog's growl. "Like he was doing me a big favor."

"What'd you say to that?"

"Nothin'. He started bragging how he was gonna get rich and famous off his paintings. Leave Buckskin. Go where artists were appreciated. Crap like that. It really hacked me. I told him not to bust a gut being accommodating and left."

Mitch was pretty sure that wasn't all that had passed between the brothers, but he couldn't prove it, not yet. Kingfisher Pigeon could stand there and lie all day and all night, and take pleasure in doing it. Mitch tried to imagine him getting rattled and contradicting himself; he couldn't. No, he'd only go in the house and slam the door in Mitch's face when he decided he didn't want to talk anymore. Probably turn that dog loose again. Mitch's leg was throbbing all the way to his knee now.

"Did you know Mary had left Joe?"

Kingfisher's eyes narrowed. "Yeah, he told me. He didn't seem too broke up about it. Never should've married her in the first place."

"Because she was white?"

"That wasn't the problem. She didn't fit in." His tone told Mitch that Mary Pigeon wasn't the only one around there who didn't fit in. "When they were first married, Joe'd bring her out here for family gatherings. She'd sit in a corner for hours. Every once in a while, her nose would twitch, like a scared rabbit. Acted like she was afraid somebody was goin' to scalp her or feed her dog stew or something. Take today, when the family left the graveyard. I know Mom tried to get Mary to come back here and eat with us, but you notice she ain't here." His square jaw hardened in resentment. "People should stick to their own kind. I tried to tell him, but you never could tell Joe nothin'."

Mitch had to get off his throbbing leg. He wasn't making any headway with Kingfisher, anyway. He'd try again later. Maybe catch his wife alone, out on that little hardscrabble farm where they lived, see what he could learn from her. "One more thing. Did Joe mention the new love in his life?"

The question seemed to demand caution of Kingfisher. "What d'ya mean?"

"Mary says he had another woman."

He hesitated too long. "He didn't say nothing to me. I hope you ain't gonna mention that to my folks. They got enough on their minds, already."

"You have any idea who might have wanted to kill Joe?"

"Wouldn't surprise me none if his wife did it because she found out about the other woman. You checked her out?"

"I'm working on it. Anybody else?"

He shrugged. "Probably a lot of people won't miss him all that much. The cocky SOB never did care for nobody but himself."

Mitch tried to read something more than contempt in Kingfisher's impassive black eyes, but he couldn't. Grimacing, he hobbled toward the front of the house. Kingfisher followed him to the car. The late afternoon sun was hidden behind the trees, and a cool breeze ruffled the leaves of a cottonwood tree, sounding like the patter of rain. "I'll leave you to your grieving, Kingfisher."

Kingfisher grunted as though he found the jibe faintly amusing and watched Mitch climb carefully into his car. He stood in the road, keeping vigil, until Mitch followed a bend in the road and was out of sight.

Sharp pains shot up Mitch's leg. He gritted his teeth and thought: If I ever get the chance, I'll splatter that dog's brains all over Going Snake Mountain.

He thought about the noise he'd heard just before the dog came after him. It had sounded like somebody stepping on a dead twig. He thought about the rope being severed so cleanly, almost as though it had been cut with a knife. He remembered something else, too. He hadn't actually seen Kingfisher get out

of one of the family cars that had returned from the graveyard. He had only seen him walking toward him from the front
of the house. Had Kingfisher come out of the church, noticed
Mitch driving away, and walked back to the house by a short-
cut through the woods while the others went on to the cemetery? He could have circled around the house through the
woods and cut the dog loose. He could have been out there all
the time Mitch was trapped in the car, watching and waiting
until the others returned.

Mitch didn't like Kingfisher, and he didn't trust him.
Thinking about Kingfisher setting that dog on him made him
so angry he hardly noticed his pain for a few moments.

"If you killed Joe," he muttered, "I'll nail you if it's the last
thing I ever do."

ELEVEN

A NIGHT'S SLEEP—interrupted several times by the throbbing of his leg—did nothing to lessen Mitch's suspicions concerning Kingfisher Pigeon. He left his house, wondering how he could pry information from the closed-mouthed full-bloods who were Kingfisher's relatives and friends.

The morning was pleasantly cool, but the temperature was predicted to climb into the eighties by midafternoon. After the August they'd had, the eighties sounded pretty good.

The *Banner* came out on Thursdays. Mitch digested it at his desk with his second cup of coffee and then threw the paper against the wall.

He limped to the coffeepot to refill his cup. Virgil was on the telephone at the duty desk. His shift had ended at midnight, as usual, but he had come back this morning to finish the calls to area pawnshops. Mitch had told him briefly what had happened at the Pigeon farm. Like Mitch, Virgil thought Kingfisher was capable of murder, if somebody made him angry enough.

Mitch glanced at Helen, who was absorbed in the story of Joe Pigeon's murder that claimed half of the *Banner*'s front page.

"Joe would have enjoyed the publicity," Helen mused, without looking up from her paper.

Mitch muttered, "Some people will do anything for attention."

Helen turned to look at him. "Grumpy this morning, aren't we?" When Mitch didn't respond, she went back to reading the article that had prompted Mitch to throw the newspaper at the wall.

The article extolled Pigeon's artistic accomplishments in detail—the honors won in high school, the Northeastern scholarship, the Gilcrease show. The high school art teacher was quoted regarding the tragic loss of a promising talent poised on the very brink of fame and fortune. Mitch wondered if Joe might not be more successful dead than if he'd lived to a ripe old age.

The article didn't mention the police until near the end, when the editor made it sound as though the department was less than competent. "When interviewed," Harrington had written, "Chief of Police Mitchell Bushyhead indicated that his three-day-old investigation had not turned up a single lead thus far." What Mitch had said was, "No comment," but Harrington was getting back at him for refusing to be interviewed.

Helen finished reading the article. "Harrington's got his stinger out for you, Mitch."

"He'll have to stand in line. I've got worse things to worry about than the likes of Harrington."

Duckworth and Roo came into the station. As usual, Duck was razzing Roo, who was walking with extreme care, like a man treading on crushed glass in his house slippers. "You been getting too much of that bedroom exercise, Roo," Duckworth observed with a cackle.

"I told you I hurt my back helping my brother-in-law move a piano," Roo protested.

Duckworth wagged his head. "My old man always told me a man has only so much joy juice in him. You use it all up in your twenties, you're gonna be one depressed dude the rest of your life."

Roo's freckled face flamed. "You're disgusting."

"He doesn't know any better, Roo. He's got no class," Helen put in before turning back to her desk.

Unruffled, Duckworth went on, "How long you gonna plow that field before you buy it, anyway?"

"Duck . . . Roo," Mitch interrupted. "Come into my office." He glanced at Virgil, who was still on the telephone, and gestured for him to join them when he'd finished his call.

"Roo hurt himself moving his organ, Chief."

"Piano, dammit!"

"He's got a catch in his getalong, or should I say his get-it-on." Duckworth clapped his leg and roared.

Mitch sighed and limped back to his desk. "Give it a rest, Duck."

"Yeah, grow up," Roo said.

Duckworth's attention had been diverted. "What's wrong with your leg, Chief?"

"Ankle's swollen," Mitch mumbled. "Nothing serious." He had no intention of telling those two how he'd received the injury. Yesterday afternoon, Doc Sullivan had cleaned and dressed the wound after giving Mitch a tetanus shot and warned him to stay off his feet as much as possible for a few days. Unwilling to trust Kingfisher Pigeon's word, Mitch had checked with the local veterinarian and been assured that Mr. Pigeon's dog, Scout, had indeed been vaccinated against rabies last April. The dog wasn't rabid, merely mean.

Virgil came in, bringing a chair with him. "The medical examiner's report arrived in the morning's mail," Mitch said as the four men settled into chairs. He removed the report from the case file folder on his desk and glanced over it again. "Pigeon died between nine P.M. Sunday and one A.M. Monday morning. He was struck on the back of the head and rendered unconscious before the neck wound was inflicted." He looked up. "Probably only seconds before. The wound was made by something less efficient than a knife. Beyond that, the M.E. didn't speculate on the weapon. Pigeon bled to death in two to three minutes. All the blood on the body was his and there was nothing under his fingernails but paint. No alcohol or drugs found in his system."

"Sounds like the stabbing was unplanned," Virgil observed. "If the killer had gone there with the intention of stabbing Joe, he'd have had a knife."

"Maybe he didn't mean to kill him at all," Duckworth added, "but things got out of hand."

"The Chevy seen at the Pigeon house Sunday evening belongs to Kingfisher Pigeon," Mitch said. "Kingfisher admits being there but claims Joe was alive when he left."

Duckworth whistled. "No kidding!"

"That neighbor saw the Chevy there about seven," Roo said, "but it wasn't there at eight-thirty when he drove by the Pigeon house. If Kingfisher did it, he went back a second time, but we didn't find anyone who saw the Chevy there later.''

''If he went back to kill Joe,'' Duckworth said, ''he probably left his car in the woods.''

''Was Kingfisher at the graveyard yesterday, Virgil?'' Mitch asked. Although Mitch had confided in Virgil that he'd been attacked by the Pigeons' dog, he hadn't yet mentioned to Virgil his suspicion that Kingfisher turned the dog loose. After thinking about it more, it did sound pretty farfetched.

''His wife and kids were there, but we didn't see Kingfisher,'' Virgil replied. He exchanged a thoughtful glance with Mitch, and Mitch decided his suspicion wasn't so farfetched, after all. ''Trudy commented that nobody seemed to know where he was. It's possible he wanted to be alone and stayed at the church rather than go with the family to the gravesite. Can't think of anywhere else he might have gone—'' His eyes widened. ''Unless he went back to his folks' house.''

''Yeah,'' Mitch responded, knowing that Virgil was now asking himself the same thing Mitch had been asking: Had Kingfisher gone back to turn the dog loose on Mitch? ''What about the pawnshops?''

''Nothing yet,'' Virgil said. ''I'm still waiting to hear from some of them. I left word for the owners to call.''

Mitch leafed through the papers in the case file until he found the report he wanted. ''Duck, it says here all the clear prints you found in the Pigeon house checked out as Joe's or Mary's. You went over the entire house?''

''Yep. There were smudged prints everywhere, but the ones that could be identified all belonged to the Pigeons.''

''I've been asking around town about Joe and another woman,'' Roo put in. ''So far, zilch. The bartender at Chick's, where Joe hung out, says he never saw Joe in the bar with a woman.''

''Duck, did you run down Jeeter?''

''I found him out at the lake. He's living in the woods like an animal.''

''His old man must have kicked him out again,'' Virgil commented. ''He'll probably let him come back for the winter, he always does.''

"He was stoned out of his gourd," Duckworth went on. "Tongue as thick as a rump roast. I don't think he even knew what country he was in, much less where he was last Sunday night. I didn't get a sensible word out of him."

The dispatcher appeared in the office doorway. "Virgil, there's a call for you on line one."

"Thanks, Helen." Virgil reached for the phone on Mitch's desk and pulled it closer. "This is Virgil Rabbit. Yes, sir. Yes, that's right. Did you get his name? What'd he look like? Uh-huh...uh-huh. Yeah, probably today. Thank you very much." Virgil replaced the receiver. "Bingo." He looked around the room with a grin.

"What?" Mitch prodded.

"That was the owner of the Jewel Pawnshop in Tahlequah. Monday afternoon a guy came in and hocked a man's wedding ring that sounds an awful lot like Joe Pigeon's. He didn't get the guy's name, but listen to this. He was about five-ten, skinny, greasy brown hair to his shoulders, wearing dirty jeans with holes in the knees. The guy didn't smell any too good and acted, and I quote, 'nervous and real weird.'"

Mitch, Duckworth, and Roo said in unison, "Jeeter Rheeves."

Mitch stood. "I know you're supposed to be off-duty, Virgil, but would you mind driving to Tahlequah to pick up that ring?"

"I'm on my way," said Virgil, scooting for the door. "I'll take it by for Mary Pigeon to identify when I get back."

Mitch wasn't even going to think about what they'd do next if Mary said the ring wasn't Joe's. "Roo, you man the duty desk." Seeing Roo's face fall, Mitch added, "Give your back a rest." Then he turned to Duck, "Come on. We'll go see if Jeeter's sobered up yet."

"How can you tell?" asked Duck, as he lumbered beside the limping Mitch to the car.

Good question. Jeeter had fried so many brain cells that, even when he wasn't under the influence, he didn't necessarily behave like a normal person.

Recalling Doc Sullivan's advice to stay off his foot, Mitch decided to take more aspirin instead and got two tablets from the bottle in the glove compartment, swallowing them without water and grimacing at the taste.

It took a half hour to reach Lake Tenkiller and find Jeeter's campsite. Duckworth thought he could go straight to the camp, using the big cedar tree he'd noticed the first time he was there to guide him. But the woods were full of cedar trees and Duckworth picked out three of them before he got the right one.

Jeeter wasn't around. They searched the tattered tent, which took about a minute since it contained only a few pieces of dirty clothing, some cans of beans, and a canteen of water. The odor inside the tent was rank, so they sat down to wait on a fallen log. Over an hour later Jeeter wandered into camp, holding his head in both hands as though it might fall off if he let go, and muttering curses.

He shuffled past Mitch and Duckworth, stopped beside the tent, and turned around before he realized he had company. He lifted his head carefully as they rose from the log. He focused on Duckworth. "Oh, man, you hanging around here again?"

"You really remember the last time, Jeeter? Geez, I'm touched."

"I ain't gonna remember when the cops come hassling me?" Jeeter whined. "Come on, man, you jiving me." He closed his eyes and groaned. "Shit, my head's gonna split right in two. You got any aspirin on you?"

"Just happen to have some in the car," Mitch said. "Go get the aspirin for Jeeter, Duck."

Not wanting to miss anything, Duckworth scowled his displeasure, but he went after the aspirin bottle. Jeeter sank down on the ground and held his head again.

"A man in Tahlequah says you hocked a ring at his pawnshop last Monday, Jeeter," Mitch said.

"Wh—what?" Jeeter dragged his eyes open and squinted at Mitch. "It's against the law to hock a ring? Hell, what next."

"If the ring doesn't belong to you, it's against the law."

Duckworth came crashing back with the aspirin. Mitch poured three tablets into Jeeter's hand, and Jeeter fumbled behind him in the tent, found the canteen, and washed them down. He wiped his mouth with his dirty sleeve, frowning as though trying to get his thoughts in some order he could rec-

ognize. "I don't know nothing about no ring," he announced
finally.

"Where were you Sunday night?" Mitch asked.

"Here, I guess. What's today?"

"Thursday."

"And you expect me to know where I was Sunday? How'm
I supposed to remember what happened that long ago?"

"Come on, Jeeter, maybe your memory will improve at the
station." Mitch bent over and took Jeeter's right arm. Duckworth grabbed the other arm and they pulled him to his feet.

"Watch it, pigs," Jeeter wailed, "you're making my head
hurt. You bust a blood vessel, and I sue you!"

"You got us shaking in our boots, scumbag," Duckworth
said.

"You can't take me in! I ain't done nothing!"

"We'll talk about it when you're feeling better," Mitch said.

"No way! Oh, man . . ."

Mitch and Duckworth resorted to dragging Jeeter to the car.
He stumbled between them, cursing rhythmically with each
step.

By the time they reached the station, Jeeter had forgotten his
headache and was demanding to see his lawyer, Jack Derring.
Mitch pointed to the phone on the duty desk and Jeeter dialed
Derring's office. "He's out of town today," he said, hanging
up and looking truly panicked for the first time.

"We'll have to wait for him to get back, I guess," Mitch observed, "unless, of course, you'd like to cooperate with us by
answering a few questions now—since you say you've got
nothing to hide."

Jeeter shook his head, his eyes darting around the room
anxiously.

Sighing, Mitch put him in a cell and went to his office to prop
his throbbing ankle on the desk.

Virgil returned at noon. "It's Joe's, all right," Virgil said,
dropping the ring on Mitch's desk. "Mary identified it." It was
obvious Virgil was pleased with the morning's work. He wanted
Jeeter to be the murderer. He wasn't fond of Kingfisher Pigeon, but Kingfisher was a Nighthawk and Virgil was worried
that if Kingfisher was found guilty of murder it would reflect

on the society. Well, Mitch also wouldn't lose any sleep if it turned out to be Jeeter. Kingfisher was his least-favorite person at the moment, but the man had a wife and four kids to support. Jeeter, on the other hand, was not exactly a contributing member of the community. Either way, Mitch wished he could get the case wrapped up before the city council really started applying pressure.

"Good work, Virgil," Mitch said. "Go home and get some sleep. We'll probably have to wait until tomorrow to question Jeeter. His lawyer's out of town."

At two-thirty, Jeeter sent word to Mitch that he had reconsidered and was ready to talk. When Roo brought him into Mitch's office, Mitch saw why. Jeeter was twitching with the need for a fix.

"Sit down, Jeeter," he said.

Jeeter lit on the edge of a chair, but seemed poised to take flight any minute. He was wound up as tight as an eight-day clock. Mitch read Jeeter his rights, adding, "Do you understand?"

"Yeah, man, I ain't stupid. Let's get this over with."

"Okay, Jeeter, where were you on Sunday night between nine and one A.M.?"

"I already told you. I was out at the lake. I always go to bed early." He was gazing at the ceiling. Mitch wondered what he saw up there besides the cracks.

"What about Monday afternoon? That man in Tahlequah swears you were in his pawnshop Monday hocking this ring." Mitch held up Joe's wedding ring.

Jeeter didn't even look at the ring. "I don't know nothing about that. How many times I have to tell you?"

"We can put you back in the cell and get the guy over here to identify you if we have to. Of course, he probably won't be able to make it until tomorrow or the next day."

Jeeter looked around the room. Roo was leaning against the wall, taking notes. Seeing no help from that quarter, Jeeter muttered, "Well, what if I did hock a ring? You can't keep me locked up for that."

"Where did you get the ring, Jeeter?"

"I found it out at the lake."

"When?"

Jeeter scrunched up his eyes. "That same morning. Monday."

"Did you know Joe Pigeon was murdered Sunday night?"

It took a moment for it to register, and then Jeeter's eyes bulged. "Is that why you keep asking where I was Sunday night? Oh, no—no, man, you ain't pinning that on me. I don't know nothing about no murder."

"A minute ago, you said you knew nothing about the ring. Now you've changed your story." Mitch dropped the ring on his desk. "This ring belonged to Joe Pigeon, Jeeter. You admit you hocked it Monday. You really expect us to believe you found it?"

"I did find it! I know I should've turned it in to the police, but I needed money, so I hitched a ride to Tahlequah and hocked it."

"Who with?"

"Huh? Oh, you mean who picked me up? I don't know. I think he said he was from New Mexico or Arizona."

Mitch leaned back in his chair. "He's long gone by now, huh, Jeeter? No way to track him down. So, you just stumbled onto that ring by accident. Is that what you're saying?"

"Uh, not exactly. See, Sunday night I heard a car. It woke me up. It sounded real close, so I got up and went out of the woods to see if it was . . . uh, anybody I knew."

"Like a drug buyer?"

"I never said that! I got friends. I thought it might be one of them. Anyway, I saw a car parked below the levee. The driver walked up on the levee and threw something in the lake. Then he got back in the car and drove away. The next morning, I went down to the lake and looked around. That's when I found the ring. You couldn't miss it. The sun was reflecting off it. It was right at the water's edge."

"Can you describe this car and driver who so conveniently woke you?" Mitch asked wearily.

"I . . . I can't remember. It was dark."

"You said 'he.' Are you sure it was a man?"

"It looked like a man but, like I said, it was dark. It could have been a woman wearing pants, I guess."

"And the car?"

"Don't know. I was watching the guy."

With someone like Jeeter, you never knew when he was lying and when he was telling the truth. The line between the two was so dim in Jeeter's own mind, he probably didn't know half the time himself. Mitch felt another suspect slipping through his fingers and resolved, Not this time, not if I can help it. "Are you willing to show us where the car was when you saw it?"

Jeeter jumped up eagerly. "Yeah, you can take me out there right now."

Mitch swung his feet to the floor and the pain stabbed his left ankle. "Come on, then," he growled. "You, too, Roo. Let's get on with it."

Jeeter, seated next to Mitch in the front seat of the car, fidgeted and sniffed all the way to the lake.

Mitch glared at him. "Can't you sit still?"

"Cops make me nervous," Jeeter explained ingenuously.

Mitch drove to the levee and they got out. Jeeter went close to the edge where the rocky bank sloped down to the lake twenty-five feet below. "He stood right here," Jeeter said, "and swung his arm out like this." Jeeter demonstrated. "The first time he swung it way out, the second time not so hard."

Mitch glanced at the tall light poles on either end of the levee, then looked away from the lake toward the woods. "Where were you?"

"Right over there." Jeeter pointed. "See that gap in the trees? I was standing right there."

If Jeeter was telling the truth, he had been less than fifty yards from where they were standing, and at night those big light bulbs would have been on. "I don't know what to think, Jeeter," Mitch said. "This guy was standing between those lights, yet you claim you didn't get a good look at him."

"It's the honest-to-God truth, man! I must have been half asleep or something. I couldn't see good."

Something nagged at the back of Mitch's mind, but it eluded him. He walked down off the levee and went to stand where Jeeter said he'd stood Sunday night. He could easily identify Roo and Jeeter from there. It would be harder at night, but with the lights.... He started back toward the levee. Something Jeeter had said continued to bother him.

The first time he swung it way out, the second time not so hard.

"Jeeter, tell me again exactly what you saw."

Agitated, Jeeter paced back and forth on the levee. "He got out of the car and walked up here. He stood right there, right on the edge. He swung his arm out in a big arc, like he was throwing in something heavy. He put his arm down for a second, and then he threw his arm out again."

There it was, the thing that had slipped by Mitch before. "You didn't see what he threw in?"

"No, but you say it was that ring I found the next morning. You expect me to see a little ring that far away at night?"

"You saw him throw twice? You're sure?"

"I know it sounds crazy, but that's what I saw. Wait a minute. He didn't have to be throwing in something heavy, like I thought. Maybe he was just making sure it went a long ways out before it dropped into the lake. Maybe there were two rings. The other one's probably still out there."

It wasn't much. Maybe nothing, but it nagged. Also, it let Jeeter off the hook, for now. "I guess you can go on back to your camp, Jeeter." Jeeter gaped at him, then scuttled down off the levee and ran for the woods before Mitch could change his mind.

Roo was incredulous. "Why'd you let him go? You know he'd lie to God on Judgment Day."

Mitch limped along the levee. Roo followed, walking stiffly with one hand on the small of his back. "I think he's telling the truth," Mitch said. "You heard what he said about two things being thrown into the lake. About the only way I can make it fit is that the first one, the one Jeeter said could have been heavy, was the hatchet that's missing from the Pigeon house."

"Could be," Roo agreed, "and the second time, he threw the ring."

"Jeeter couldn't know about the hatchet, so why would he say the guy threw twice if he didn't see it?"

"He'd know about the hatchet if he killed Joe."

Mitch shook his head. "I don't think so. If he's the killer, he wouldn't let on that he knew two things were thrown into the lake. Jeeter may be nuts, but he's not stupid, especially when it comes to saving his own hide."

"What about Joe's fingers?"

"Yeah, I'm wondering that myself."

"Do you think Jeeter really didn't see whoever it was well enough to identify him—or at least describe him?"

"I don't know. He could be saying that because he doesn't want to get involved. Or he could have taken something that dilated his eyes so he couldn't focus."

Roo took a step toward the rim of the levee, grabbed his back with one hand, and grunted.

Mitch made a humorless sound. "Talk about the halt leading the blind. Neither one of us is in any shape to climb down there. I'll send Duck back to look around. But the lake drops off fast here. Twenty feet out it's forty or fifty feet deep." Mitch halted. "Hey, Virgil's oldest boy took diving lessons last summer."

"Yeah, and I'll bet the kid would be thrilled to help in a police investigation."

Maybe they'd get lucky and find the hatchet. They might even find the fingers. The ring must have been separated from them when they were thrown into the water. The killer had evidently driven straight to the lake, after murdering Joe, to dispose of the evidence that would incriminate him if found in his possession. Another nagging question: If the killer hadn't cut off Joe's fingers because he wanted the wedding ring, then why had he done something so bizarre?

They returned to the car. Mitch sighed. "Well, I had serious doubts all along about Jeeter being the killer. Can you picture Joe letting Jeeter in his house, much less turning his back on him?"

Roo admitted that he couldn't picture it. They drove back to town in morose silence.

JACK DERRING INTERCEPTED Mitch on the sidewalk later that afternoon as he was leaving the station. "My secretary says I had a call from Jeeter Rheeves this morning. Jeeter wanted me to come to the station as soon as I got back. What are you holding him for this time?''

As usual, Derring's accusing manner irritated Mitch. "You're too late, Jack. Jeeter decided to cooperate with us, and we let him go.''

"Then you had nothing to hold him on in the first place,'' Derring shot back. "I'm getting hacked at you people harassing my client every time the law's broken in Buckskin.''

Mitch was just too tired for Derring's crap. "He wanted out of jail so he could get some dope. I read him his rights, and he said he understood. He ought to, as often as he's had 'em read to him. Your client hocked Joe Pigeon's wedding ring in Tahlequah Monday afternoon. He claims he saw somebody throw it into the lake Sunday night but he says he doesn't know who it was. Now, Derring, this person, if he exists, was standing on the levee between two big lights. I think Jeeter knows who it was.'' He planted a finger in the middle of Derring's chest. "You can advice your client that as long as he's withholding evidence, he's going to see a lot more of us.'' It wouldn't hurt to shake up Jeeter, in case he knew something else. Pushing Derring a little was just an added bonus.

Derring brushed Mitch's hand away. "You shouldn't have questioned him in my absence,'' he fumed. "You took advantage of his illness. I may advise him to bring charges against the police department for harassment.''

"Oh, hell, Derring, tell it to the judge.'' Mitch walked away, leaving the lawyer standing on the sidewalk. As he drove off, he looked back to see Derring staring after him with a look of mingled anger and speculation. *Bushyhead's desperate*, he was probably thinking, *he has no leads so he's picking on poor Jeeter*.

Well, he'd like to see Derring and the other members of the city council do any better. He'd made *some* progress. *Sure* he had. He'd pretty well satisfied himself that neither Mary Pigeon nor Jeeter Rheeves was the murderer. The council wasn't likely to give him a medal for that, though. Besides Derring, he'd run into almost all of them this week and each time he'd felt he was being weighed and found wanting. It was unreasonable, but the council members tended to crumple under any criticism from the townspeople. For the first time in his life, Mitch thought he could be in danger of losing his job, if he didn't solve this case. A few months ago, he wouldn't have cared except for how it would affect Emily. Now he found he cared very much. His professional pride was involved.

Kingfisher Pigeon remained the prime suspect. Maybe he should question Kingfisher again tomorrow. No, better to wait another day or two, give him time to work up a sweat over how much Mitch knew. A little war on Kingfisher's nerves. He almost laughed aloud. What nerves?

TWELVE

FRIDAY NIGHT. A snap of autumn chill in the air. Enticing smells of popcorn and hot dogs. Excitement in the stands. The Buckskin Bears were about to play their arch rivals, the Warriors, in the first football game of the season.

Mitch arrived as the opposing team kicked off. The home-side bleachers were crowded. Mitch squeezed in on the end of a row behind the pep squad. The pom-pom girls were directly below him.

"Daddy!"

Emily waved a red-and-gold pom-pom over her head. Mitch winked at her and thought proudly, She's the prettiest girl on the squad. Why be modest? She was the prettiest girl in town. The blatantly paternal thought made him chuckle to himself as he settled back to watch the game.

On the third play, the Bears fumbled the ball, and the Warriors recovered. The groans all around Mitch turned to roars when the Bears recovered on the next play. Mitch picked out Lowell Rabbit's number; Virgil's second son was playing halfback.

Six rows below him, Mitch noticed Lisa Macpherson sitting with Janet Harden, another teacher. Lisa's blond hair was easy to spot in the crowd, and he found his gaze returning to her again and again.

When the teams retired to the dressing rooms at halftime, the score was tied 13–13. Mitch left the bleachers for a soft drink and popcorn. Spotting Virgil in the crowd at the concession stand, Mitch worked his way to him.

"Lowell's looking good," Mitch said.

Virgil looked up with a proud grin. "Duck took over for me so I could come to the game. I'm going back to the station when it's over."

Mitch nodded.

"Donald's going to dive for that hatchet Sunday," Virgil said. A thorough search of the area below the levee had turned up nothing. "I'm going out with him in the boat. Come to lunch and we'll both go."

"Emily made other plans with a girlfriend, and I think I've taken enough advantage of Trudy's hospitality for a while."

"Come on, Mitch, you know Trudy likes having you as much as I do."

"Thanks, but not this time. George Turnbull and I are going fishing Sunday morning. I'll check with you when I get back to town."

Mitch got his food and returned to the bleachers. The seat beside Lisa Macpherson was now vacant. Lisa was turned away from him, speaking to the high school girls seated on the row in front of her.

She turned and noticed Mitch. She smiled. "Hello, Mitch. The pom-pom girls look good, don't they?"

"I'm not an impartial observer." For some reason he felt conspicuous, standing there. "I think somebody got my seat. Is this one taken?"

She shook her head. "Janet Harden was sitting here, but she was getting one of her migraines, so she decided to go home." She patted the bleacher. "Sit down if you like."

He sat beside her with mixed feelings. This was the first woman he'd noticed in the way that a man notices an attractive woman since Ellen's death. He thrust the popcorn sack toward her. "Help yourself."

She accepted. "Umm, that's good. Thank you." In jeans and a bulky sweater, she didn't look much older than the members of the high school pep squad seated around them. During the first half, she'd rooted for the Buckskin team with as much enthusiasm as a teenager. One of the girls called to her, and she turned aside to answer, giving Mitch a chance to study her long legs and firm thighs in the tight jeans. She was wearing something that smelled like lilacs.

She turned and reached for another handful of popcorn from the bag he'd set between them, flashing him a smile.

"You like Buckskin, Lisa?"

"Fine so far. There's a close, small-town feeling. The people are friendly."

"Not much to do on a Saturday night, though."

She shifted her shoulders. "I suppose that depends on how resourceful you are."

He chuckled. "Yeah, and whether or not you bore easily."

"I haven't had time to get bored."

She wouldn't have any trouble finding male companionship, even in Buckskin, if that's what she wanted. Questions crowded into his mind. Was there somebody special in her life since her divorce? Did she still love her ex-husband? Why would a man let a woman like this get away? Recalling how he'd embarrassed himself at the sandwich shop by blurting that her husband was a fool, he didn't give voice to any of these questions.

He realized she was watching him. "I accepted the job in Buckskin because I wanted a fresh start," she said.

"You make it sound easy to start over."

Her blue-gray eyes were open, honest. "It wasn't at first. I was depressed, felt like a failure, felt . . . oh, all the things most people must feel after a divorce."

"How long has it been?"

"Eighteen months. The time comes when you have to get on with living."

He nodded. "You have to turn that corner."

"It's a matter of choice. You can choose to keep looking back with regret, or you can look ahead." She gazed at him gravely. "I heard about your wife's long illness. The guidance counselor thought I should know, since Emily's in my sophomore English class. She seems to be handling it pretty well. I wonder about you, though."

"We're both making it." He looked down at Emily on the field.

"Does Emily look like your wife?"

"Quite a lot. I was always glad she didn't take after me." The band had finished its halftime routine and was marching off the field. The teams ran on, and the cheers of the hometown fans made it impossible to continue the conversation.

Lisa jumped up and down and yelled as loudly as any member of the pep squad. During a lull, she said, "It'll get better, Mitch."

"I'm sure it will. It is already, in fact."

They didn't talk much during the remainder of the game, which the Bears won with a field goal in the last minute of play.

As the fans began filing out all around them, Mitch felt awkward suddenly.

"Thanks for sharing your popcorn," she said.

"You're welcome." Then in a rush, he added, "Would you like to go somewhere for something to eat?"

She looked carefully at his face. "Sure, sounds good. Where?"

"Judy's, out east on Highway Ten. Do you know it?"

She nodded. "I have my car. I'll meet you there."

She was waiting for him in a booth at Judy's, a roadhouse that catered to lake visitors by staying open twenty-four hours a day. He didn't know any of the dozen or so customers.

She grinned as he slid into the booth across from her. "Excellent idea you had." She perused a menu. "I think I'll have a steak. I didn't have time for dinner."

"Great. Me, too."

As they waited for the food, she said, "Did Emily go to the sock hop at school?"

"Of course. I think she had plans to meet Kevin Hartsbarger there. I guess that's a date, or do they call them dates these days?"

She laughed. "It's a date. Kevin's a good kid."

"So I keep hearing from various quarters."

"You've been investigating him?"

"Unofficially," he admitted. "You won't tell Emily, will you?"

"Heavens, no. Speaking of investigations, have you caught that artist's murderer yet?"

"We have a suspect." A trip with Virgil to Kingfisher Pigeon's house that afternoon had gained them nothing. Kingfisher's wife said her husband was home Sunday night by nine, that he hadn't gone out again, and that she herself hadn't talked to Joe in a year or more. She rarely got into town, she said, and so had heard nothing about any extramarital affair Joe might have been having. Her husband, she told them, was gone, she knew not where, and she didn't know when to expect him. In other words, See no evil, hear no evil, speak no evil. Mitch and Virgil had waited outside for nearly an hour before they gave up and returned to town. "Not enough evidence to make an arrest yet," Mitch told Lisa, "but we're working on it."

Their food arrived and they ate as though it were a serious business for several moments. "Are you originally from Kansas City?" Mitch asked.

"No. A little town in central Missouri." She dribbled ketchup on her steak. "My parents are still there."

They talked about brothers and sisters, of which Mitch had none and she had two, both sisters. About higher education. Mitch had managed three years on loans and grants before he married and took a job with the Oklahoma City police department. She was a few hours short of a master's, which she intended to finish in summer sessions at Northeastern State. She was working on a thesis proposal on Christian symbolism in the poetry of John Donne, a name that Mitch vaguely remembered hearing at some point during his three years at college. She loved Mexican food and hated sushi.

A half hour drifted by. When they left the restaurant, she tucked her arm companionably into his and he walked her to her car, a blue Honda Civic. She opened the door. "Thank you, Mitch."

He was reluctant for the meeting to end, and it came as a bit bit of a jolt to realize that he wanted very much to kiss her. "Lisa, wait—"

She stopped the words by placing a finger on his lips. "It's too soon, Mitch."

He tucked his hands into his jeans pockets to keep from touching her. Was she right? he wondered, as he watched her drive away.

THIRTEEN

AT SEVEN-THIRTY SUNDAY morning, nothing stirred on the main drag. The store windows were dark. A green-sweatered, black-wigged department store dummy gazed blindly from the shadows at a mangy brown dog who appeared suddenly from between two buildings, chasing a Mr. Goodbar wrapper across the street. After chauffeuring their offspring to Sunday School, a few men would appear when the Downtown Coffee Shop on the corner of Sequoyah and First Streets opened at eight.

Other than the dog, the only living thing in sight at the moment was a dejected-looking form huddled on the bench in front of the post office, elbows on knees, hands dangling, head bent. Mitch pulled over and stopped.

"Hey, Jeeter, you okay?"

Jeeter raised his head and squinted through straggly hair. For an instant there was a glimmer of fear in Jeeter's bloodshot eyes, but then bravado replaced it. "Can't a man sit in a public place without the cops jacking him around? You ain't my keeper." He made an obscene gesture. "Lemme alone, pig, or I'll get a restraining order." Evidently Jeeter had been talking to his lawyer and was spoiling for a fight.

Mitch wasn't interested in postponing the fishing trip long enough to pick up the gauntlet. His ankle was healing nicely and he wasn't going to concern himself right now with why Jeeter was sitting in front of the post office early Sunday morning, trying to pick a fight with an officer of the law.

"Don't sweat it, Jeeter. Have a good day." He pulled away, shaking his head. Did Jeeter ever have a good day?

He continued south on Sequoyah, past the First National Bank where George Turnbull had been president since his father's death fifteen years ago. It was a solid-looking sandstone building, one of the oldest in town, a Buckskin landmark.

The Turnbull family had been prominent in town affairs almost from the beginning and had made a lot of money from banking and oil. Like his predecessors, George Turnbull appeared to have about everything a man could want. The bank was probably holding some farm notes that were past due, considering the bind farmers had been in the past few years; but George was shrewd enough not to have all his eggs in one basket. Mitch was confident the bank would continue to be solid and solvent, even if agriculture remained depressed. If one judged from outward appearances, George was a man to be envied; but Mitch knew too much about his family problems to envy him.

Mitch drove all the way to the south edge of town where all the houses had been built within the past ten years and the streets bore names like Wildwood Lane and Rosehill Drive. Buckskin's four doctors and two dentists lived there, along with thirty or forty other families. The Turnbull house was a red brick colonial structure with white pillars across the front. It looked impressive, standing there, the early morning sunlight sparkling the dew that adorned its manicured lawn.

Mitch followed the circular drive around to the back and turned off the engine. To his right, the swimming pool glimmered. To his left, turned off the engine. To his right, the swimming pool glimmered. To his left, Valerie Turnbull's baby blue Mercedes 550 SL, which had been the talk of Buckskin when her father gave it to her last spring, sat in front of one of the garage's triple doors.

Ordinarily Mitch would be unreservedly eager to be going fishing with George, but when George had phoned him yesterday and suggested it, he'd added, "We can both use a few hours' relaxation, and there's something I need to talk to you about." That had sounded more like a councilman than a friend.

Mitch suspected the council was pressuring George to get a reading on the progress of the murder investigation, and Mitch hoped they could get that over with first so he could let down his guard and enjoy the morning.

He waited in his car for a few minutes, but Turnbull didn't appear. Mitch got out and knocked on the back door. Two or

three minutes passed before the door opened to reveal Valerie
Turnbull, wearing a pink satin robe that lapped in front, without quite covering all of her ripe, rosy breasts. If the robe had
been dripping wet, it couldn't have clung more revealingly to
her body, and what was revealed had made several men lose
their heads.

"Good morning, Chief," she trilled.

He had supposed Valerie lay abed until noon, and her
cheerful reception threw him for a minute. She leaned forward
to hold the glass storm door open for him. In so doing, she
thrust her pert little behind out and exposed even more of her
breasts to Mitch's view. "Come on in." She was fully aware of
her effect and pleased with it. "Daddy will be down in a little
while. You can sit on the sun porch and have a cup of coffee
with me while you wait. How do you like yours?" The slow
sideways look she gave Mitch as he walked past her hinted that
the question didn't necessarily have to do with coffee, depend-
ing on how he chose to interpret it.

"Black will be fine."

"And strong, right?" She led him through the kitchen to a
glassed-in porch floored with chocolate brown Mexican tile.
The furniture was rattan, the low table in front of the sofa,
glass. Pots of greenery were scattered about. The room was cool
but humid and smelled pleasantly like a greenhouse. Mitch sat
in a rattan chair, thinking that he could easily put his head back
and go to sleep; he'd had another restless night.

She brought two steaming brown mugs and handed one to
him before settling cozily in a corner of the sofa. She crossed
her legs and the robe fall apart above her knees. Clearly she had
on nothing beneath the robe.

Mitch wondered what she was up to. Valerie was pretty in the
way that all healthy, young women are pretty, but few people
noticed that. They were too busy noticing Valerie's sex appeal,
which oozed from every pore. She was a reckless flirt. As a re-
sult, men were fascinated while being a little wary of her, and
women despised her.

Valerie could be charming when she wanted to be. From what
Mitch had observed, she wanted to be when it suited some
mysterious female whim that might never be comprehended by

anyone but herself. To Mitch, she was an enigma. She'd never worked a day in her life. She'd even botched college, having been enrolled four years without coming close to earning a degree.

Valerie's interests at Northeastern State had been outside the classroom. Then, as always, she had majored in good times. Since Mitch could not conceive of anyone—even Valerie, who had perfected the art—filling all her waking hours with play, he wondered what she did the rest of the time.

"Did you enjoy your trip?" Mitch asked.

She cocked her head and eyed him with amusement. "What trip is that, Chief?"

"Your father told me that you'd gone to Tulsa to pick out your wedding gown last week."

"Oh." The flicker of amusement in her eyes went out. "He told you that?" She gazed at the backyard thoughtfully as though she saw something out there that nobody else could see. "Daddy's so quaint."

What's going on behind those big blue eyes, Mitch was thinking. "You didn't buy your gown?"

She smiled tolerantly, a smile that invited him to share the secret—whatever it was. "Oh, yes, I bought it. It's lovely. Virgin white silk with lace and millions of seed pearls. A traditional as all get-out." A dimple winked at the right corner of her mouth. "Do you think of me as a traditional bride, Chief?" He could almost have sworn she gave him a conspiratorial wink.

Mitch took a slow swallow of coffee. "I'm sure you'll look real nice."

She chuckled, a low, delighted gurgle. "My little trip cost Daddy the earth. I spent more than three thousand dollars for the gown and accessories, and my trousseau cost a few thousand more."

"Easy come, easy go," Mitch observed.

She chuckled again. "You're cute, Chief." She leaned toward him. Mitch expected her breasts to bounce out of that robe any minute. "Anyway..." She straightened and stared out at the yard again. Beneath her playful manner, Valerie seemed abstracted this morning. Was she having second thoughts about giving up her freedom? After a moment, she went on. "I don't have much patience with tradition. Most of the time I was away, I was otherwise engaged."

I'll bet, Mitch thought. He could easily imagine Valerie spending a few days in a motel with one man while she was supposedly outfitting herself to marry another in six weeks. One last fling.

Her father must be counting the days until the wedding. Folks said George Turnbull was his father made over—methodical, prudent, conservative, exactly what you wanted your banker to be. But he'd married a St. Louis girl who had chafed at the provincial restraints of small-town life and finally found her escape in the bottle. They had rarely agreed on anything, including how their daughter should be raised, and Valerie had early learned to play one of her parents against the other to get what she wanted.

By the time Valerie was fifteen, she was snagging masculine attention wherever she went, and reveling in the sense of power it gave her. The world was Valerie Turnbull's oyster—the male half of it, anyway. All she had to do to get her way was show a bit of leg, hitch her saucy little behind, and flash her white teeth in a smile that managed, at once, to mock and promise boundless sensual delights. Did Jack Derring have any idea what he was taking on? Mitch wondered. For an instant, he almost felt sorry for Derring.

Valerie stirred and brought her gaze back to Mitch, as though she'd momentarily forgotten he was there. "So, how is the big murder investigation going?"

"Slowly. Why?"

"Well, I'm interested. I mean, there's a murderer out there somewhere." She waved a slender hand vaguely. Sunlight flashed off the diamond solitaire. Derring probably thought the two-carat stone was sufficient warning to other men that she belonged to him, but Mitch doubted it had cramped Valerie's style much. "For all we know, he might be picking his next victim right now."

"What makes you think there will be another murder?"

"I read an article once about murderers. It said they acquire a taste for it. Isn't that true?"

"Sometimes, if it's a psycho."

"Obviously, whoever killed Joe Pigeon is deranged. It'll be easier for him to take another life, now that he's done it once."

"You're assuming he's deranged because of the fingers?" Mitch asked resignedly. By this time, everybody in town must be speculating about the missing fingers.

"Aren't you?" She shivered. "It's creepy."

He shrugged. "Maybe." On impulse, he asked, "Do you have any thoughts about who the kook might be?"

"You really want to know what I think? I think it's somebody who has failed in life, somebody who never got the respect he feels he deserves. Think about it. This summer, Joe's talent has been getting a lot of recognition. Maybe the murderer thought, Why him and not me? And he exploded."

"Interesting," Mitch said, remembering that Virgil had put forth a similar theory at one point. "I'd forgotten. You were attending Northeastern last year when Joe was there."

"Yes," she said eagerly. "Joe was something of a campus luminary. He really was a great artist. Oh, I know people in Buckskin didn't understand or appreciate him, but at Northeastern everybody knew he'd be famous someday, even the professors."

"Did Joe have any friends at Northeastern?"

She thought it over a minute. "I suppose he was close to the other art students. They always hung out together."

"Did you ever see him with a woman?"

She caught her bottom lip between her teeth. "His wife? No. Maybe she didn't visit him there. I don't know."

"I'm not talking about Mary Pigeon. Did you ever notice him with anybody else?"

She looked at him from beneath half-closed lashes. "You mean, like a girlfriend? Well, I can't say that would surprise me. Artists aren't bound by traditional mores." What's *your* excuse, Mitch thought wryly. "Let me see now," Valerie went on. "There was one woman that I saw him with several times. I think she was an art student. She was Indian, but I don't know if she was Cherokee. I'm sure she wasn't from Buckskin, though."

"Do you know her name?"

"Janet...or Janis. Janis something, I think." She shook her head. "I can't remember. Why? Is it important?"

"Probably not." Janis, he thought, storing the name.

At that moment, they heard someone descending the back stairs to the kitchen. "Here comes Daddy," Valerie said. "You two meanies are going to run off now and leave me here all alone. Jack's not coming by until this evening. What will I do with myself?"

"You'll think of something."

"Are you being naughty?" She wagged a finger at him. "I'm an engaged woman, Chief, and Jack is very possessive."

Turnbull came out on the sun porch and frowned his disapproval of Valerie's attire. It didn't faze Valerie. She flitted past her father, saying over her shoulder, "Bye, now, Chief."

"Good-bye, Valerie. Thanks for the coffee." Already, he was wondering when he could go to Tahlequah to get a lead on the Indian girl, Janis. The name might lead to something. Valerie had been helpful, although that had probably not been her intention. Valerie wasn't helpful unless there was something in it for her.

MITCH TOOK the country road around Going Snake Mountain.

"I thought we were going to the lake." Turnbull had already killed one beer and was reaching into the cooler on the backseat for another. Mitch had opened a can when they left the highway and was nursing it along.

Turnbull peered at Mitch over the gold-framed glasses perched halfway down his narrow nose.

"I heard the bass are biting at the mouth of Spider Creek."

"I'm not sure it's worth what you have to go through to get there," Turnbull said, flipping the tab on his beer can and tipping it to his mouth. "This road will jolt the hell out of your shocks—not to mention my kidneys." He took another swig.

"Anything for a mess of fresh bass," Mitch said cheerfully.

Turnbull wiped his mouth with his shirt sleeve. "It's your car. How's the investigation coming?"

"There's nothing I can tell you."

Turnbull looked morosely out the window. "Mitch, something...anything would help."

"To placate the council? You're expected to exploit our friendship to find out where I'm going with this, right?"

Turnbull released a long breath. "That's a bit strong. The mayor did speak to me yesterday. He was out of town for a few days, and when he got back there were messages from most of the councilmen, asking for a report on the investigation. They're antsy, Mitch. They're all getting calls at home. I told Bob I could only ask you, so that's what I'm doing."

"Devay's a horse's ass."

"True, but he can be a thorn in your side."

Mitch glanced at his friend. Turnbull was starting to look his age, he thought. Mitch wondered what the latest news on Opal was, but he didn't want to ask in case it wasn't promising. George gave him a sheepish smile, obviously regretting his role as the council's go-between. "Okay, George, I'll make a deal with you. I'll talk to you in confidence. You go back to the council and tell them I'm following some promising leads and you can't say any more than that."

"It's worth a try," Turnbull said. "I hope it's true."

"Leads, yes. Promising is in the eye of the beholder."

They had reached the section of deeply rutted road bordering the Pigeon farm, and both men fell silent as they bounced past the house of Joe Pigeon's parents. There was no sign of anyone. A crudely lettered warning—BEWARE OF BAD DOG—had been nailed to the gate post, but Scout didn't show himself to live up to his advance publicity.

"The going has to be rough for them now," Mitch commented.

"It never rains but what it pours," said Turnbull. "The bank's holding the mortgage on the Pigeons' farm. They're a year behind in their payments."

"You'll have to foreclose?"

"Not as long as they can make a payment now and then. Many of these small farmers are in the same boat. If we foreclosed on every farmer who's in trouble, all we'd have would be a lot of land that's worth maybe half of what's been borrowed against it. *If* we could sell it, which is questionable."

"Times are tough." Mitch was thinking of Kingfisher Pigeon and others like him who had a wife and four or five kids to feed.

The Pigeon house disappeared as Mitch followed a bend in the road. "About these leads . . ." Turnbull said.

Mitch emptied his beer can and tossed it out the window. It disappeared in the brush. "Joe was having an affair," he said, finding it a relief to talk freely. "I've got a lead on a woman who was seen with him in Tahlequah when he was attending university there." He realized that he was making it sound like more than it was because of the council's pressure.

Turnbull's forehead was furrowed. "You don't think he was killed by a woman, do you?"

"I'm keeping an open mind."

"Have you checked out Mary Pigeon? Did she know about the affair?"

"Of course we checked her out. She knew Joe had another woman, but nothing else, not even the woman's name. She doesn't want to know anything else, and I hope she doesn't have to. I'm ninety-nine percent sure she's clean, but my bones tell me there's some connection between the other woman and Joe's murder. I'm going to Tahlequah Monday to see what I can turn up."

Turnbull wedged his beer can between his legs and took off his glasses. He began to polish the lenses with his handkerchief. "How much do you know about this woman in Tahlequah?"

"She's Indian, and her name's Janis."

Turnbull replaced the glasses on his thin nose. "I'm no detective, but if that's all you have, the feeling in your bones may be wishful thinking."

"Could be," Mitch admitted, "but I'll follow it up, anyway. Also, Joe's wedding ring turned up in a Tahlequah pawnshop. We're working on that angle, too." Mitch decided not to mention Jeeter Rheeves or the guy Jeeter saw throw the ring into the lake.

"Maybe you'll get lucky there," said Turnbull hopefully. "Anything else in the way of hard facts?"

"Not yet. Get the council to lay off and give us the time we need, George."

Turnbull reached for another beer. He was really tossing them back this morning. "I'll do my best. I had to ask, Mitch. Don't hold it against me."

"I understand you're just doing your job. We're all doing our jobs. I don't have any problems with that."

"Good. Now we can forget that and get down to the serious business of fishing."

But Mitch was thinking about something Turnbull had said. Bob Devay had been out of town for a few days. Valerie Turnbull had returned from Tulsa Friday morning. Coincidence, probably—but a little over a year ago Valerie and Devay had had a pretty heavy relationship going. It was merely idle curiosity, but Mitch wondered if Devay had been in Tulsa while Valerie was there. Another nagging little question to pursue. No connection with the murder investigation, but Mitch liked to know what was going on in his town. If you turned over every rock that made you curious, sooner or later you're bound to find something interesting. He was faintly pleased by the thought of Valerie and Devay sowing a few wild oats behind Derring's back.

THE PRICKLING at the base of Mitch's skull was so persistent he could no longer dismiss it. It had been a disappointing morning, as far as the fishing went. They were packing up their gear. They'd polished off the beer—George had drunk most of it—and caught nothing worth keeping. A drowsing, uneventful morning until now. Mitch bent to set his tackle box down, certain they were being watched.

He straightened and whirled around.

Twenty feet in front of him the clearing surrounding the mouth of Spider Creek ended. At the edge of the clearing, the trees crowded close together, almost close enough to be a log fortress. Tangled underbrush made the narrow spaces between the trunks nearly impassable. In there were pathless acres of woods and high scrub covering hill after hill, deep green cedars and yellowing elms and cottonwoods and blackjack oaks, and wild plum and sumac bushes. These hills were riddled with natural caves, their mouths screened by scrub and buckbrush, keeping their secrets well.

Deeper still were narrow ravines where the Little People of Cherokee legend cavorted in the rocky depths.

Very few people lived this far into the woods. In Indian Territory days, outlaws had disappeared in that ghost-ridden forest for months at a time. Mitch scanned the trees. Not a leaf moved.

Turnbull's back was to Mitch as he arranged his flies in his tackle box. Finishing, he snapped the lid shut.

"Shh," Mitch cautioned.

Turnbull turned around. "What's wrong?"

"Somebody's out there."

Turnbull pushed his glasses up his sweat-glistened nose and squinted at the woods. "I don't see anything."

"Neither do I, but I feel him."

Turnbull glanced at Mitch dubiously. "You trying to scare me?"

"Put the gear in the car and wait for me. I'm going to look around."

"Mitch, there's nobody in that jungle. You probably heard a deer. Or a rattler."

Shaking off the slithering image Turnbull's words created, Mitch walked toward the woods.

"Don't go too far," Turnbull whispered urgently. "You can get so lost in there you'll never find your way out."

Mitch put his hand above his head and made a circle of thumb and forefinger to indicate that he'd heed the caution. Taking high, deliberate steps, he struggled through the undergrowth, thinking that if a snake should cross his path, it could strike before he knew it was there.

Holding his arms over his face to ward off slapping limbs, he slogged slowly through the thick, yellowing trees. A light breeze came from somewhere and stirred the high limbs overhead, and a few dead leaves floated down. Mitch's healing left ankle began to ache dully. He zigged and zagged, choosing what appeared to be the path of least resistance. He hadn't gone far before he was breathing heavily. It was, he decided, as hard as wading through five feet of chilled honey. Around him, insects hummed and grasshoppers jumped away as he plodded past. Thorns and nettles snatched at the legs of his jeans.

He stumbled and realized he was going downhill now. He had entered the back of beyond. Here nature still fought human intrusion, and the stillness was almost suffocating. He could sympathize with people who dropped out, went to live in the woods and never returned to civilization. It was the enervating peace; it captured and sapped you.

He saw no sign of anyone having been there before him. Had he imagined they were being watched? Mitch's ankle gave without warning and he staggered and his hand shot out to grab at the nearest tree trunk. He barely kept himself from falling. He cursed in frustration and looked back the way he had come.

Turnbull struggled after him, about a hundred yards behind. He waved for the other man to go back. Turnbull was almost twenty years older than Mitch and not very physically fit. If Turnbull understood Mitch's gesture, he ignored it and kept coming, huffing and puffing. Irritated, Mitch hoped Turnbull didn't have a heart attack over this. He decided he would go on a little way, and if he saw no one, he would turn back.

A few steps farther along, he glimpsed a patch of sky ahead of him, across the green-brown brush and through the low tree branches. Minutes later, he staggered to the edge of a clearing roughly the size of a football field.

"Mitch, where are you?" Turnbull was still following, had even managed to gain a few yards on Mitch. His voice was breathless and anxious. "Dammit, Mitch, answer me!"

"Here." About twenty feet into the clearing, directly in front of Mitch, sat a battery-powered lamp, the kind people took camping or kept in their car trunks for emergencies. It was shiny, new-looking. "Look at this, George."

Turnbull hauled himself to Mitch's side, gasping and cursing and slapping at a spider's web. The two men stood there for several minutes, getting their breath. It was a relief just to be still, and Mitch didn't think about the trek back or about his ankle. He wanted to give Turnbull plenty of time to recover before returning to the car.

There was nothing unusual to be seen in the clearing, except for the lamp. "What's that doing here?" Turnbull asked when he had enough breath to speak.

"Maybe a camper left it behind," Mitch said. "An odd place to make camp, though. You'd have to walk in, carrying your gear." His gaze drifted over the trees on the other side of the large clearing. Suddenly, from the corner of his eye, he caught a glimmer in the woods opposite, sunlight reflecting off metal. Before he had time to react, a shot pinged into a tree to the right of where he stood.

Turnbull froze. "Sweet Lord!"

Mitch's mouth had gone as dry as tumbleweed. He seized Turnbull's shoulder and shoved him to the ground. They sprawled on their stomachs, their faces pressed into dying weeds and brush. A thorn pricked Mitch's neck and he pushed it away, feeling a tiny welling of blood where his skin had been broken.

"Ouch!" Turnbull yelped.

Mitch ran his tongue over the parched roof of his mouth. "Keep still," he said urgently. He'd left his gun in the trunk of his car. A rank rookie would have known better than that. They were defenseless against an armed man, and if they tried to get away through the woods, they'd never make it to the car. Oh, God almighty...

Mitch lay without moving, his senses on full alert. Finally he realized that someone was moving through the woods on the other side of the clearing, away from them. They lay in the scrub for long moments, dry twigs and thorns pricking painfully wherever there was bare skin. When Mitch lifted his head, he saw nothing beyond the clearing but vegetation. Whoever had shot at them had hidden himself well and was at this moment making his getaway by going deeper into the woods. Mitch could no longer hear the sounds of his retreat. Silence, broken only by the buzz of insects, engulfed them.

Mitch sat up shakily. "He's gone, George." Collecting himself, he got his feet under him and hunkered down in the weeds as he continued to scan the clearing.

Turnbull crept close to Mitch and positioned himself behind a tree before standing. He peeped around the trunk. "It could've been a hunter. Maybe he didn't see us." He didn't sound very convincing. "God knows why anybody would try to hunt in here, though. That must be his light."

Mitch stared at the lamp, thinking it didn't fit. The Indians who hunted in these woods wouldn't come in the dark, and they'd carry their game out before nightfall. Beside him, he heard Turnbull suck in a breath.

"Mitch, I think we've stumbled into something here we shouldn't have. Do you know what this is?"

"What?"

"This is where the Nighthawks meet. Has to be. A hidden clearing deep in the woods, a light for night meetings. We better get the hell out of here while we can still navigate."

Mitch hesitated. It would be a waste of effort to go after the sniper. He wouldn't find him. The Nighthawks knew these woods, Mitch didn't.

If Turnbull was right, they were desecrating holy ground. The sniper had probably been posted to guard it and warn off intruders. And he wouldn't hesitate to shoot at a lawman, Mitch thought angrily.

He glanced at Turnbull, whose face was pale and perspiring. "Are you all right?"

"I'll be a lot better when I'm out of here."

"Let's rest a few minutes longer. You don't look any too good."

"I'm fine. Let's go."

Mitch nodded grimly and led the way slowly back through the woods, limping to favor his throbbing left ankle.

FOURTEEN

BEFORE DAWN on Sunday, Crying Wolf had walked to a spring deep in the woods behind his house. Wrapped carefully in a clean handkerchief in his pocket was the tobacco he would remake. His heart was full of the gravity of his mission; it was so grave, in fact, that, mixed with the Cotton Bowl Twist and dried bits of cedar was a precious pinch of *tso:lagayv:li*, the powerful Grandfather Medicine.

Crying Wolf's store of *tso:lagayv:li* had dwindled to a few spoonfuls, which he kept in a tightly sealed fruit jar beneath his bed. It was the last of the small supply sent to him by a North Carolina medicine man, through his daughter who'd visited in North Carolina three years ago. Crying Wolf used *tso:lagayv:li* only on momentous occasions because he might never be able to get another supply. Even on the Cherokee reservation in North Carolina it was exceedingly scarce because of the stringent requirements for growing it.

Tso:lagayv:li had to be planted in the woods in a secret place, for if anyone other than its sower should see it while it was growing, its power would be lost. Furthermore, it had to be planted on Christmas Day or St. Valentine's Day in ground that had been prepared by burning lightning-struck wood upon it. The original planting dates had been lost in the dim past. Influenced by Christian missionaries, later medicine men had adopted Christian holidays.

This occasion warranted its use.

As Crying Wolf walked to the spring, his boots scattering bright, fallen leaves, he thought about the previous afternoon when Virgil Rabbit, a good man and a Nighthawk, had come to his cabin. While Crying Wolf wanted as little contact as possible with the white man's law, he held no animosity for those who felt otherwise, and so he had welcomed Virgil to his house. Virgil asked permission to bring the chief of police,

Mitchell Bushyhead, to see him. Virgil's explanation for this unusual request had alarmed Crying Wolf.

Bushyhead had found a homemade cigarette in Joseph Pigeon's yard Monday morning, after Callie Roach's son discovered Joseph Pigeon's body and Callie had called the police. Bushyhead had asked Virgil if the cigarette could have been used in a Cherokee medicine ceremony. Not only that, the police had learned that Kingfisher Pigeon visited his brother the same evening he was killed. They suspected Kingfisher of being involved in his brother's murder, perhaps even of actually doing the deed himself. Virgil's explanation had strengthened Crying Wolf's own suspicions.

Now, Bushyhead wanted to talk to a medicine man. As keeper of the fire on Going Snake Mountain, Kingfisher was a highly respected member of the Nighthawk Keetoowahs. Since Crying Wolf and Virgil Rabbit were also Nighthawks and because Virgil knew that Crying Wolf was the medicine man for most of the society's members, Virgil had come to Crying Wolf.

Virgil had not asked him directly if he had made medicine at Joseph Pigeon's house at Kingfisher's request; but Virgil knew that, if such a ceremony had taken place, Crying Wolf had performed it.

Crying Wolf was not afraid of talking to the police, but he feared what the police might discover in their investigation. Had a murderer infected the Nighthawk Keetoowahs with evil? If that were the case, the evil must be removed. For that to happen, the truth had to come out. Therefore, Crying Wolf had agreed to see Bushyhead.

In the meantime, he would prepare himself well for the meeting.

Sunday night he would sleep in the woods because the spirits were more accessible out-of-doors. He hoped to receive a message in a dream that would either clear Kingfisher Pigeon and all other Nighthawks or convict one of them of involvement in Joseph Pigeon's murder.

To ensure success, Crying Wolf would fast today. To protect himself he would use the tobacco he was about to remake to trap and kill any night-walkers who tried to harm him as he slept.

By the time he reached the spring, the sky was white with early dawn. Spreading pecan trees grew near the small circular mouth of the underground spring, and the ground was littered with rotting pecan hulls from past years. Crying Wolf took the folded handkerchief from his pocket, and carefully emptied its contents into the palm of his hand. He faced east and lifted the tobacco to the rising sun. He kneaded the tobacco as he chanted the *idi:gawe:sdi* for destroying night-walkers.

"Now! No one is to climb over me!
His soul itself over there will be broken as the
     Sun rises, this Thinker of me: in the very
     middle of the light of the setting Sun he
     will be broken, this Thinker of me!
I will have emerged from the Seven Clans.
Then I have just come to strike you with
     Small Arrows, with Small Arrows I have just
     come to strike you!
Then I have just come to strike you with Lightning!
Then I have just come to strike you with Thunder!
Then with Clay your soul will be broken!''

AFTER REPEATING the incantation four times, he transferred the tobacco to the handkerchief and returned it to his pocket. He bent and, cupping spring water in his hands, threw it over his head. The water would purify and increase the power of the incantation.

He walked back to his cabin through the first sparkling newness of day but, because such an important issue was at stake, he would return to the spring at midday and at dusk to repeat the ceremony.

AFTER TAKING TURNBULL home, Mitch drove to the lake. He parked not far from Jeeter's campsite and identified Virgil's bass boat among several others by the figure in diving gear. He honked and the shorter figure waved and pointed to the small pier, indicating that they were headed for shore.

Mitch met them at the pier. While Donald tied up, Virgil jumped out. He was carrying a hatchet in one hand and something in a scrap of terry cloth toweling in the other.

Returning Virgil's grin, Mitch clapped him on the back and said, "About time we got lucky. Good job, Donald." Cupped in the toweling were the still recognizable remains of human fingers. Fish had nibbled away most of the flesh.

"Looks like Jeeter was telling the truth," Virgil said. To Donald, he added, "I'll back down to the ramp and help you load the boat, son."

Mitch and Virgil walked toward Virgil's car. "I'll take this stuff by the station for safekeeping," Virgil said, "and write the report tomorrow."

"Virgil, do you know where the mouth of Spider Creek is?"

"Vaguely. That road past old man Pigeon's place will take you to it, I think. Why?"

"George and I were out there fishing this morning. Somebody was in the woods with a shotgun. I went to investigate and found a good-sized clearing hidden in the woods. Have you ever been there?"

Virgil's dark eyes studied Mitch's face in puzzlement. "No."

Mitch frowned. "Whoever was in the woods took a shot at us."

Virgil's black brows shot up, then dropped like tiny sails tossed in the wind. "The hell you say. Did you get him?"

Mitch shook his head. "Didn't even get a look at him. He hightailed it deeper into the woods. There was a battery-powered neon lamp in the clearing, like somebody might've been there recently after dark. George thought we'd stumbled on the Nighthawk meeting ground. Obviously George was wrong."

"The Nighthawks meet on top of Going Snake Mountain," Virgil said gravely but without hesitation. "I figured about everybody in Buckskin knew that. I'm not telling any big secrets, but you'd have trouble finding the place unless you knew the way."

"Yeah, so I wonder why that guy was so antsy about us being out there?" A few of the full-bloods resented all whites, especially law officers, particularly when they trespassed on what was considered Cherokee turf. But taking potshots at people seemed a pretty extreme reaction. Besides, Mitch had fished that creek several times with no problems before.

"Beats me," Mitch."

"Dad!" Donald shouted. "Bring the boat on down here. I have to get home."

"Go ahead," Mitch said. "Maybe I'll drop by this evening for a beer, if you're going to be home."

"We'll be there. Oh and Mitch, about that cigarette you found. I've been asking around, and there's a man you probably ought to talk to. I can take you out to his place this week sometime."

"Thanks, Virgil. See you later."

Mitch got home before Emily, who'd gone to church. As he fried a couple of breaded minute steaks, instead of the fish he'd hoped to be cooking, he puzzled over the lamp in the clearing and the warning shot. No reasonable explanation came to him. Abandoning that, he thought about Valerie Turnbull and Bob Devay and their being absent from town at the same time. Of course, he could simply call Bob and ask him where he'd gone, but Bob would lie if he actually had been in Tulsa with Valerie. He'd have to think of something a little more subtle.

He folded three thicknesses of paper toweling on a plate and transferred the golden, batter-fried steaks to it for draining. He chopped salad vegetables and put two potatoes in the microwave for baking.

The luncheon preparations made, Mitch went to the phone and called an acquaintance on the Tulsa police force. "Harry, it's Mitch Bushyhead over in Buckskin."

"Hey, Mitch, I haven't seen you in a coon's age. What've you been up to?"

"The usual thing. How about you? How's the family?"

"Family's fine. I've been working undercover in vice for a while. I prefer my old duty in homicide, but vice is better than some other assignments I could've drawn."

"Harry, I'm calling to see if you can do a little checking for me, whenever you can find the time." Mitch's credentials as a small-town cop would carry no weight in Tulsa, whereas people would be willing to talk to one of the local boys.

"Sure, what's up?"

"I want to know if a couple of Buckskin people stayed in one of your hotels or motels last week."

"Just a minute, let me find a pen. Got it—what are the names?"

"Bob Devay, that's D-e-v-a-y, and Valerie Turnbull."

"This have anything to do with that artist's murder?"

"No, just a loose end that keeps bugging me."

"I know what you mean. Making any progress in the murder investigation?"

Thinking of the hatchet and bones Donald had fished out of the lake, Mitch said, "A little. Still too many of the pieces missing, though."

"Good luck with it. I'll get on this other thing early in the week if I can. I'll call you."

"Thanks, Harry. If I can ever return the favor..."

"Don't mention it."

Mitch heard Emily's arrival as he hung up. She came into the kitchen, looking as fresh as a tree-ripened peach. She sniffed the air. "I thought we were having fish."

"Sorry to disappoint you, but I didn't catch a thing."

"I had my mouth all set, too." It was one of Ellen's expressions, and Emily's eyes grew cloudy for an instant as she remembered, and Mitch shared the moment of regret. "Is that chicken fried steak?"

"Sure is, and we're having baked potatoes and a salad to go with it."

She smiled. "You're getting to be a pretty decent cook, Daddy."

"Self-preservation. I couldn't stand to look another omelet in the face." He watched her take off her high heels and dangle them by the straps on two fingers. She was wearing a pink skirt with a white ruffle at the hem and a white blouse with lots of lace. "I like that outfit. I don't remember seeing it before."

She glanced down, as though she'd forgotten what she was wearing. "Oh, I've had this skirt since last year. This is Temple's blouse. She liked my denim jumper, so we traded for a while."

"Interesting way to add to your wardrobe."

"All the girls do it." So, of course, she and Temple had to do it, too, Mitch thought. "I'll change and set the table." In the hall, she added, "Oh, and I'm supposed to play tennis with Temple this afternoon. Her mother's taking us to the park. That's okay, isn't it?"

"I guess." Mitch removed the potatoes from the microwave. "I sure don't see much of you since school started."

"What?" she called.

Mitch already regretted his words. He raised his voice and asked, "What time will you be home?"

She came back down the hall to stand in the kitchen doorway, tugging the blouse from the waistband of her skirt. "About nine-thirty or ten. Some of the kids are going over to Temple's house later to watch a movie." Would Kevin Hartsbarger be among them? Mitch wondered. If he asked, would Emily resent his interest? Ellen would have already been on the phone with Temple Roberts' mother and would know all the details. "No later than ten, okay?"

"Okay."

"You know, honey, you can invite your friends here sometime."

"I know. Maybe I will later." She disappeared down the hall again and he heard her padding barefoot up the stairs.

Mitch wondered if he should call Mrs. Roberts while the girls were at the park, offer to bring over some soft drinks or something. She'd understand his paternal curiosity. He'd do it, he decided, and immediately felt better.

EARLY SUNDAY EVENING, Crying Wolf rolled two blankets and tied them with twine. Carrying the bedroll on his shoulder, he locked his cabin and walked west through the woods.

Several times before he had spent the night camped on a flat, relatively open circle of ground midway between his cabin and the dirt road that wound past Spider Creek to the south and north to the highway. When he reached the familiar spot, he unrolled the bedroll and spread it between two cottonwood trees. Newly fallen leaves provided a cushion for his bed.

He took out the cigarette rolled from the remade tobacco containing the Grandfather Medicine. He lighted it and blew the smoke as he circled the bedroll seven times.

Before sleeping he announced aloud that he sought the truth concerning Joseph Pigeon's death, that in particular he wished to learn if Kingfisher Pigeon or any other Nighthawk Keetoowah was guilty of the murder.

He lay down then and, before dropping off to sleep, said a divining prayer in his mind, invoking the help of Thunder, friend of the Cherokee:

> "Now! Listen! I am the doer of Your Will:
> You love me, You Ancient Red One!
> I say to You, 'Your Food!'
> You possess me overnight: I am filled with life.
> Nothing can alight upon me.
> Freely let me be turning over and over;
> I have appeared like the Water Strider.
> Ha! I have to finish that which I am keeping.
> I am Crying Wolf."

Sleeping rolled in his blankets, Crying Wolf dreamed of the *Uk'ten'*, the huge horned and clawed reptile who, long ago, had preyed on man. The *Uk'ten'* flew across the sky, trailing fire. In the odd manner of dreams, Crying Wolf knew that he lay sleeping in the woods beneath the cottonwood trees, yet at the same time he could see himself and his surroundings. Four times, the monster hovered in the sky to the south of where he slept, to look down at the woods as though searching for someone to devour, and Crying Wolf was conscious of drawing his body in upon itself, to make himself small. Then, with a far-off cracking of the sky, Thunder came and chased the *Uk'ten'* away. The fire left behind by the monster turned to rain.

Crying Wolf awoke while it was still night. Above him the cottonwood boughs nodded and sighed, tossed by a chilly wind, and his blankets were damp. He rolled out of them and returned to his cabin through the darkness, knowing his way as well as the animals who inhabited the woods.

FIFTEEN

WHEN MITCH ARRIVED at the station Monday morning, Jeeter Rheeves sat on the bench in front of the post office two doors down, head in hands. Mitch hadn't thought it possible for Jeeter to look more dejected than he had yesterday morning when he passed on his way to pick up George Turnbull; but Jeeter did. He couldn't possibly have been sitting there for twenty-four hours, could he? He wore the same dirty jeans and shirt, but Jeeter often seemed to wear the same clothes for days.

Mitch walked over to the bench. "Jeeter, are you sure you're okay?"

Startled by the sound of Mitch's voice, Jeeter looked up, wild-eyed and terrified for an instant. The poor guy evidently had a full-blown case of drug-induced paranoia. Seeing Jeeter like that reminded Mitch of something that happened when he was sixteen years old. His mother, aware that several neighborhood teenagers were getting heavily into drugs and alcohol, had taken Mitch to the psych ward of the hospital where her sister worked. There, he'd seen addicts going through the agonies of withdrawal. As he and his mother left, she said, "When you choose the beginning of a road, Mitchell, you choose the end of it as well." She had never mentioned it again, but that had been enough; he'd never forgotten it.

Jeeter looked around as though fearing Mitch had brought reinforcements in white coats. "Whatcha staring at, pig? I'm gonna do a drug deal here any minute. Ain't you gonna arrest me?"

Still in a churlish mood and looking for somebody to blame, Mitch noted with a sigh. "You do anything that stupid, Jeeter, and I'll oblige you. You know that."

"You cops are all mouth," Jeeter sneered.

Shaking his head, Mitch turned and walked into the station. He stopped at the dispatcher's desk. "Helen, I'll be in Tahlequah most of the day. Anything important I need to take care of before I leave?''

"The mayor called," Helen said. "He says he needs to talk to you before the council meeting Thursday night."

Devay undoubtedly wanted to turn the screws a little tighter, Mitch thought. Maybe he hadn't talked to George yet or, if he had, what Mitch had told George about the Pigeon case hadn't satisfied him. "If he calls back, tell him I had to go out of town on police business. You don't know when I'll be back."

Helen nodded in sympathy. "Got it. I have no idea how you can be reached by phone while you're gone, either. Right?"

Mitch patted Helen's shoulder. "What would we do without you, Helen?"

"It'd be pathetic. This place would go to rack and ruin in a week."

Duckworth was at the duty desk. Mitch waved and went into his office to look over the Pigeon case file before he left.

A few minutes later, Duckworth lumbered into the office. "Look out your window, Chief! Jeeter's taking a leak on the sidewalk!"

Mitch swiveled around. Jeeter stood not ten feet from Mitch's window, relieving himself as unconcernedly as if he were alone in the woods. A stream of yellow urine splattered on the concrete and ran off the curb into the street.

"Good God!" Mitch shot out of his chair. "At least he didn't wait until the stores opened and women were everywhere." Followed by Duckworth, he rushed outside and grabbed Jeeter's arm as he fumbled with his jeans. Jeeter had his shirttail caught in the zipper. "Come on, Jeeter. We've got a nice, private room inside just for you."

Jeeter went berserk, jerking and punching and yelling. "Pigs! Commies! Police brutality!" It took both Mitch and Duckworth to drag him into the station. Jeeter hollered accusations and epithets all the way; his repertory even included a few Mitch hadn't heard before.

"Cuckoo City," Duckworth panted after they'd managed to shove Jeeter in a cell.

"Sure seems so," Mitch agreed. "Charge him with exposing himself, creating a public nuisance, resisting arrest, and what-

ever else you think will stick. When he calms down, let him call
his lawyer."

"I ain't calling nobody," Jeeter shrieked, "and you swine
can't make me!"

"He's really flipped this time," Duckworth observed.

"When he's in enough pain, he'll make his call," Mitch said.
"Probably threaten us with a suit because we didn't let him do
it sooner."

AT MIDMORNING, the tree-lined walks traversing the campus of
Tahlequah's Northeastern State University were crowded with
students hurrying to classes. Mitch's uniform elicited a few curious glances. "Where's the art department?" he asked two
gangly, shorts-clad young men who stared at him suspiciously.

"Over there," one said, pointing, "in the Fine Arts Building." The three-story, red-brick building was directly across the
street from the University Center.

"Thanks." Mitch gave them a mock salute and took a walk
angling in the direction they'd indicated.

Northeastern was one of the oldest institutions of higher education in the state, having evolved from the Cherokee Indian
female seminary. The seminary was built in 1851 a few miles
away, at Park Hill; but when that building burned to the
ground in 1887, the seminary was moved to Tahlequah. By
1909, two years after statehood, the seminary had developed
into a normal school for training teachers. Several years after
that, it became a four-year college.

The university's older buildings surrounded a block-square
yard, which was crisscrossed by concrete walks. The yard was
well-shaded during the growing season by venerable old trees,
and in mid-September red begonias and white periwinkles still
bloomed in carefully tended beds bordering many of the
buildings. It was a beautiful campus and Mitch hoped that
Emily would decide to enroll there after high school. For one
thing, it was only an hour's drive from Buckskin.

The Arts and Letters Department occupied half of the Fine
Arts Building. The entry doors led into a large reception area.
A woman sat at a desk, sipping coffee and scanning the com-

puter screen in front of her. She glanced absently at Mitch, and back to the screen. "May I help you?"

"I'm Mitchell Bushyhead, chief of police from Buckskin. I'd like to talk to one of the art teachers."

She typed a couple of words, then gave Mitch her full attention. She frowned at his badge as though noticing it for the first time. "Which one?"

"Whichever one happens to be free at the moment."

"Dr. Halprin is in his office, I think. I'll check."

She went to one of the doors opening off the reception area, returning after a few minutes to say that Dr. Halprin could see Mitch now.

Halprin lounged behind an oak desk. Stacks of books and papers were lined up around the walls of the office. Sunlight entering through venetian blinds barred the ceiling. Halprin was fortyish, long-limbed, bearded, with deep-set, serene green eyes. He unfolded his considerable length and half-rose to shake hands with Mitch.

"Thank you for seeing me without an appointment," Mitch said, taking the chair facing Halprin across the desk. "I'll try not to take up too much of your time."

Halprin settled back in his chair, one argyled ankle propped on a corduroyed knee, and tented his long fingers in front of his chest. "You're a break from students trying to cajole me into lowering my minimum passing grade requirements. Miss Zoller said you're from Buckskin, so this must have to do with Joseph Pigeon's murder." He shook his head sadly. "Tragic loss, that. Tragic."

"Yes," Mitch agreed, recalling what Valerie Turnbull had said about Joe being something of a luminary on the Northeastern campus. "Did you have Joe in class?"

"Oh, yes. Several classes during the two semesters he was with us. We're not a large department, only two other full-time teachers—another professor and an associate professor. Recently we've added two part-time instructors."

"Then you knew Joe pretty well."

"I would say so, yes. I urged him to stay on for at least another year, but his scholarship was only for the one and he had no money, you see." He sighed audibly. "He said he'd work hard on his own, and I knew he would. He wasn't like so many of our younger students—passable craftsmen, but lacking the discipline and passion needed to produce great art. Discipline alone will take one a good ways along the road to success, but passion is what separates the technician from the artist, and that can't be taught. A teacher gets only five or six students like Pigeon in his career—if he's lucky.''

Mitch was impressed and wished he'd taken a closer look at those paintings in Joe Pigeon's shed. ''I'm looking for a woman, an art student. Joe was seen with her a number of times while he was here. My informant thinks she was called Janis.''

Halprin perused Mitch over his tented fingers. ''You don't know her last name?''

''No.''

''Did your informant describe her?''

''She's Indian. That's about all I know.''

Halprin gazed at his blunt fingertips for a moment. ''Can't think of an Indian art student named Janis. In fact, I don't recall that we had any student named Janis last year. I suppose it could be someone who was enrolled for only a class or two with one of the other instructors.''

''Any idea how I might track her down?''

He gazed at his fingertips again. ''Let me call the NASA office—that's the Native American Student Association.'' He reached for the phone and dialed. ''Betty, this is Tom Halprin in the art department. I need to locate an Indian art student named Janis. I don't know her last name. She was in school here last year, but it might have been for only a class or two. No, I don't know if she's back this year or not. Yes. Yes, all right. I'll be in my office until noon. Thanks.''

Halprin told Mitch, ''She'll check and get back to me. It shouldn't take long for her to go through her card file. Do you suspect this woman of being involved in Pigeon's murder?''

''Probably not. It's just something we have to chase down.'' Since it was obvious that he had admired Joe Pigeon, Mitch decided to tell him a little more in the hope that his confidence would elicit anything Halprin might be holding back. ''I'd like to tell you something, but I'd have to be assured you'd keep it confidential.''

''By all means.''

''We have reason to believe that, for some time before his death, Joe was intimately involved with a woman other than his wife.'' Halprin gazed at him, his green eyes as placid as before. ''You don't seem surprised.''

''To tell you the truth, I suspected it.''

''Did Joe mention it to you?''

''Oh, no, nothing like that. But this is a small town and Northeastern still has a small school atmosphere, in spite of our burgeoning enrollment. Word of such things gets around among the students. I overheard a brief conversation between two of my students last spring. Only a few words, but Joseph Pigeon's name was mentioned. My impression at the time was that they were discussing Joseph and a woman. One of the students said Joseph wanted to keep it quiet because he was married.''

''You didn't hear the woman's name or anything else about her?''

''No, nothing more than I've told you. I wish I could be of more help to you, Chief Bushyhead. Anyone who was in any way involved in this terrible tragedy must be brought to justice.''

''Can you give me the names of the two students you heard talking about Joe?''

He deliberated before saying, ''One of them, Nancy Rice, got married and left school. I don't know how you could reach her. The other was Donna Tandy. She's in my one o'clock class. If you like, I'll explain the situation to her and let you know what she says.''

''I'd appreciate that.'' Mitch handed him a business card.

They chatted inconsequentially for another fifteen minutes until Betty at the Native American Student Association office called back. She had no record of an Indian student named Janis who was currently enrolled at the university or who had been enrolled the previous year.

''That's not absolute proof she wasn't here for a class or two,'' Halprin said. ''Registering with NASA is voluntary, though virtually all of our Indian students do so because the association's newsletter gives them useful information—scholarships or loans available to Native Americans, for example. When I talk to Donna Tandy this afternoon, I'll ask her if she remembers this student from last year."

Mitch thanked the professor and left. Walking across the campus, quiet and almost deserted now between classes, he reflected that it had been an unproductive morning. About all he'd accomplished was hearing Halprin confirm his conviction that Joe was having an affair. He stopped for lunch at the Sizzlin' Sirloin on the main highway through Tahlequah, then headed back toward Buckskin.

In no hurry to get back to where Devay could find him, he decided to stop for a visit with Charley Solomon a few miles out of Tahlequah. Solomon's quarter horse ranch bordered the highway. A couple of years ago, Solomon had retired from the Oklahoma State Bureau of Investigation. While he was with the bureau, he and Mitch had worked on a couple of bootlegging investigations together. Like Mitch, Solomon was a fisherman and every year or so the two men fished the coves and hidden crannies of Tenkiller Lake together.

The road leading from the highway to the ranch house edged Solomon's private landing strip. An orange wind sock fluttered in the light breeze. Flying and horses were Charley's passions. He had a Piper Cub that he used for transportation to horse auctions; and he provided hangar space for other small plane owners in the area, mostly crop dusters. The hangar, a corrugated steel building with two gas pumps beside it, sat in the corner formed by the county road and the graveled drive leading to a white, two-story frame house with black shutters and deep porches in front and back. Charley and his wife, Nell, were sitting on the front porch.

"Wall, look what the coyotes drug up," Charley said as Mitch got out of his car.

"Hi, Charley. Hi, Nell." Mitch grabbed Charley's hard, tanned hand, then hugged Nell, who smelled pleasantly of cinnamon. On her five-feet four-inch frame she carried fifty pounds more than her husband's rail-thin five-feet-eight.

"How's the horse business?" Mitch asked, leaning back against the porch railing.

Solomon's grin crinkled his tanned, leathery face. "Why, we're making money hand over fist out here. We'll probably come out with enough to pay the horses' feed bills this year."

"I keep telling him we could get rid of the horses and sleep late and be better off," Nell said.

"She doesn't understand." Solomon patted Nell's plump knee. "That'd be like selling our kids."

Nell snorted. "Our three kids put together never cost us as much as those horses do. But as long as the stud fees cover their upkeep, Charley might as well be doing that as hanging out in bars with wild women."

Solomon slapped his forehead. "Hell's bells, she's on to me. Musta heard about that blond, spitting image of Dolly Parton."

"Hah!" Nell chided. "Dream on, Charley Solomon."

Mitch laughed and turned to watch an old Cessna 170 taxi out of the hangar along the grass runway and take off.

Solomon followed the Cessna's flight. "Gregory finally woke up."

"I heard him coming in about two this morning," Nell said. "How he can sleep in that hot hangar is beyond me." She sniffed disdainfully.

"Nell's got her feather's ruffled 'cause Gregory turns down her invitations to sleep at the house."

"It's ridiculous," Nell said. "All those empty bedrooms upstairs, and he beds down on the hangar floor."

"Now, Mother," Solomon said, "he wants to keep an eye on his plane. Some men are like that." To Mitch he said, "Gregory and his brother recently started a little freight-hauling business down in South Texas near Brownsville. They make some long hauls. Gregory stopped here once before, about a month ago, to rest and refuel. I think they're just managing to hold things together—they sure can't afford to have some joy-riding kids damage one of their planes."

"Joy-riding kids, my foot," Nell said.

"Just be glad we don't have to dun him for the gas money like some of the other pilots. Last time he left money in a coffee can in the hangar."

"So he pays his bills," Nell admitted, "but he hates people. He's plain weird, if you ask me."

"Nell's mad 'cause Gregory won't come up to the house and jaw with her and let her stuff him with fried chicken and apple pie, like the other pilots do."

"That's weird, all right," Mitch said with a chuckle. "Anybody who would turn down Nell's chicken and apple pie has to be one brick short of a load."

"Speaking of food, Mitch," Nell put in, "we just finished lunch. It's pot roast, not chicken, but there's plenty left. I'll fix you a plate."

"No, thanks, Nell. I ate in Tahlequah."

"Surely, you'll take a glass of iced tea."

"No, I really couldn't hold it right now."

"Well, I'm going in and get you a couple of jars of the apple butter I've been putting up this morning."

"That I won't turn down," Mitch said as Nell went into the house.

"What brings you out this way, Mitch?" Solomon asked.

"I thought I had a lead in the Pigeon case, but it looks like it's fizzled out."

"That artist? Do you know who did it?"

"Confidentially, I think it was his brother, but I can't prove it yet."

They talked for another half hour, planning an October fishing trip. After a while, Nell came out with two pint jars of still-warm apple butter, a loaf of fresh baked whole wheat bread, and some T-bones and a roast from the freezer.

Mitch arrived back at the station at two-fifteen. Duckworth had just returned from a routine patrol and Roo was taking a late lunch break. Duckworth followed Mitch into his office and Mitch gave him the disappointing results of his morning's work.

"Did Jack Derring come after Jeeter?"

"Jeeter still refuses to call him."

Mitch gaped at Duckworth. "What's going on with that guy?"

"I can't figure it."

Struck by a sudden frightening thought, Mitch sat straight in his chair. "When was the last time you checked on him?"

"Before I went on patrol, but if he wants anything, we'll be able to hear him for a block."

Frowning, Mitch rose and left the office. "All we need is for him to go into convulsions or a coma and die in that cell. Did you search him for drugs?"

"Sure. What do you think . . . ?" Duckworth ran to keep up with Mitch's long strides. "He had a bag of grass in his pocket, and I confiscated it."

Jeeter was lying on the cot, legs drawn up, a blanket pulled up to his chin. His eyes were squeezed shut and he was shaking so hard the cot rattled. "Get the key," Mitch said and when Duckworth handed it to him he unlocked the cell and they went in. "Jeeter?"

Jeeter opened his eyes. "Lem-mee a-a-lo-ne." His teeth snapped together between syllables, and his face was the color of dead ashes. He was obviously in agony.

"If you don't want Derring," Mitch said, "tell me who to call."

"No-oo!"

Mitch exchanged a bewildered look with Duckworth. "Why won't you let me call somebody?"

"Lo-ook at me, ma-an," Jeeter got out between clenched teeth. "I'm go-oing cold turk-key. Can't do it un-unless I'm lo-ocked up."

Mitch's worry heightened. Did Jeeter even know what he was saying? From the bizarre way he'd been acting, Mitch had his doubts. Whether Jeeter knew or not, if he died in a cell, Derring would claim Jeeter wasn't responsible and that Mitch should have realized it. He'd talk Jeeter's father into filing suit.

"He didn't eat any lunch," Duckworth said.

"Ca-an't stand smell of fo-ood," Jeeter chattered. "Lemmee 'lone, stinkin' cops."

Mitch gestured for Duckworth to follow him out of the cell. "If he's serious about getting off drugs," he said as they reached the duty desk, "he's going to need medical help. Call his father and tell him to get Derring and come and take Jeeter to the hospital."

"What about the charges?"

"We'll worry about the charges later. I don't want him in here like that."

A little after three, Halprin phoned from Tahlequah. The small spark of hope Mitch felt as he took the call was quickly smothered. The student Donna Tandy remembered the conversation with another student about Joe Pigeon, but she had merely been passing on second- or third-hand gossip. If Joe had been involved with a woman last spring, Donna Tandy didn't know her identity. She had never heard of an Indian art student named Janis, either. Halprin had even questioned a couple of his other students about it, but had come up with nothing.

Fighting an urge to call it a day and go fishing, Mitch thanked Halprin and hung up. Derring and Jeeter's father showed up a few minutes before five. Mitch and Duckworth had to remove Jeeter from his cell by force. "I can't go! I gotta stay here!" Jeeter kept screaming. "They're after me, I tell you!"

"He's hearing voices," Mr. Rheeves explained calmly, as though he'd seen Jeeter in this state too many times before to find it upsetting or even surprising. "Dr. Sullivan will give him a tranquilizer."

Before leaving the station at five, Mitch and Virgil had a cup of coffee in Mitch's office. Virgil had talked to the Pigeon family's medicine man again and reminded Mitch to let him know when he wanted to go out to the old man's house. "He's John Irons," Virgil said. "His Cherokee name is Crying Wolf. I think he'll cooperate with you if he can."

Mitch was not particularly cheered by this news. "It's probably another wild goose chase like everything else we've tried. The council is on my back to make some progress in the case." He stared glumly into his coffee mug. "Maybe I should have followed my instincts when Ellen died and told them to shove this job."

"If you'll remember, you wanted to shove everything. That's the easy way, Mitch."

Mitch grunted. "Easy. Hard. Words, Virgil, just words."

"It'll get better, man. You may not be able to see it yet, but you're a lot better off than you were at first. And we'll crack this case, too. Maybe not this week, but we'll crack it." He paused. "In time there will be someone else, Mitch. You're only thirty-nine. That's not over the hill."

Mitch glared at his coffee, knowing Virgil meant well but knowing also he had no idea what it was like to lose the center of his life, the core that held it all together. He tried to imagine being with someone else, making love to someone else. When Lisa Macpherson's face swam in front of him, it gave him a distinctly uncomfortable jolt.

"Tell me something," Virgil was saying. "Did Ellen ask you to die with her?"

Mitch gulped the rest of his steaming coffee. It burned as it went down. He shoved back his chair impatiently. "What kind of damned fool question is that?"

Virgil's black eyes were calm, persistent. "Did she?"

"Hell, no."

"Then don't do it."

"I appreciate your concern, Virgil, but I'm not in the mood for a pep talk right now. I'm going home. Call me if you need me."

WHEN MITCH GOT HOME from the station, Emily and her friend Temple were in the kitchen, making dinner.

"Don't come in here, Daddy," Emily called. "We want to surprise you."

Temple ran to the kitchen doorway to greet him. She was a petite girl with a thick halo of curly copper-colored hair framing her milk-pale face. Her wide blue eyes were startling in contrast to the almost translucent redhead's complexion. She put Mitch in mind of a baby owl who'd been dipped in flour and was wearing a Halloween wig.

"Hi, Temple. Good to see you."

"Temple's spending the night," Emily yelled.

"Glad to have you." Temple was the first friend Emily had invited home since Ellen's death. Evidently she had taken to heart Mitch's suggestion. "Hey, what smells so good?"

"It's a secret," Temple said. "You read the newspaper or something. We'll bring it in on a TV tray in a minute." She dimpled and ducked from sight.

"It" proved to be lasagna and garlic bread and a tossed salad. They watched anxiously as he sampled the meal and broke into smiles when he heaped lavish praise on their efforts. A few minutes later, they returned carrying two more TV trays.

Mitch felt his tense muscles relaxing and his depression easing as he listened to their girlish chatter. After a few minutes, they seemed to forget he was there.

"Did you know Rosalee Sturgeon was back in school today?" Temple asked.

"No! Really? How did she look? I mean, could you tell?"

"She looked the same as always to me."

"I suppose she would," Emily murmured. "I mean, I guess it's not a major operation or anything."

"Who is Rosalee Sturgeon?" Mitch asked.

Emily and Temple exchanged furtive glances. "She's kind of new," Emily said with an elaborately casual shrug. "She moved to town last spring."

"Is she in your class?"

"She's a senior," Temple said.

"And she's been in the hospital? The way you girls are acting, she must have had an extra head removed."

Temple was unable to repress a nervous grin as she and Emily exchanged another glance. Finally Emily said, "I guess they did it in a hospital. Not in Buckskin, though."

"Had that pesky extra head chopped off, huh?"

Temple giggled and Emily smiled this time. "I guess we might as well tell you, Daddy," Emily said. "It's all over school, anyway." She looked at Temple for confirmation. "Everybody is saying that Rosalee had an abortion."

"I see." What was he supposed to say now? These things happen? No, that might sound as though he didn't take it seriously. I hope you girls have learned a lesson from this? Worse, much worse. "She must be feeling pretty low right now."

"I bet," Temple agreed earnestly. "The kids are all kind of tiptoeing around her. You know what I mean? I wanted to talk to her today, but I didn't know what to say. So I just said Hi, and left it at that."

"Maybe that was the best thing you could have done on her first day back," Mitch said.

"You think so? I hope she doesn't think I'm stuck-up or something."

Emily groaned. "Yeah, I hear that all the time, Temple. Everybody is always saying, 'Temple is *so* stuck-up.'"

"I love you, too," Temple said, laughing.

After dinner, Mitch volunteered to wash dishes and the girls went up to Emily's room to style each other's hair and listen to Madonna tapes. Later, Mitch watched a baseball game on television. The news came on after the game and then an old movie, which finally put him to sleep. He awoke with the muscles in his neck and back protesting painfully about their cramped position. He stumbled upstairs, barely awake enough to notice that Emily's room was silent and there was no light around the door. He stripped to his briefs and dropped like a stone into bed. He knew nothing more until the telephone woke him at six A.M.

He groped blindly for the receiver. "Yes?"

"Chief?"

Duckworth had been the officer on call last night. Mitch sat up groggily. "Yes, Duck."

"I got a call just now from old man Jordan—lives about a mile west on Highway Ten. He went out to milk the cow this morning and says he saw something in the ditch alongside the road. Says it looked like a body to him, but he was afraid to go any closer because he has a bad heart. I thought...well, the old fart's senile but I thought I'd better call you and see if you want to go out there with me."

"I'll meet you at the station in fifteen minutes."

After a quick shower and shave, Mitch dressed and slipped a note under Emily's door, saying he'd try to be back in time to take her and Temple to school. If he wasn't there, they'd have to make other arrangements. He suggested they could walk, but knew that suggestion would be greeted with groans. They'd probably call Mrs. Roberts to pick them up.

Duckworth was leaning against the brick wall of the police station, yawning and looking disgruntled at being rousted out before breakfast. He climbed into the squad car, grumbling. "Old man Jordan's mind is over in Arkansas half the time. Besides having a bad heart, he can't hear it thunder. His kids have been trying to get him to go into a nursing home. Once they got the doctor and a couple of orderlies to try to take him by force. He ran them off with a shotgun."

"Good for him," Mitch said. "How would you like it if other people were trying to take control of your life?"

Duckworth stared at him. "What's eatin' you? They're gonna go out there someday and find him dead or vegged out from a stroke."

"So, he'd rather die at home instead of hooked up to machines. Everybody ought to be allowed to make the choice. People should mind their own business."

Duckworth gave him another hard sideways glance. "You're grumpy this morning."

"Yeah. Well, the last week hasn't exactly been a picnic. We could all lose our jobs if we don't come up with *something* in the Pigeon case, and soon."

Duckworth's head jerked around like a turtle coming out of its shell. "You really think so?"

"Aw, I'm exaggerating. I'll probably take most of the flak. Devay and the council will want a token sacrifice if the case ends up in the unsolved file."

"That'd be real bright," Duckworth grumbled. "Can the only officer in the department with experience in homicide investigation."

"That was over ten years ago."

"What difference does that make? Geez, it'd be about Devay's speed to fire you, the grinning jerk."

Vere Jordan was watching for them from the porch. He came out in the yard as the police car turned into the drive.

"Morning, Mr. Jordan," Mitch called as he got out.

The stoop-shouldered old man was reading his lips. "Morning, Chief." He watched Duckworth waddle around the car, then shifted his gaze back to Mitch. "It's down that side road about a quarter mile," he said, pointing. "I keep Clementine—that's my milk cow—in that field, so that's how I happened to see it when I went out to milk."

"What time was that?" Mitch asked.

Jordan cupped his ear. "What say?"

Mitch stepped closer and shouted, "What time did you go out to milk Clementine?"

"Oh. 'Bout five forty-five. I hurried right back here and called the police station. Clementine's been bawling for me to come milk her for the last little while, but she'll just have to wait. I hope it ain't one of them dang optical illusions. I been having 'em lately. Cataracts."

"We'll go on down there, Mr. Jordan," Mitch yelled. "You did the right thing to call us."

Back in the car, Duckworth gave Mitch an I-told-you-so look. "Optical illusions. The old coot didn't mention that before."

Mitch backed the squad car out of the drive and continued west to the graveled section-line road. "You have something more important you should be doing?"

"Yeah, eating breakfast. My stomach feels like my throat's been cut."

A Holstein cow with a tight bag came over to the fence and bawled at them. "Must be right about here," Mitch said, pulling up. The ditches on either side of the road, called bar ditches in this part of the country, were deep to accommodate runoff from heavy spring rains. Oklahoma got most of its rain all at one time, usually in the spring, sometimes in the fall. They left the car and walked over to the ditch bordering the Holstein's pen. Clementine chewed her cud and watched them with huge, placid brown eyes.

A body lay crumpled in the bottom of the ditch. It was clothed in jeans and a dark-colored windbreaker. The corpse lay facedown, the back of the head a bloody mess. A veil of weariness settled over Mitch. He didn't have to see the face to recognize Jeeter Rheeves.

Jeeter had been shot at the base of the skull at very close range. A small-caliber gun, Mitch judged; otherwise half Jeeter's head would be gone.

"Gawd help us," Duckworth said in an awestruck voice, "it's Jeeter. I thought they took him to the hospital."

"He must've checked himself out." Mitch hunched his shoulders; the weariness was still there, weighing him down. "Go back to Jordan's house and call an ambulance. I'll wait here."

The squad car tires threw gravel as Duckworth took off in a hurry. Mitch climbed down in the ditch and went through Jeeter's pockets. He'd apparently been dead for several hours; rigor mortis had set in.

The pockets gave up nothing but a tattered wallet containing Jeeter's social security card and an expired driver's license.

Mitch sank down to sit on the rim of the ditch. The last time he'd seen Jeeter, he'd been kicking and fighting being taken from the jail cell. *They're after me, I tell you.* Those were the last words Mitch had been able to distinguish as Jack Derring and Jeeter's father wrestled him into the car. His father had assumed Jeeter was having a psychotic episode, hearing threatening voices; they'd all assumed that. After all, Jeeter's behavior for the twenty-four hours prior to that had been bizarre. He'd practically begged to be thrown in jail. He'd refused to make a phone call. He'd preferred suffering the pain of drug withdrawal to being out on the street.

Now he was dead, murdered, and Mitch was left to deal with the last time he'd seen Jeeter alive, to deal with it in an entirely new light. If Jeeter hadn't been in a psychotic state, but instead had been in legitimate fear for his life, then his behavior became comprehensible. Mitch had made the decision to take Jeeter out of the cell. Frustration knit through with regret lurched sickeningly in his empty stomach.

"Dammit, Jeeter," he muttered, "why didn't you tell me?"

Too many years of seeing cops as the enemy? Too many scrambled brain cells to think clearly?

After the ambulance attendants had removed the corpse, Mitch and Duckworth drove back to the station. Duckworth went out for doughnuts and coffee while Mitch phoned Jeeter's father. In spite of all the grief Jeeter had given them, Mr. Rheeves's voice broke on the telephone and Mitch could hear his wife sobbing in the background.

"He begged us not to take him to the hospital," Rheeves said in answer to Mitch's questions. "He pleaded with me to bring him home instead. I couldn't force him to go to the hospital when he was so set against it. Mr. Derring agreed with me. Dr. Sullivan came to the house and gave him a shot, and he went right to sleep. We were trying to let him rest as long as he could, so we didn't check on him until a few minutes ago. That's when we first knew he was gone. I was getting ready to phone Mr. Derring when you called."

"You don't know when he left the house, then."

"No. We didn't hear a thing." Rheeves paused to compose himself. "He was a sick boy, Chief. Who could have done this terrible thing?"

"We'll find out," Mitch promised, wishing as he hung up that his words didn't sound so hollow. The easy conclusion was that Jeeter had been killed in a disagreement over a drug deal. But that conclusion didn't sit right with Mitch. There had been two murders in Buckskin in a week. Jeeter had found Joseph Pigeon's wedding ring. The likelihood that the killings were connected was inescapable. Unlike Pigeon's, Jeeter's murder hadn't been a spur of the moment decision; the murderer had come prepared with a gun. Did the killer know Jeeter had found Pigeon's ring? Did he think Jeeter could identify him? Hell, Mitch himself had as much as told Jack Derring that Jeeter could identify the man who threw the ring into the lake. He'd known Derring would repeat his words to Jeeter and had hoped to shake Jeeter up and make him reconsider if he was withholding information.

Something had shaken Jeeter up, all right. The murderer, too.

Duckworth and Roo entered the station together. Duckworth was answering Roo's questions about the discovery of Jeeter's body.

Mitch came out of his office. "Duck, let's go out to Jeeter's camp." He fished a doughnut out of the box Duckworth carried. "We can eat on the way."

They had no trouble finding the camp this time. It looked about the same as it had when they'd been there the previous week. Mitch started searching through clothes and bedding.

"What are you looking for?" Duckworth asked.

"Nothing. Anything."

Mitch tossed the clothing aside and picked up a crumpled quilt. When he shook it, a wadded piece of paper fell out. He smoothed it out. It was an ordinary piece of cheap letter-size white paper, the kind sold in dime stores for typing paper. Words and some individual letters had been cut from a magazine and pasted on to read: "Be at phone booth outside post office Sun morn at 7. IMPORTANT."

Mitch handed the note to Duckworth. As he read it, his brow wrinkled above the mismatched eyes. "Druggies don't usually go to so much trouble to contact their pusher."

"Yeah. I saw Jeeter sitting outside the post office Sunday morning about seven-thirty. He looked worse than I've ever seen him. He must have just taken the phone call from whoever sent that note, and he was terrified. He tried to pick a fight with me then, and again Monday morning when I got to work. He was probably hiding somewhere all night."

"They must've told him they were gonna kill him!"

"That's the only thing I can imagine that would make Jeeter *try* to get himself arrested. When insults didn't work, he urinated on the sidewalk in front of the station, where we'd be sure to see him."

"The poor jerk. He knew they were after him. No wonder he didn't want out of jail. Geez, he must've got crossways with some heavy dudes in the drug trade."

"I don't think so," Mitch mused.

Duckworth's eyebrows slanted downward steeply toward the bridge of his nose, deepening his frown. "If he wasn't in trouble with drug traffickers, who shot him?"

"Whoever killed Joe Pigeon. Jeeter found Joe's ring. The murderer thought Jeeter could identify him."

Duckworth whistled. "Wow! We've got us a serial murderer on our hands."

Mitch started back to the car. "A full-scale panic is what we'll have on our hands if you say that where anyone else can hear you. I want something understood. As far as anybody outside the department is to know, we're convinced Jeeter's murder resulted from a quarrel over turf with out-of-town drug dealers." Before he started the engine, he looked over at Duckworth and added sharply, "I mean it, Duck. Not a word about Joe Pigeon or anything connected with the other case."

"Not even to Geraldine?"

"Especially not to Geraldine. You know how those gals at the Three Squares gossip."

"Yeah, I guess you're right." Duckworth slumped down in the seat. "She'll know I'm holding back something. I can't put anything over on that woman."

"Tell her you're worried about your health or your job— anything to divert her."

SIXTEEN

By THE TIME they got back to town, word of Jeeter's murder had already reached at least two members of the city council. Devay and Derring were waiting for Mitch, pacing his office like two pit bulls raring to get into the ring.

Devay hit him with the big guns the second he stepped into the office. "Mitch, you have to find the murdering maniac who's running loose in Buckskin."

Wordlessly, Mitch walked around his desk and lowered himself into his swivel chair. Devay looked scared, he noted, and he might have found that amusing if he hadn't been fully engaged in holding onto his temper. Why wouldn't they keep out of his hair and let him do his job?

"What do you think I've been trying to do for the last week, Bob?" Devay waved that aside with an impatient grumble.

"Going fishing, for one thing," Derring snapped. "Spending a full day out of town for another."

Mitch ignored Derring. "Bob, you said 'maniac,' singular. You got a hot lead or what?"

Devay looked even more alarmed. "Are you saying there are two killers loose?"

"We have to proceed on that assumption unless we turn up evidence to the contrary. There are some real bad people in the illicit drug business—"

"Bullshit," Derring interrupted. "Jeeter saw Joe Pigeon's murderer. He was killed to make sure he didn't talk. You know it and we know it, Bushyhead, so cut the crap. Jeeter knew the killer was after him, that's why he wanted to stay in jail. Didn't he tell you that?"

Mitch bolted half out of his chair and, bracing himself with his hands, leaned across his desk. "Watch my lips, hotshot. I begged Jeeter to tell me what was wrong with him. All the dumbhead would say was that he was trying to kick his habit, cold turkey. I was afraid he'd go into convulsions. I had a responsibility to get him medical attention." Derring flinched, giving Mitch fleeting satisfaction.

"You know no more about the Pigeon murder than you did a week ago," Derring snarled. "As for Jeeter, if you'd had any experience in this kind of thing, you'd have known he was afraid to leave that cell. You're incompetent!" Derring's face was red with righteous indignation. "I should have been notified of Jeeter's arrest as soon as he was brought in."

"Why? So they could have killed him sooner?" Suddenly weary beyond words, Mitch sank back into his chair. He gripped its wooden arms in frustration. "Jeeter refused to make a call or tell me who to contact. Oh, hell, will you two go and let me get to work."

Neither of them moved. Devay cleared his throat. "I conferred with other councilmen before we came here, Mitch. We'll get out of your way, at least until Thursday night, but we expect to receive a complete report on the two murder investigations at the council meeting. I don't think I have to tell you that if you've still made no progress, we may feel obliged to bring in outside help on this."

Mitch stared at Devay, and he looked away. As though following some unspoken command, Derring and Devay stood at the same time and left the office. Neither of them said goodbye.

Mitch reached for the Pigeon case file, then slammed it back on the desk violently. He stood at the window and scowled at the main street. An elderly woman entered the post office, and a couple of young women who worked at City Hall came out of the drugstore carrying coffee in Styrofoam cups. They were talking intently, and he would bet money they were talking about the murders. That would be everybody's topic of conversation today.

Hands clenched at his sides, Mitch spent a brief moment fantasizing a fistfight in which he punched Derring and Devay about the head and shoulders until they begged for mercy. Unless he'd made an arrest before the Thursday night meeting, he had no intention of revealing any part of the investigation. If they confiscated the file or decided to bring in outside help, he'd give them his resignation on the spot.

Mitch cursed under his breath and turned away from the window, wondering what "outside help" Devay had in mind. The county sheriff's department? Oklahoma State Bureau of Investigation? A private investigator? He gazed at the Pigeon case file for an instant, then shoved it, backwards so the label was hidden, in the bottom drawer of his file cabinet, then locked the drawer.

He pushed thoughts of the council meeting out of his mind in order to concentrate on the latest murder. Who knew that Jeeter found Joe Pigeon's wedding ring? Mary Pigeon, certainly; Virgil had asked her to identify the ring. Jack Derring knew, and there was no telling how many people Derring had told. Even one of his own officers might have let the information slip. They weren't accustomed to being guarded in what they said about police investigations. Most of the cases they dealt with weren't that sensitive. Did Kingfisher Pigeon know? Mitch wondered. The question filled him with a sense of urgency to be out of the office, doing *something* to further the investigation.

He found Roo at the duty desk and told him where the file was. "Nobody is to know where it's kept except you, Duck, and Virgil. If anybody else asks for it, you can't find it. Understood?"

Roo, who had seen Devay and Derring leave Mitch's office, gulped and squeaked, "Understood, Chief."

"When Duck gets back from patrol, you two go out to Highway Ten where we found Jeeter and interview people who live in that area. Also anybody who lives between there and town. Ask them if they saw Jeeter walking along the highway last night, or if they noticed a car turning off the highway on that county road bordering Jordan's farm. Everybody was probably in bed, but maybe we'll get lucky. Maybe somebody had insomnia or was up with a crying baby. Maybe somebody, at least, heard a gunshot."

"Okay, Chief."

"I'm going over to Virgil's and the two of us will be talking to some people out in the Going Snake Mountain area. If you need me, you can reach me on the radio." After giving Helen the same information, Mitch drove to Virgil's house.

Trudy answered his knock. "I hate to wake Virgil," Mitch said, "but I need to talk to him."

"He's already up, Mitch," Trudy said. "Come on in. He's in the kitchen, eating his breakfast."

Virgil sat at the big oak table, wolfing link sausages and pancakes drowned in maple syrup. "You look like a man who just ran over his faithful old dog," Virgil observed as Mitch dropped into a chair. "Don't blame you, either."

Trudy set a cup of coffee in front of Mitch and left the room quietly, sensing that Mitch wanted to talk to Virgil alone. "You heard about Jeeter?"

Virgil nodded, chewed, and swallowed a bite of sausage before he said, "Heard the ambulance and called the station. Helen didn't know what had happened yet, but when Duck came in and told her, she called me back. Of course a few minutes after that, Trudy's friends started calling with the news."

Mitch ran a restless hand through his hair. "Duck and Roo are going out to Jordan's neighborhood, see if anybody saw or heard anything suspicious last night. For lack of any other logical avenue of investigation, it seems as good a time as any for us to talk to that medicine man."

"Don't see how he can help us, but I admit it's as good as anything I can think of."

"I had another visit from Devay and Derring this morning. They gave us until Thursday night to come up with something or the do-do is going to hit the fan."

Virgil mopped a bite of pancake around in maple syrup. "That figures. Most of those guys will crumple at the first sign of public pressure."

"I'm sorry to keep asking you to help when you're not on duty, Virgil. I'll try to get you some overtime pay."

Virgil scooped up a soggy forkful. "I won't hold my breath," he said philosophically. "Let me finish this and get dressed."

MITCH TURNED OFF the highway and followed the road around Going Snake Mountain. "I've always wondered about something, Virgil," Mitch said. "When you decided to become a police officer, did your family or friends try to talk you out of it?''

"A few of the Nighthawks made some cracks about me upholding the white man's law," Virgil answered. "It made me mad at first, but I finally hit on an explanation that shut them up. I stood up at a Nighthawk meeting and told them that my gunbelt was my loincloth and my badge was my war paint. I asked if anyone there could tell me another way, in this day, for a young man to be a warrior like our ancestors were. They couldn't, and I didn't hear any more criticism after that."

Mitch laughed. They passed the elder Pigeons' farm, and after that there were a few houses and the gravel grew sparser and finally gave out. They continued on the dirt road.

"Turn off up ahead there," Virgil said. "The other side of that big cedar."

Mitch detected no sign of an opening until the car reached the cedar, and then he saw a narrow dirt lane, hardly wider than a footpath. "Can we take the car down that?"

"Most of the way," Virgil said. "Just go slow."

Mitch turned in and the car crept along, amid the call of jays, between thick-growing wild cedars and blackjacks that were shedding their leaves. Eventually they reached the end of the lane and were forced to stop. Ahead and on both sides of them was unbroken forest.

"What now?"

"Now we get out and walk."

Mitch killed the engine and locked the car. He followed Virgil through tall, shedding elms, a light wind rustling treetops. Dead leaves crunched beneath their feet. Occasionally they walked into spiderwebs and slapped the clinging threads from their faces and clothing. It wasn't hard for Mitch to imagine dislodging a black widow or deadly fiddleback and knocking it into a fold of clothing. They were too busy finding their way to talk. After about ten minutes of this, they came to a clearing with a small shack in its center.

"This is it," Virgil said.

Mitch could hardly believe that someone actually lived in the shack. It appeared to have only one room—two if they were very small—with a porch in front.

"Should we call to him, let him know we're here?"

"He's known for the last five minutes," Virgil said. "He's been listening to our approach."

They walked up on the porch, which creaked with their weight, and Virgil rapped at the closed door. From inside, a voice called, "Come in."

Virgil opened the door and stepped inside. Mitch hesitated, his hand on the rough door facing. The faint smell of tobacco drifted out of the house; the interior was dim and shadowed. Mitch entered. Rough-woven curtains were drawn over the room's two windows, but a single shaft of light shone between the curtain and edge of one of the windows. The light illuminated a brown, wrinkled hand. Mitch waited an impatient few moments for his eyes to adjust well enough for him to make out the man to whom the hand belonged. An elderly Cherokee sat cross-legged on the floor. His long gray hair was plaited in a single braid that hung over one shoulder. Mitch couldn't guess his age: somewhere between seventy and ninety was as close as he could come.

"Thank you for seeing us, sir," Mitch said, and even though the words were low they shattered the silence like gunshots.

The old man looked up and Virgil said, "Crying Wolf, this is my boss, Chief Mitchell Bushyhead."

The old man nodded and looked directly into Mitch's eyes. "I told Virgil he could bring you here." He spoke gruffly and with dignity, and from his accent Mitch knew that he spoke more often in Cherokee than in English.

"I hope you'll be able to help us," Mitch said. "Virgil says you might be willing to talk to me about medicine."

"Virgil has told me you can be trusted," Crying Wolf said. His eyes, as black as space, gazed penetratingly at Mitch. "You have Cherokee blood?"

"Yes, sir. My father was a full-blood. He left Cherokee County as a young man. My mother was white." He watched the old man's face for an indication that his white blood lowered him in the medicine man's estimation. He saw none.

Crying Wolf merely nodded and said, "I can see that you have white blood, but you are Cherokee, too." He raised one hand to indicate that they were to sit on the floor with him.

Mitch followed Virgil's example, but he felt awkward and a little silly seated, Indian fashion, face-to-face with the old man.

Before speaking again, Crying Wolf took advantage of Mitch's proximity to examine his face with his penetrating black eyes. Few people had ever looked at him so closely, and it made Mitch want to stir or speak, but he forced himself to remain silent. The old man's face was as wrinkled as a terrapin's. As he examined Mitch, the wrinkles shifted, rearranging themselves into new patterns. Then the medicine man said, "I am known in the white world as John Irons. I am known to my people as Crying Wolf. I will help you if I can."

Not knowing where to start, Mitch said hesitantly, "Virgil says you're a medicine man."

Crying Wolf inclined his head. "Any Cherokee can use medicine. I am a member of the Nighthawk Keetoowahs, the medicine clan of the Cherokee people, one of the original seven clans. Virgil is a member, too." He glanced at Virgil gravely. "Not all of our members make medicine. They have forgotten or they never knew the rituals. So they ask me to make medicine for them. It is also true that Cherokees who are not Nighthawk Keetoowahs can use medicine."

"Is their medicine accepted by the Nighthawks?" Mitch asked, finding himself intrigued with what the old man was saying.

"Yes," Crying Wolf said slowly. "Any Indian can learn Cherokee medicine from people within the society. You understand, I mean by medicine how to use tobacco."

"I'm not sure I do understand," Mitch admitted.

"The way the tobacco is remade is what makes the medicine," Crying Wolf said patiently.

"There must be a ceremony, you mean."

"Yes, and the words that are spoken must be in Cherokee. When the tobacco is remade, it can be used for many purposes. These purposes are not for you to know."

"Isn't Kingfisher Pigeon a member of the Nighthawk society?"

Crying Wolf searched Mitch's face again before he responded. "Yes, he is."

"If Kingfisher knew how to remake tobacco, could he use it for evil purposes?"

Mitch was watching the old man closely, and he saw that his question caused a spasm of uncertainty to unsettle the wrinkles around Crying Wolf's eyes. "It is possible, but any man who does that will condemn his soul forever."

"Sir, we found the remains of a homemade cigarette outside Joseph Pigeon's house after he was murdered, and we know Kingfisher went to Joe's house the evening he was killed."

"Virgil has told me this. That is why I agreed to see you. If the Nighthawks are harboring a murderer, the man must be punished and the society purged."

Mitch wondered if he meant that the society would punish the killer, or that they would allow the white man's law to do it. He didn't ask for fear of spoiling the rapport that seemed to be developing between him and the old man. He chose his next words with care. "Let me tell you what we are faced with, sir. A week ago we had several suspects who might have had reason to kill Joe, but since then we have pretty well eliminated all of them, except Kingfisher Pigeon. We know Kingfisher disliked his brother intensely and that he went to Joe's house the evening Joe died. I questioned Kingfisher, but I don't think he told me the truth about much of anything. I suspect the cigarette we found was used in a medicine ceremony, performed by Kingfisher or by somebody acting for him."

Virgil's eyebrows drew together as he listened to Mitch practically accuse Crying Wolf of performing the medicine ceremony. Mitch sensed that Virgil was trying to catch his eye to caution him, but he didn't look away from the old man. "Sir, at this moment you are our last source of information. I know I'm asking you to talk of sacred matters, but if you don't help us, the murderer may never be caught. Whatever you tell us will not be repeated to anyone without your permission. I give you my word."

Long moments of silence passed and none of the three men moved. Mitch felt slightly uncomfortable at first; most people couldn't stand that much silence and would say something, anything to break it. Crying Wolf seemed to have little awareness of time passing as he pondered Mitch's words. He's comfortable with silence, Mitch thought; he probably can't conceive of speaking merely for the noise.

At last, Crying Wolf said, "I don't think you have faith in Cherokee medicine."

"I don't know anything about it, so I'm in no position to judge."

Crying Wolf nodded, as though he approved of Mitch's answer. "I understand. You have Cherokee blood, but you were raised to be white."

"Yes," Mitch said.

"No man can help the way he was raised," said Crying Wolf, surprising Mitch with his tolerance. "But both of us want to see justice done. I will tell you something now that should only be talked of in Cherokee. But you do not understand your father's language, so I will speak in your tongue. There are times when a good man must choose between two things that are right."

"Yes, sir."

"Sunday night I slept in the woods. I dreamed of the *Uk'ten'*. Do you know about the *Uk'ten'*?"

Mitch shook his head and Crying Wolf continued. "The *Uk'ten'* was a monster, like a very big snake. He had spots on his body and horns and claws and his breath was poisonous. When the *Uk'ten'* lived on earth long ago, a man could even be killed by walking in the *Uk'ten'*'s path. At that time men had to live in caves, they say, to be hidden from the *Uk'ten'*, because the *Uk'ten'* roamed about looking for people to kill and eat."

The old man's voice was deep, rhythmic, and Mitch could easily imagine him sitting beside a campfire telling such stories to his people. "What happened to this monster?"

"A brave man who lived in that long ago time decided that the *Uk'ten'* had to be killed or men would always live in caves like animals and fear to walk on the earth. This man—I do not know his name—was told by the old men of his clan that he would have to hit the *Uk'ten'* on his seventh spot to kill him. The first time he drew his bow, he missed. The second and third time the arrow went under the *Uk'ten'*. The fourth time he drew his bow, the arrow hit right upon the seventh spot."

Mitch was mesmerized by the story with its sacred regard for the number seven, the theme found in the myths and legends of many cultures.

"Then," Crying Wolf said, "the *Uk'ten'* fell over and floundered about and thunder came, louder than any we hear in these days, and lightning flashed all around, they say. Thunder and the *Uk'ten'* had a fight to decide which one would live among people. The *Uk'ten'* caused it to rain hot fire, and the fire rained until he was completely dead. The people came from their hiding places after that. Since that time Thunder has been the Cherokee's friend." Crying Wolf was watching Mitch, as though to gauge his reaction. "I told you the story of the *Uk'ten'* to help you understand my dream."

"The *Uk'ten'* was in your dream?" Mitch couldn't say the monster's name with the same guttural roll as the old man.

"Yes. You see, I have been worried that Kingfisher Pigeon or some other Nighthawk might have killed another human being. Before I slept, I asked to be given a message in my dream so I would know if this is true. In my dream, the *Uk'ten'* was in the sky, flying back and forth, and bright streaks of fire flew out from his body. He crossed the sky four times not very far from where I was sleeping. Then Thunder came and the *Uk'ten'* flew away. When I woke up, it was raining and my blankets were wet."

Virgil spoke for the first time since the conversation between Mitch and Crying Wolf began. "I don't understand the dream's message, Grandfather."

"Dreams must be interpreted by the dreamer," Crying Wolf said slowly. "I didn't understand right away, either. I thought about it all day. Later, I understood. When Thunder chased away the evil one it meant that the person who killed Joseph Pigeon was not a Cherokee."

Mitch stirred restlessly and Virgil said quickly, "Is it possible that you could have misinterpreted the dream?"

For a moment, Crying Wolf closed his eyes as though to think more deeply. "It is possible, but I do not think so."

"Sir," Mitch interjected, feeling another potential informant slipping away from him. "If you refuse to help us and it turns out you're wrong about the dream, then you could be shielding a murderer."

"You are a determined young man, Mitchell Bushyhead."

"Sir, I am desperate."

"I have thought, too, of what you say. If I misunderstood the dream and the murderer is a Cherokee, I may be guilty of helping an evil man go unpunished."

"If you are right about the dream, wouldn't you be helping to clear Kingfisher Pigeon by telling us what you know? Truth can't hurt an innocent man."

For the first time, a whisper of a benign smile touched Crying Wolf's wrinkled lips. "That is a good argument. Yes, what you say is true."

Mitch breathed a sigh of relief. "*Did* Kingfisher Pigeon ask you to make medicine at his brother's house?"

The old man bowed his head as though to pray. After a few moments, he looked up and said, "Yes. Kingfisher Pigeon came to see me Saturday, a week ago. He asked me to make medicine to separate his brother and Joseph's woman. He did not ask me to make medicine to send his brother's soul to the Nightland. If he had, I would have refused."

"I apologize for my ignorance, sir, but is the Nightland death?"

"Yes. Nobody who knows me would ask that. They know I would not do it."

Mitch nodded. "The woman that Kingfisher wanted to be separated from his brother, was it Mary, Joe's wife?"

Crying Wolf stiffened slightly. "I do not make medicine to separate a man and his wife. That would be a misuse of my medicine."

"I'm sorry," Mitch said hastily. "I didn't understand. I thought, because Mary is white—"

"She is Joseph's wife," Crying Wolf said. "Color has nothing to do with it."

Mitch realized that he was suddenly alert. Beside him, Virgil tensed. "Did he tell you the woman's name?" Mitch asked.

"Of course," said Crying Wolf, no longer surprised by Mitch's abysmal ignorance of the ways of his father's people. "I could not do the medicine properly without both names."

Mitch glanced at Virgil and saw the excitement in his expression, the same excitement that was making Mitch's heart beat faster. "Will you tell us the woman's name?"

"Before you came here, I would have said no. I took a vow, you see. But I also took a vow to uphold what is right, and as you say it is always right to tell the truth."

Mitch was afraid to speak, afraid to move, almost afraid to breathe, for fear he might do something to change the old man's mind. He gripped his knees with taut fingers, waiting.

"You must understand that I will not speak in a white man's court. Even if you give me one of your white man's papers I will not come."

Mitch believed him. They could subpoena Crying Wolf till hell froze over, but he would not appear. This proud old man would sit in a cell the rest of his life before he would go against his conscience. "I understand."

"Then I will tell you what you ask. The woman's name is Valerie Turnbull."

SEVENTEEN

HALFWAY ACROSS the clearing, Mitch could contain his amazement no longer. "Valerie Turnbull! How do you like them apples?" It was the first time either of them had spoken since leaving Crying Wolf's cabin.

"It blows me away," Virgil said. "I can't believe it, but I know he wouldn't lie. If he hadn't wanted to tell us, he'd have said so."

They left the clearing and entered the woods, single file, Virgil in the lead.

"That was my impression." Mitch pushed a branch out of the way with one arm. "But what in tarnation does it mean?"

"Beats me, partner. It doesn't fit with the other things we know." Virgil grunted as he swerved to avoid a thorny tangle of wild blackberry vines.

Mitch was looking away and plowed into the thorns before he saw them. He muttered a curse and extricated himself with extreme care. They gave up trying to talk in order to concentrate on weaving their way back to the car.

The interior of the closed squad car felt like a blast-furnace. Windows down and air-conditioner blowing full force, Mitch threw his left arm across the back of the seat and backed the car slowly over the narrow trail.

Upon reaching the county road, Mitch stopped the car and rolled up the windows. He turned to Virgil. "Okay, let's lay out what we have. For weeks, maybe months, before Joseph Pigeon died, he was having an affair that he managed to keep hidden. Even his own wife didn't know about the other woman for sure until two nights before Joe was killed, and she claims she doesn't know the woman's identity."

"Assuming that's true," Virgil said, "how did Kingfisher know? As far as we've been able to find out, he'd had nothing to do with his brother for months until he went to Joe ten days ago. That was Sunday, so how did he know about Valerie Saturday when he went to see Crying Wolf?''

"Maybe he only pretended to know the woman's identity for some unfathomable reason." Mitch knew that made even less sense, but he was still reeling from hearing the old man say Valerie's name.

"He wouldn't use a made-up name for a medicine ceremony. You don't play games with medicine."

"Okay, then maybe he saw Joe twice, the first time on Saturday after Mary moved out, and that's when Joe told him about Valerie," Mitch reasoned. Almost immediately, he shook his head in frustration. "Even if Joe and Kingfisher talked on Saturday, I can't see Joe telling Kingfisher about the affair when he'd taken such care to conceal it before that."

"Neither can I. Joe and Kingfisher weren't on speaking terms. Even if they were trying to mend their fences, I don't think Joe would've trusted Kingfisher enough to confide in him."

"There was no fence mending," Mitch said. "When I talked to Kingfisher the day of the funeral, he didn't have a kind word to say about his brother."

"Something else that doesn't make sense. If Kingfisher *did* know about Valerie, why would he care enough to try to separate them?"

"I don't get it, either. He makes no bones about the fact that he doesn't like Mary and didn't approve of Joe marrying her. So what difference would it make to him if Joe was carrying on with another woman, white or Indian? But, dammit, he cared enough to ask Crying Wolf to make medicine to separate Valerie and Joe."

Both men sat in morose silence for a minute. Then Virgil said, "We're missing something. I can't think of a single reason for Kingfisher to take it so seriously he'd use medicine. What would he have to gain by separating them?" He scratched his head. "When you think about it from Valerie Turnbull's point of view, having an affair with Joe Pigeon makes even less sense."

Mitch snorted. "It doesn't have to make sense for Valerie to do something that reckless. Maybe that's what she liked about it, the recklessness."

"She's supposed to get married in six weeks. Would she risk screwing that up?"

Mitch thought about it. When he had spoken to Valerie, she had seemed truly to believe that Joe had great talent. That might have intrigued her. Of course, the fact that Joe was off-limits by her parents' standards might have appealed to her, too. Joe was unemployed, a full-blood from a conservative Cherokee family, and married. He had "Don't touch" signs all over him. Valerie was the kind of woman to whom that would be a challenge, not a deterrent. Mitch didn't think she was crazy enough to dump Jack Derring and his future for somebody like Joe. That wouldn't have been a factor; it was the risk of getting caught—the danger—that she thrived on. She must have loved the scheming, breaking the rules and getting away with it. She must have loved feeding Mitch that cock-and-bull story about Joe being involved with an Indian girl named Janis in Tahlequah, and watching him fall for it, hook, line, and sinker.

"Jack Derring has an ego that won't quit," Virgil said. "If this got out, the humiliation would kill him. And *he'd* probably feel like killing little old Valerie."

The two men stared at each other as the next step in the chain of logic burst upon them simultaneously. "Yeah," Mitch said, "or maybe he'd feel like killing Joe Pigeon."

"He might be cocky enough to think he could get away with it, all right."

"Having gone that far, he wouldn't hesitate to take out Jeeter, too." Absently, Mitch tapped the steering wheel with his knuckles. "I told Derring myself that Jeeter could identify the man who threw the axe and Joe's fingers into the lake." Mitch's mind cringed at the thought that his lie could have motivated Jeeter's murder. "Derring encouraged Jeeter's dad to take him out of jail, against Jeeter's wishes, and then he didn't insist that they take him to the hospital. It would've been much harder to kill Jeeter in the hospital and get away without being seen."

"Jeeter must have known," Virgil said. "No wonder he refused to call Derring from jail."

"It all fits, doesn't it?"

"Except for one thing. Why did Derring cut Joe's fingers off?"

Tired of putting the puzzle together again and again and always ending up with at least one piece too many, Mitch rubbed both hands over his face as if he could wipe away the extra piece in that way. "I haven't figured that one out yet."

"The other stuff, we can make fit, theoretically," Virgil said, "but we better have iron-clad evidence or he'll never be convicted. He probably wouldn't even be brought to trial. Derring's a big man in this county."

"Tell me about it. Our theory doesn't explain how Kingfisher Pigeon fits into it, either. I didn't think he even knew Derring or Valerie, beyond maybe knowing their names."

"I wouldn't have thought Joe knew Valerie well, either. They didn't exactly move in the same circles."

"They *were* at Northeastern at the same time," Mitch pointed out, "and maybe she saw him differently at the university. According to one of Joe's professors, he was considered a great talent on campus." He started the engine again and reversed the car's direction. "As long as we're this close, we might as well rattle Kingfisher's cage. You mind using up another hour of your off-duty time?"

"You're kidding. I wouldn't miss this for anything."

Mitch stepped on the accelerator and headed for Kingfisher Pigeon's house about a mile farther along the road. The house was a simple six-room affair, living room, dining room, and kitchen, front to back. No available space was taken up with a hallway. Each of the family rooms had a door leading to one of the three bedrooms, and there was a single bathroom between the front two bedrooms. On his previous visit, Mitch had been surprised at the neatly trimmed, fenced yard and what appeared to be a fresh coat of yellow paint on the exterior.

Mitch made sure the Pigeons' two coon hounds were confined to a separate yard before opening the front gate. Kingfisher Pigeon himself came to the door.

"Hello, Kingfisher," Virgil said. "Maybelle." He nodded to the trim, compactly built Cherokee woman who hovered behind her husband.

Clearly not in the mood for pleasantries, Kingfisher snarled, "What do you want?"

"We'd like to ask you a few questions," Mitch said.

"You already asked me a few."

"Something new has come up in your brother's case. We need to talk to you about it." Noticing Maybelle Pigeon's anxious expression, Mitch suggested, "Maybe you'd like to come outside where we can talk in private."

"I got nothing to hide from my wife," Kingfisher said, not moving.

"Then may we come in?"

Kingfisher glanced at his wife. It was obvious he didn't want to let them in, but perhaps he thought a refusal would carry more weight, coming from her.

"Let them in," Maybelle said. "They'll keep bothering you until you talk to them."

Wordlessly, Kingfisher turned and walked away from the door. His wife opened the screen and Mitch and Virgil stepped inside.

The house was tidy and meticulously clean, the linoleum floor waxed and gleaming. The living room furniture—brown vinyl with wagon wheel designs on the arms and legs of the occasional tables—though not expensive, appeared to have received little use. Since there were four school-age children in the house, the furniture was obviously a recent acquisition. The house was quiet now; the kids would be in school at this time of day.

"You can sit on the couch," Maybelle said as she closed the door, but there was no hospitality in her tone. A fan in the living room window was turned on to circulate air.

Kingfisher sat in the big vinyl armchair, arms folded across his chest, closed, resentful, uncooperative. His wife took the pine rocker and leaned forward, clutching its arms. Ignoring Mitch, she said, "Virgil, why do you want to keep pestering us? You know Kingfisher. You know he wouldn't have anything to do with murder."

Virgil shifted uncomfortably. "Nobody's accused Kingfisher, Maybelle. Look, I know Joe and Kingfisher didn't get along, but surely you both want the killer caught and punished.''

"We can't help you,'' Maybelle said impatiently. She glanced at Mitch. "We've told you all we know, but you keep badgering us.''

Maybelle Pigeon's accusing eyes made Mitch wish they had caught Kingfisher alone. He was not welcome in her well-cared-for home, and for her sake he felt faintly embarrassed about being there. "Kingfisher, would you prefer to have a lawyer present when we question you?''

"He doesn't need a lawyer!'' Maybelle responded for her husband. "Besides, we don't even know one. What use do we have for a lawyer?''

"Don't you know Jack Derring?''

Maybelle looked at him in puzzlement. "No, not really. I've seen his name in the paper, but I'm not sure I'd know him if I saw him.''

"What about you, Kingfisher? I was under the impression you'd had some dealings with Derring.'' It was the only thing that made the pieces fit. Derring must have paid Kingfisher to go to Joe and tell him to stay away from Valerie. It would explain where Kingfisher got the money for the new furniture and the paint job. Being the man he was, Kingfisher went to Crying Wolf for medicine as added insurance. When Derring heard about Joe's refusal, he wouldn't have expected Cherokee medicine to do the job—even if Kingfisher told him about the ceremony, which was doubtful. So Derring lost no time in killing Joe. A logical theory, but still only a theory.

Kingfisher grunted contemptuously. "I don't know where you got your information, Bushyhead, but it's wrong. I don't know the man. What has this got to do with Joe's case?''

"We have reason to believe your brother was having an affair with Derring's fiancée, Valerie Turnbull.''

"Valerie Turnbull!'' Maybelle blurted. "You mean the daughter of Mr. Turnbull, at the bank?'' She laughed. "That's the craziest thing I ever heard. What would a girl like that want with Joe?''

No point in trying to explain to Maybelle Pigeon. She was an uncomplicated woman; she'd never understand about people who found their comfortable, affluent lives so boring they thrived on crazy risks, living on the edge.

Mitch had been watching Kingfisher for his reaction, but there was none, at least none that was detectable. He couldn't tell Kingfisher how he knew about Valerie; he'd given Crying Wolf his word.

Virgil said, "Kingfisher, we need your help on this, if we're going to catch Joe's killer. Tell us what you know."

Angrily, Kingfisher pushed himself from his chair. "Virgil, I already told Bushyhead. I went to see Joe to talk to him about forgetting our quarrel for the folks' sake." His hands were balled at his sides, and his feet were spread, as though he were bracing himself for a fight. "That was when he told me Mary had left him, and it was the first I knew about it. He didn't say nothing about Valerie Turnbull or any other woman. Hell, I don't believe it, anyway. A woman like that, looks, money, everything going for her. She wouldn't even notice somebody like Joe. If he was standing nose to nose with her, she'd look right through him. People like us don't even exist for people like her. Did you *see* them together?" His blazing dark eyes bored into Virgil, then scorched Mitch. "Answer me that."

"No," Mitch said, "we didn't see them."

"Have you talked to somebody who did?"

"No."

"Then get the hell out of my house."

It was useless, Mitch realized, but then he'd known it would be. He rose. "Sorry to bother you, Mrs. Pigeon." At the door, he turned back. "Have you been away from home any night this week, Kingfisher?"

"I told you to get out!" Kingfisher shouted and stalked from the room.

Maybelle Pigeon rose, looking anxiously up at Mitch. "Why do you want to know that?" She waited for his answer, absolutely still, like a deer alerted by an unfamiliar sound.

Mitch wished again that they'd found Kingfisher alone. "There's been another murder, Mrs. Pigeon."

"That drug addict who wanders the streets—yes, I know. My sister called this morning to tell me." Her head came up, her nostrils flared. "You can't think my husband had anything to do with *that*! We don't have anything to do with drugs!"

"No, ma'am."

She was visibly upset. "That boy who was killed...*that's* why you want to know where Kingfisher was last night! You've got it in for him, for some reason. You—"

"Mrs. Pigeon, I don't think Kingfisher killed Jeeter Rheeves, but I think he might have an idea who did."

"That's ridiculous. I can tell you where he was any night you want to know about. Sunday night he played cards with friends, men he grew up with, at Gene Smith's house. They get together every month or two like that. Last night, when that Rheeves boy was killed, Kingfisher was here with me and the children—all night. I can swear to that."

"Thank you, Mrs. Pigeon." Mitch left the house quickly. Virgil was waiting for him in the yard. "She says he was here last night," Mitch said. "She'll swear to it."

Virgil looked at him thoughtfully. "I thought Derring was our prime suspect."

"Still is, but we have to tie Kingfisher to Derring to figure out why Kingfisher wanted Joe to stay away from Valerie." Driving back to town, Mitch said, "One of them's lying, Kingfisher or the medicine man, and we both know who we'd bet on."

"I was afraid you were going to tell Kingfisher what the old man said."

"That wounds me, Virgil. I gave my word."

"We also have no case against Derring. If we could connect him to Kingfisher, we'd at least have a starting place. It's a tough dilemma."

"If I have to, I'll explain it to Crying Wolf first and ask him to release me from my promise."

"There aren't many more like him."

"Medicine men?"

"No, there will always be medicine men, I guess, but not men who've remained virtually untouched by the twentieth century."

"You stayed in the house with him for a few minutes, after I'd gone outside. What did you say to him?"

"I told him you'd found Jeeter's body this morning." Mitch was trying to sort this out when Virgil continued. "According to his beliefs, you contaminated his house today because you were near a corpse. I wanted him to know so he could do whatever he needs to do to get rid of the contamination."

Mitch experienced a mixture of surprise and interest. Finally, he asked, "Do you believe in the *Uk'ten'* and all that stuff about Thunder and getting messages in dreams?"

Virgil was silent for a long moment. "It makes about as much sense to me as some of the things our preacher says."

Mitch glanced over at him, hugely startled, since he knew that Virgil attended the Baptist church in town faithfully with his family. "You better be careful where you say that. The Baptists have been known to de-church heretics."

"I don't disbelieve, either. I keep an open mind. I figure two insurance policies are better than one."

Mitch hooted. "I see your point."

He let Virgil out at his house, then used the car radio to ask Helen if Duckworth and Roo had returned to the station. They hadn't, and he told her he'd probably be back within the hour, but if not he'd check in again. He drove to the Turnbull house, turning into the drive and following it to the back of the house. Valerie's car wasn't parked there, nor in the garage. He went back to his own house for lunch, leftover lasagna heated in the microwave.

Emily called as he was eating. "Daddy, I'm glad I caught you. Helen said you'd be back at the station pretty soon, but I only have a few minutes left of my lunch hour. I wanted to tell you we're having pom-pom practice after school, and at seven they're having tryouts for the all-school play...so Temple and I thought we'd go over to her house for dinner and Mrs. Roberts can bring us back here for the tryouts. When she comes back after Temple, she can drop me by the house. Is that okay?"

"If I follow you, yes."

"Oh, and Mrs. Roberts said it was okay. Temple already called her."

"When do you think you'll be home?"

"Nine or ten. It depends on how many people try out."

"Did Mrs. Roberts take you to school this morning?"

"No...uh, Kevin Hartsbarger goes right by our house, so we called him."

"I see."

"Daddy, did Jeeter Rheeves really get shot in the head?"

"Really. That's why I had to leave so early."

"I figured. What's going on in this town, Daddy?"

"Honey, I wish I knew."

"Well, I have to go now."

"Good luck with the tryouts."

"Thanks, Daddy. Bye."

Mitch hung up, wondering where fifteen-year-olds got their energy. If he were honest with himself, he'd have to admit that Emily's plunge into high school activities left him feeling a bit neglected, and that made him feel selfish. *Loosen the reins*, he told himself. *Would you rather she had no friends and no interest in extracurricular activities?* Of course, he didn't wish that. He couldn't expect Emily to fill the void in his life left by Ellen's death.

He finished the lasagna and his mind went back to the meeting with Crying Wolf. The Cherokees were one of the five "civilized tribes," among the first to embrace the white man's culture. True, they had done so out of necessity, seeing it as the only way to preserve their tribal identity and remain a separate nation. In spite of their efforts to do whatever was necessary to earn the federal government's recognition and respect, they hadn't been a nation with their own territory since statehood in 1907. As a group, Cherokees had probably intermarried with whites more extensively than any other North American Indian tribe. There remained pockets of conservatives who continued to fight assimilation, but even after living in this rather isolated corner of Cherokee County for ten years, it still surprised Mitch how many Cherokees continued to put their faith in Cherokee medicine. He had never felt any affinity with that kind of Cherokee; and he hadn't expected to come away from the meeting with Crying Wolf with such a strong feeling of respect for the old man and his beliefs.

He thought about Crying Wolf's dream of the *Uk'ten'* trailing fire across the sky and being chased away by the Cherokee's ancient friend, Thunder. He did not doubt that the old man had had the dream and that he believed he'd been given the message he sought: The Nighthawk Keetoowahs were not harboring a murderer. At this point, Crying Wolf's interpretation of his dream seemed to be true. Mitch was convinced that Jack Derring was the murderer, as convinced as he had once been that the killer was Kingfisher Pigeon. Unfortunately, conviction and proof were poles apart.

He had to admit that he'd rather pin the crime on Derring than on some poverty-stricken Indian with a family to feed. He would have to guard against letting that color his investigation. Valerie was the nut he had to crack, and a tough nut she would be. Maybe it was just as well that he hadn't found her at home earlier. If he had more facts, he would have a better chance of shocking her into telling the truth when he questioned her.

For the first time he thought about George Turnbull and what it would do to him if Mitch's current theory proved to be correct. George had had more than his share of grief, and Mitch wouldn't enjoy adding to his burden. When he questioned Valerie, he'd do it without George's knowledge, Mitch decided. George would find out soon enough if the investigation turned up the evidence to bring Derring to trial; but if not, George might never have to know. Being Valerie's husband would be a punishment of sorts if Mitch couldn't pin the murders on Derring, he told himself, but that would give little consolation. If this ended with Mitch convinced Derring was a murderer who got away, it would never stop eating at him.

By God, he wasn't going to let that happen.

Mitch left his dirty dishes in the sink and drove to the station. A few minutes after he walked in, Detective Harry Baker phoned from Tulsa.

"Mitch, I asked a couple of gals at the station to make some phone calls for me. They can't find any Devay registered at a local hotel or motel last week, but Valerie Turnbull was at the Sheraton from September ten to September thirteen."

"I already knew Valerie stayed somewhere in Tulsa; but the other was a long shot."

"Something else came up that might mean something, or it might not. One of the clerks misunderstood the assignment. She checked hospitals as well as hotels. A Valerie Turnbull checked into a local hospital on September ten and out on September eleven. That was all the clerk could get from the records department without a court order, except that this Valerie Turnbull was in Room Fifty-one-oh-nine. Thought I'd mention it. There are twelve Turnbulls listed in the Tulsa phone directory and there are probably a few more in outlying suburbs."

"I guess the name isn't all that rare," Mitch said. "Thanks for your help, Harry. Next time I'm in Tulsa, I'll buy you lunch."

"I'll hold you to that, Mitch."

Mitch replaced the receiver and leaned back in his swivel chair with his hands behind his head. Valerie Turnbull in the hospital? Why? She might have gone into the hospital without telling anyone, if she didn't want people to know what she was there for. Maybe she'd had plastic surgery. Boob enhancement? Mitch laughed at the thought. Talk about carrying coals to Newcastle. Valerie had been well-endowed since the age of fourteen. What about some other kind of plastic surgery, like removal of fat from stomach or thighs? The only thing was, he had seen Valerie since her return from Tulsa and she had looked the same as always. Voluptuous curves in all the right places. Anyway, she couldn't have checked into both the hotel and the hospital on the same day. He was grasping at straws, as desperate men were prone to do.

Duckworth and Roo came back at one. "Wasted trip," Duckworth told Mitch. "Nobody heard or saw a thing."

"Jeeter could have been shot somewhere else," Roo said, "or the gun could have had a silencer on it."

"Have you heard from the medical examiner yet, Chief?" Duckworth asked.

"No. We probably won't before tomorrow or the next day. You two better take your lunch break now. I'll hold down the duty desk until you get back."

Mitch took some blank forms out to the duty desk with him and filled out reports on the morning's interviews with Crying

Wolf and the Pigeons. He marked the reports "Confidential to Rabbit, Duckworth, and Stephens only," and signed his name. If the reports fell into the wrong hands, the information they contained would hit Buckskin like a bomb, and the fallout would alter a number of lives. Everything would come out at the trial—if there was a trial. Until then, Mitch put the two reports in a separate folder that he locked in the trunk of his squad car. He would brief Duckworth and Roo orally on the contents of the file after lunch and stash the written reports at home.

He spent the latter part of the afternoon in his office, staring at the earlier reports in the Pigeon file, hoping that if he reread them often enough, two pieces of the puzzle might suddenly fall together in a new way. It didn't happen, even after he'd batted the evidence around with Virgil when he came on duty at four. By six-thirty, Mitch was thoroughly sick of the cracked ceiling and institutional gray plaster walls of his office and sicker still of the whole Pigeon investigation.

He was almost home when he remembered that Emily wouldn't be there before nine o'clock. The thought of scaring up something for dinner and then eating it alone depressed him. The thought of eating in a restaurant in Buckskin, where at least a dozen people were bound to seek him out to talk about the murders, didn't thrill him, either.

Driving slowly, he turned a corner, and then another, reversing his direction and heading away from his house and back toward the business district. He passed up the restaurants on the main drag. That left the drive-through windows of the two fast food places, but he merely glanced at them as he passed without turning in. Neither fried chicken nor a burger appealed. He left the business district and cruised slowly through residential neighborhoods on the west side of town, debating whether to drive out of town for dinner or go home and hypnotize himself with television.

On Oak Street, he recognized Lisa Macpherson's blue Honda Civic parked at the back of a lot beside a detached two-car garage with rooms above it. Reflexively, his foot eased off the accelerator, and he pulled over to the curb in front of the next house.

He sat there for a few minutes, wondering what he thought he was doing. She had invaded his mind several times since their last meeting, fleeting impressions of golden hair and a sunrise smile that he had pushed aside because they made him feel uncomfortable. Okay, they made him feel guilty, like an adolescent sneaking peeks at the *Playboy* centerfold in the drugstore, and snatching looks over his shoulder to see if his lecherous absorption was being observed.

He realized that the meeting with Lisa at the roadhouse had left him with a sense of something hanging, unfinished, and he wanted to see her again. His refusal to recognize that before now was absurd, he told himself. Holding that thought, he walked to the driveway and down it to the garage apartment.

She answered the door wearing jeans and a gray sweatshirt with "Patience, hell! I'm going to kill somebody!" emblazoned in red letters across the front. On her feet were white cotton socks.

Holding the edge of the door with one hand, she placed the other on her hip as she smiled at him. "So you finally caught up with me, Officer. Put away the handcuffs. I'll come quietly."

He relaxed and grinned. "Smart lady. Now I won't have to get out the rubber hose."

She laughed and made a sweeping gesture for him to enter. The small living room seemed to be almost entirely filled with books. In three bookcases crowded in among chairs and a brass-armed daybed that, with bolsters propped against the wall, doubled as a sofa, between bookends on tables and a small television set, and stacked on the floor at either end of the daybed. Apart from the books and daybed, there were a couple of comfortable-looking, blue-padded rattan chairs—one with a brass pole lamp beside it—and double windows with white ruffled curtains and a view of a chunk of sky and the driveway.

The pictures on the walls were prints of famous paintings; Mitch recognized one as Van Gogh's *Sunflowers*, another as Wyeth's *Christina*.

"You look tired," she said. "Want some coffee?"

"I want dinner," Mitch said. "Put your shoes on and come with me."

"Like this?" She held her arms out and looked down at the words lettered across her chest. There was a yellow pencil tucked behind her ear and her shining gold hair was mussed as though she'd been running the pencil through it. She looked comfortable and relaxed. "I don't think so."

"We'll sneak out of town."

"In your police car, I presume."

"That would draw some attention. Okay, I'll go get my own car."

She thought about it. "I only came home a few minutes ago. I really don't want to go out again today. Would you settle for a sandwich?"

He'd take whatever he could get. "What kind?"

She laughed. "We'll find something."

"You have plenty of mayonnaise?"

"A brand new jar."

"You sold me."

She cleared a place for him at the kitchen table among books and student papers.

"Have you made an arrest in the murder investigations?" she asked, as he crunched his way through rye bread, a pile of crisp bacon, lettuce, tomato, and American cheese.

"No, but I have some new evidence and a new suspect."

"I'm curious as all get-out." She linked her fingers on top of her head and leaned back in a cane-bottom chair. "If you'd prefer not to talk about it . . ."

He studied her for a long moment. She looked at him, her eyes alight with interest and her full bottom lip caught softly between her teeth as though to keep herself from asking more questions. God, he missed talking over cases with Ellen. He found himself wanting to talk to Lisa about the investigation, a woman he barely knew. Odd that it didn't feel like "barely."

"Can you keep your mouth shut?"

She sat forward eagerly. "Absolutely."

His instincts told him he could trust her, and it might help to talk it through with someone who knew none of the parties involved and could therefore be objective. He hoped he didn't live to regret relying on instinct in this particular case.

"Well..."

"Wait." She rose, opened the refrigerator, and took out two beers. "Let's go into the living room."

They sat on the daybed-sofa, he sprawled back against a bolster, his feet stretched out in front of him, she with a pillow on her drawn-up knees to rest her chin on.

She listened with great absorption and when he had finished, she said, "Whooee... I've heard some of the teachers mention Jack Derring and Valerie Turnbull. I've gotten the idea they're sort of local gentry."

"The closest thing to it in Buckskin. Makes it tough to get the evidence I need. At this point my whole case is suppositional and theoretical."

She made a rueful face, her eyes full of understanding and intelligence. "Jack Derring must be sharp and very clever to have reached where he is. But murdering two people seems really stupid to me."

"Emotions can blot out intelligence and common sense for a few seconds, and that's all it took. The first murder was probably accidental. It was at least unpremeditated. The second murder was to cover up the first. I think Derring went to Joe Pigeon's house to tell him to stay away from Valerie, but Pigeon laughed in his face and Derring lost his head."

"Hmmm. Derring will know exactly how to conduct himself on the witness stand, won't he?"

"If I ever get him there."

"Poor Mitch. I wouldn't want to be in your shoes right now."

He reached out and touched the toes of a stockinged foot. "You couldn't keep them on, unless you put both feet in one shoe." He lifted his head and, because he didn't want to stop touching her, he let his fingers brush her cheek. "Talking about it helps me get my thoughts in order. Thanks."

She went very still, her eyes wide, solemn. He smoothed her shining hair and leaned toward her slowly. The kiss was gentle and easy, and it sent shock waves along all his nerves. Breaking the kiss, he caught her face in both hands. "I don't want to go."

"Oh . . ." She took a shaky breath. "I know that. But I still think it's too soon. It's—"

He stopped the words with another kiss, this one longer and deeper than the first. "It's exactly the right time."

Her eyes fluttered open and she stared at him for a long moment. Then, without a word, she rose from the sofa and took his hand.

IN LISA'S BEDROOM, waning daylight was a muted white edge around the window blinds.

As she rose above him, he placed his hands on her hips and guided her down. Except for a single soft shuttering of dark lashes, her eyes didn't leave his. Her pale skin seemed to glow from within, rosy and luminous. Yet her eyes were darker than he'd ever seen them. Deep inside her, he shuddered, as if he had plunged into a molten lake and had to fight the compulsion to let go and seek oblivion beneath its surface.

"When I first saw you at the door," she whispered, "I wanted you inside me like this."

He turned her on her back and thrust deeper. She rose to meet him, wrapping her legs around him, and her hands splayed on his hips pressed him deeper.

Outside, dusk crept slowly, silently. Inside, the light around the blinds dimmed and grayness crept along the walls. The room smelled of sun-dried sheets and the faint lilac scent of her skin and sex.

Her arms and legs enclosed him, and his flesh slid smoothly against hers on a film of perspiration. She was all around him, and with a groan and surrender he buried himself in her.

In that moment, all strangeness fled, and legs, hands, rose-tipped breasts, the faint trembling of parted lips were made familiar by the rightness of things. She kissed his damp shoulder and sat up, cross-legged on the bed. "Did you banish any ghosts?"

"I did that before I came here." He wasn't sure it was true, but he wanted it to be. "What about your ghost?"

"My ex?" She turned her head, no longer meeting his eyes. "I got over him a long time ago."

He pulled her down beside him and held her close. After a long silence, she went on in a careful, quiet voice, half muffled against his skin. "I wasn't enough for him...he wanted an heir."

He cradled her head in the hollow of his shoulder. Her breath was warm on his skin. "I had all the tests, and we were told I'd never bear a child. Adoption was out of the question. He wanted a child with his blood flowing in its veins. He raved on and on about the unfairness of it, as though I'd married him under false pretenses." She swallowed. "So, anyway, it was never right between us after that, and when he found someone else, I was glad, really..."

"He sounds like a spoiled brat."

"Yes..." She pressed her face into his neck. "He is."

"But you loved him."

"At first—for a long time. Later I hated him for making me feel deformed, like a freak."

He heard the utter vulnerability in her voice. "Lisa, you are a completely beautiful woman, inside and out."

She lay still for a moment, and then she rose up on one elbow. "You're a sweet man." She watched her fingertip trace his eyebrow and the strong line of his nose, her lips pressed together, her expression grave, until he pulled her head down and opened her mouth with his.

EIGHTEEN

DEEP IN THE NIGHT, Mitch came awake with Lisa's question in his mind: *Did you banish any ghosts?* Is that what he'd hoped to accomplish by taking her to bed? Certainly not consciously.

But he couldn't rid his mind of what Virgil had asked him: *Did Ellen ask you to die with her?* Virgil's question had irritated Mitch at the time, perhaps because he'd sensed an implicit accusation that in some sick way he was becoming too comfortable with his sorrow. God, fate, whatever, had done him wrong and Virgil seemed to think Mitch meant to get even by refusing to let it go. Evidently, Virgil saw a tendency in him to wallow in his grief, feed off it, and he'd been trying to make Mitch confront the tendency.

He hadn't gone to Lisa with any conscious intention of using her to exorcise his demons. Yet he wasn't sure that the unconscious motivation hadn't been there. Nor had he totally convinced Lisa, for as he was leaving she had said, "Mitch, I don't regret what happened, but it could become a habit I'd find hard to break. I don't think we should see each other again until you know in your heart that you're free."

After what she'd been through, he understood her need to say it, and he had to respect her wishes. She'd been deeply hurt by her ex-husband. What kind of man blamed a woman for her inability to bear children? What kind of man discarded a woman like so much trash when he discovered she couldn't serve his purposes?

As Mitch asked himself these questions, there was a nameless shifting at the back of his mind, like the colors of a kaleidoscope starting to fall into a different pattern. He tried to free his mind of thought, to see the new pattern. When that didn't work, he sent his memory back over the past two weeks until he found the connection he'd been searching for. Mary Pigeon. He could still hear the pain in her voice: *Maybe if Joe and me could've had children...* She had left Joe with the cruelest words he could have uttered echoing in her ears. *He said she was more a wife to him than I ever was.*

Valerie? Trying to fit Valerie into any man's idea of the perfect wife was so ludicrous to Mitch that his mind boggled at accepting the thought. But if not Valerie, who?

There was another soft click back in the nether regions of his mind where the pieces were still trying to settle into place. He groped for the bedside lamp, turned it on, and sat up. He reached for the telephone, got the number he wanted from information, and dialed.

A woman's voice answered. "Five West. Mrs. Dorsey speaking."

Mitch said the first thing that came to mind. "A friend of mine is on your floor, at least she was. I'm trying to reach her, but I can't remember her room number. She was in Room Fifty-one something. Her name's—"

"That's Five East," the woman interrupted. "I'll transfer you."

Another woman answered, this one sounding harried. "OB-GYN. This is Miss Carter."

Mitch was still trying to decipher the letters she'd reeled off. "Hello? Is anybody there?"

He held the receiver to his ear another moment until, finally, he comprehended. He replaced the receiver without speaking.

It didn't make sense. *That* Valerie Turnbull could not be George's daughter.

Too tightly wired to go back to sleep, he pulled on a robe and went downstairs where he could pace without disturbing Emily. He tried to abandon the line of thought upon which he was embarked, but it was too intriguing. Sometimes things only seemed impossible because you didn't have all the facts.

What *did* he have? Fact: A Valerie Turnbull had been in the Obstetrics and Gynocology Unit of a Tulsa hospital overnight during the time George's Valerie was registered at the Sheraton in the same city. Fact: When Mitch had talked to Valerie Sunday morning, she'd seemed abstracted, certainly not high with excitement as you'd expect a young woman preparing for her wedding to be. It was as though, Mitch thought, she'd had something besides the wedding at the forefront of her mind.

Suppose she'd left her luggage at the Sheraton and sneaked into the hospital for the night. If so, why was she in the OB-GYN Unit? One thing he could discard. Valerie was out and around Buckskin all summer, right up until the day she went to Tulsa, so she hadn't gone there to have a baby. She hadn't been pregnant. He backed up and tried to get a rein on the rush of suppositions. All he actually knew was that Valerie hadn't been far enough along to show. Could she have checked into the hospital to abort a fetus? It happened all the time. According to Emily and Temple, a student at the high school had recently had an abortion.

He let his mind turn that over for a bit. Then he added another floor to the already shaky house of cards. If the two Valerie Turnbulls were one and the same, and if she'd undergone an abortion, she had been bent on secrecy. Knowing Valerie, Mitch didn't think she'd care much if people found out she'd had an abortion unless…unless her fiancé didn't know she was pregnant. Since Jack Derring was marrying Valerie in a few weeks, Mitch thought Derring might not take kindly to Valerie's getting rid of his child. So, if it was Jack's baby, he knew nothing about it. Or if he did, Valerie didn't *know* he knew. The other possibility was that the baby wasn't Derring's.

Suppose it was Joe Pigeon's baby. That made Joe's parting remark to his wife more understandable; the pregnancy might have been so important to him it made Valerie more of a wife to him than Mary. But the last thing Valerie would want would be to have Joe Pigeon's baby, or for Derring to find out she was pregnant; it would be impossible to pass off a half-Indian child as Derring's. So secrecy would have been essential.

The house of cards, if outrageous, remained erect. But it was all supposition and built on an assumption that was itself hard to swallow. Mitch couldn't imagine Valerie getting pregnant without intending to. She had been lifting her skirts since the age of fourteen. Mitch knew this because once, during Valerie's sophomore year in high school, George, while in his cups, had poured out the story of the latest crisis with his daughter.

They had been fishing the lake from George's boat, a cooler full of beer on the boards between them.

Having suspected for some time that Valerie was what in earlier generations was called "easy," Opal had waited up for her daughter the previous night. By the time Valerie came home at two A.M., Opal was in a frenzy of worry and anger. A condition further fueled by several stiff drinks, Mitch had thought at the time. Opal met Valerie as she tiptoed through the door and all the suspicions that had built in Opal for months gushed out. Valerie's reaction had not been what one might expect of a fifteen-year-old girl.

She had merely laughed and said, "Of course I let boys do it to me, Mother. I have been for a year. Why shouldn't I?"

Stunned, Opal had reached back in her memory for an argument that must have been effective in her tender years. "You're in for a rude awakening, you little tramp! You'll end up an old maid. Men don't marry the women they sleep with."

Valerie had been amused. "Poor Mother, you're so Victorian. Why, I'll have my pick of men when I decide to get married, don't you worry. Until then I'll have as much fun as I can. I *like* it, don't you understand that?" At Opal's wordless, choking sound, her daughter had added, "Oh, Mother, don't you like for Daddy to do it to you? I'm sorry."

In a state of near-apoplexy, Opal had rushed into the bedroom she shared with George, slamming the door hard enough to shake the house. While Valerie slept peacefully, Opal was awake the rest of the night, and she kept George awake, too. After Opal stopped raving, they hashed out their options, all but one of which were untenable, given the daughter they'd been blessed with. The next day Opal took Valerie to a doctor in Tulsa, who told her horror stories about venereal disease before prescribing contraceptive pills.

Mitch shook his head and kept on pacing. No contraceptive was 100 percent effective, of course. As fantastic as the theory was, it provided a possible explanation for how Jack Derring discovered that his fiancé was sleeping with Joe. A man notices even small changes in the body of his lover. If Derring was the killer, it followed that he knew about the pregnancy and—

however he'd reached his conclusion—he believed the baby was Joe Pigeon's.

The ironic implications of his theory were not lost on Mitch. On the one hand, you have Mary Pigeon and Lisa Macpherson feeling inadequate because they're barren. On the other, a high school girl and Valerie Turnbull aborting unwanted fetuses. The world had its own crazy scale of balances.

How was he going to get any hard evidence? He couldn't get a court order for Valerie Turnbull's hospital records on the flimsy basis of a wild, middle-of-the-night construction of events. Even if he could, the records might not tell him whether the patient and George's Valerie were the same woman. Valerie would have thought of the possibility of the records falling into the wrong hands, so she might have used another address. She could have rented a Tulsa post office box specifically for receiving hospital mail.

It was a sure thing that Kingfisher Pigeon wasn't going to admit *anything*. Valerie probably wouldn't, either, but Mitch knew he had to take a stab at her today.

He waited until nine o'clock to go to the Turnbull house, knowing George would have left for the bank by then and that he should be able to find Valerie at home that early in the morning. If she was still in bed, he'd ask the housekeeper to wake her.

Valerie's car wasn't parked in the driveway at the back of the house, but Mitch didn't bother checking the garage before he rang the bell. After a minute, he heard hurried footsteps and Mrs. Nuttall, a widow in her sixties who had been the Turnbulls' live-in housekeeper for more than fifteen years, opened the door.

"Why, good morning, Chief Bushyhead."

"'Morning, ma'am."

"You've missed Mr. Turnbull."

"I didn't come to see George. I'd like to talk to Valerie."

Her shoulders seemed to slump as though in resignation. She had always reminded Mitch of his first-grade teacher, a tall, big-boned woman who'd worn her dresses to the ankles, regardless of current fashion, and whose graying hair was always slicked back and bound in a tight coil at the back of her head.

From the rear, they could have been the same woman. But his teacher's face had been smooth and serene. Mrs. Nuttall's was lined with care. She had been with the Turnbulls so long that she felt like a member of the family and, being a natural worrier, she fretted about their problems. "Don't tell me she's gotten another speeding ticket," she said.

"It's not urgent," Mitch said, preferring to let her think what she chose, "but I really do need to talk to her, even if you have to wake her."

"Oh, she isn't here. She left about an hour ago."

"Do you know when she'll be back?"

"She didn't say."

"Where did she go?"

"She didn't tell me that, either."

"Mrs. Nuttall, may I come in and talk to you?"

His request seemed to trouble her, but she invited him into the kitchen. "I don't like talking about my employer's family behind their backs," she said severely. "Whatever you have to say, I'd prefer you say it to Miss Valerie."

"I understand perfectly. I'd be disappointed in you if you felt any other way, Mrs. Nuttall." The ramrod straight line of her mouth relaxed a little. "Is that a fresh blueberry coffeecake?"

She relaxed a little more and began to bustle. Mrs. Nuttall's blueberry coffeecake was famous in Buckskin, the recipe carefully guarded. "It surely is, Chief. If you have time, I'll cut you a piece."

"Mrs. Nuttall, I'd have time for your blueberry coffeecake if I was on the way to a fire," Mitch flattered shamelessly as he made himself comfortable at the kitchen table. She brought him the still-warm coffeecake with a cup of coffee. She had unbent enough to sit at the table with him and she flushed with pleasure when he sampled the cake and flattered her some more.

Her wariness returned when he asked casually, "Was Mr. Derring here Monday night?"

"Mr. Derring is here almost every night," she said primly.

"I wouldn't ask, if it weren't important," Mitch told her. "Mr. Derring's whereabouts Monday night may have some bearing on a police investigation."

She stared at him, and there was a flicker of unease in her eyes. "This isn't about a speeding ticket, is it?"

"No, ma'am. It's a bit more serious than that."

"Mr. Derring was here Monday night," she said reluctantly. "He came about eight to pick up Miss Valerie, and he brought her back a little after eleven."

"How long did he stay after that?"

"Not long. I'm sure no longer than a half hour." She gripped her hands together on the table, but her eyes never left Mitch. "That Rheeves boy was killed Monday night."

"Yes, ma'am." She looked frightened now. "I don't want to upset you. I have a long list of people whose activities Monday night I'm trying to pin down. Most of what we learn in the investigation of a crime leads nowhere. It's a matter of eliminating as suspects people who were connected to the victim. It's routine."

"I know Mr. Derring was that boy's lawyer, but . . ."

Mitch nodded. "He was one of the last people who saw Jeeter alive. He and Jeeter's father picked Jeeter up at the station and took him to Mr. Rheeves's house late Monday afternoon."

"Oh, I see." Her clasped hands relaxed somewhat. "I didn't know that."

"How did he seem when he came to pick up Miss Valerie? Did he seem nervous or worried?"

"I didn't notice anything like that. Of course I only saw him for a minute or two. I let him in and went upstairs to tell Miss Valerie he was here. While he waited, I asked if he'd like something to drink, and he said no. I went on back to my bedroom, and I heard them leave a few minutes later."

"When they returned, did he seem all right—I mean, did he seem about the same as always to you?"

"I didn't see them. I was already in bed, but I wasn't asleep yet and I heard them come into the house. They were talking low because Mr. Turnbull had already retired. I think they were in the den."

"And Derring left about thirty minutes after that?"

"Yes. He usually stays later. Of course I'm asleep by then but sometimes the sound of his car starting up wakes me. He parks beside the house near my window. He must have been tired or he needed to get up early Tuesday morning. Unless—'' She caught herself, but not in time.

"Unless what, Mrs. Nuttall? Anything you think of might help me cross Derring off my list and go on to the next name.''

"Well, I was just thinking that they could have argued. I didn't hear an argument, but Miss Valerie hasn't been the easiest person to get along with lately...snapping at everybody.''

"Why do you think that is?''

She lifted her hands, palms up, then let them drift back to the table. "Miss Valerie is the last one I'd expect to have prewedding nerves, but that must be what it is. She's been all jitters the last few days. Lord knows how she'll be five weeks from now for the wedding.''

"When did you first notice this?''

She frowned. "I guess it was before she went to Tulsa to buy all those new clothes. Yes, I remember, it was right before that. She and Mr. Derring were supposed to go to a party in Muskogee. Some friend of Mr. Derring's was having it, another lawyer, I think. Anyway, she called him at the last minute and said she couldn't go. She said she wasn't feeling well. She went up to her bedroom, but she didn't go to bed. I heard her walking around half the night. It kept me awake. I went up there— oh, it must have been about one A.M.—to see if I could do anything for her. She said she was all right, but she was as nervous as a cat. Her hands were shaking.''

Was that the day Valerie found out she was pregnant? Mitch wondered. "How long was it, after that, when she went to Tulsa on that shopping trip?''

"The very next day. Up and decided on the spur of the moment and she was off. I think she wanted to be alone for a few days, away from the house and Mr. Derring. Between you and me, I wondered if she was considering breaking off her engagement.''

"She didn't.''

"No. She came back with a wedding gown and trousseau, but she's been a bundle of nerves ever since. She's always been a late sleeper, but not now. Half the time she's up at dawn, and she roams around this house like a caged animal and then she'll fly out of here and jump in her car and take off somewhere. She might be back in an hour, or she might not be back all day.''

''Do you think she's still having second thoughts about getting married?''

She sighed. ''I suppose I do. Tuesday morning I heard her on the telephone in the study. She was talking to Mercy Becker. Mr. Derring rents the first floor of Mercy's house. Ever since Mercy's father died she's lived in the upstairs apartment and rented out the ground floor. Miss Valerie was talking real friendly like to Mercy and naturally I thought that was strange because Mercy Becker is no friend of Miss Valerie's. They have nothing in common. Mercy's fifty years old if she's a day and she's a staunch Mormon. Won't even drink coffee. Why, I've heard Miss Valerie make fun of Mercy.''

''Did you hear what she was saying to Mercy?''

''Not all the words, and what I caught didn't make much sense. At the time, I thought she was trying to find out what time Mr. Derring got home the night before. When she hung up, she muttered something about the old biddy lying through her teeth and something else about Mr. Derring catting around on her and she'd scratch his eyes out if she found out he was. Then she stormed out of the house and was gone all day. She was off again this morning. Honestly, I don't know what's come over that girl. I don't think Mr. Derring would be sneaking off with other women behind her back. Why would he do that? If he's changed his mind about marrying Miss Valerie, I think he'd come right out and tell her. Mr. Derring is a man who speaks his mind. Don't you think so?''

''I've never noticed him mincing many words,'' Mitch agreed.

''Well, I'll just be glad when that wedding's over with and this house can get back to normal. The way that girl is behaving, Mrs. Turnbull doesn't need to have to deal with it when she comes home. And if anybody can make Miss Valerie settle down, it's Mr. Derring.'' She rose to pick up Mitch's empty plate and cup and carry them to the sink. She turned from the sink and went on worriedly, ''I wouldn't want Miss Valerie to find out I've said any of this.''

"I won't tell her," Mitch said. At the door, he added, "I don't see any point in either of us mentioning this visit to George, either."

"Gracious, no. I wouldn't want to give Mr. Turnbull something else to worry about."

"Neither would I. Thanks for the coffeecake, Mrs. Nuttall, and for answering my questions."

"Anything I can do to erase Mr. Derring's name from your list, I'm glad to do."

Mitch pondered the interview with the Turnbulls' housekeeper as he drove to the station. It sounded as though Valerie didn't think Derring went home after leaving her Monday night. Maybe Derring said something earlier in the evening that made her suspicious. What the landlady told her the next morning—presumably that Derring had come home soon after eleven-thirty—had not allayed her suspicions, either.

He found Roo at the duty desk and sent him to question Mercy Decker about what time Derring came home Monday night and to warn her about the potential penalties for obstructing justice if she so much as hinted to Derring that she'd talked to the police. Less than an hour later Roo was back in Mitch's office.

"She tried to tell me he was home by eleven-thirty," Roo said, "but when I mentioned obstruction of justice, she admitted she didn't know what time he came in. She went to sleep after the ten o'clock news and didn't wake up until the next morning. She said Valerie Turnbull had been nosing around and she didn't want to get Mr. Derring in trouble. I don't think she has a very high opinion of Valerie. She as much as said she thought Derring would live to regret marrying Valerie, but it wasn't her place to interfere."

"What does she call lying to Valerie?" Mitch snorted.

"She said she thought Valerie was drunk when she called. Said it seemed to run in the family, but if that's the kind of people Mr. Derring wanted to marry into, then he was free, white, and twenty-one."

Mitch slumped down in his swivel chair. "I think Mrs. Nuttall would have told me if Valerie had been drinking. That's probably what Mercy Decker wants to believe. Some people get some kind of satisfaction from knowing the rich have problems, like everybody else.''

"She won't tell Derring I was there," Roo said. "I scared her good. I'll go write the report while it's still fresh in my mind, if you don't need me for anything else."

"Go ahead." Mitch waved him away. When Roo was gone, he continued to sit slumped down in his chair with his head down, thinking about what his next move should be. If he questioned Derring, he'd learn nothing. Derring knew too much about police interrogation techniques and his own rights under the law to be tripped up. Questions would only tip Derring off that Mitch was closing in on him.

If he was the murderer.

NINETEEN

By WEDNESDAY AFTERNOON, Mitch had decided to question Jack Derring, after all. Upon reflection, he came to the inescapable conclusion that the investigation was hopelessly stymied. He had to risk talking to Derring without further delay. He'd say it was Jeeter Rheeves's movements Monday night that he wanted to pin down. It might work.

Derring's office suite was above the drugstore at the corner of Sequoyah and Second Streets. Two years ago Derring had had the space completely gutted and the interior restructured into four rooms—a large reception area where two secretaries worked, Derring's office, and two conference rooms. The walls were ash-paneled, the floor covered with deep green pile, the windows shuttered with green-and-white striped vertical blinds.

The reception area was deserted when Mitch entered. He heard somebody operating a copy machine back in one of the conference rooms and had started in that direction when he heard a woman's angry voice. Mitch retreated quietly until he was standing a few feet from the closed door of Derring's office.

"Stop lying to me, Jack! I know you didn't go straight home Monday night!" It was Valerie Turnbull.

"You don't know any such thing, sweetheart." Derring's voice was low, reasonable, a man trying to calm a hysterical woman.

"Who is she?" Valerie demanded shrilly.

"Valerie, what in the world has gotten into you? How can you think I'd even look at another woman?"

"Never mind how, just tell me who she is!"

"You're too upset to listen to anything I have to say right now. I'll come by after work." Mitch heard movement. It sounded as though Derring had moved closer to the door.

"Keep your hands off me! If you think you can get away with this, you're crazy. I won't put up with it, Jack. Not now. Not after the wedding—if there is a wedding."

"Listen to me, Valerie. There's no other woman. What do you want me to do? Take a lie detector test? Say the word and I will."

A long silence. "You probably know how to beat the machine."

"That's ridiculous."

Another silence. "All right then, if you weren't with another woman Monday night, where were you? I *know* you didn't go home until after three A.M."

"You don't know that because it isn't true."

"Oh, yes, I do, Jack. I talked to somebody who swears your car wasn't parked outside your apartment until after three. She looked every fifteen minutes."

"Are you telling me Mrs. Decker—"

"Not Mercy Decker, that witch. Another neighbor, and I have no intention of giving you her name."

"What the hell were you doing questioning my neighbors!"

"I had to know. I could tell your mind was on something besides me during dinner. Then you couldn't wait to leave me at the house, and I got mad. I spent all day yesterday and this morning trying to find out something from somebody. I won't be played for a fool! I finally found a neighbor who couldn't sleep Monday night. She sat up reading."

"And watching my driveway? Come on, sweetheart."

"That's what she says, and I believe her. Jack, I don't intend to marry somebody I have to worry about every time he leaves the house."

"It seems to me if I'm willing to trust you, you damned well ought to be willing to trust me," Derring said grimly.

"What do you mean by that?" Valerie's voice had risen another notch. "Let's just clear the air here, shall we? If you've got something stuck in your craw, Jack, spit it out right now. Don't wait till after we're married."

"I'm saying that trust is a two-way street, Valerie."

"Now it comes out, what you really think of me. Maybe we should postpone the wedding again, or call it off completely."

Derring cursed. "I knew it. You've been thinking about calling it off for weeks. You created this stupid scene so you'd have an excuse. For once in your life, shoot straight."

"Talk about the pot calling the kettle black!"

Before Mitch could move, Valerie threw open the door and stormed out, barely glancing at Mitch as she tore past. Jack Derring stood in the center of his office, red-faced, looking mad enough to throw the furniture. When his eyes lit on Mitch, his face turned redder except for the area around his mouth, which went chalk white. "How long have *you* been eavesdropping?" he demanded.

Mitch sauntered into the office. "I'd guess everybody in the building has been eavesdropping, Derring. They'd have to be wearing earplugs to miss that little lovers' spat."

Derring smacked his fist down on the desk. Mitch thought he might have broken a bone. "Dammit to hell!" Nursing his aching right hand in his left, he wheeled and flung himself into the leather chair behind his desk. "What do you want?"

After what Mitch had just heard, dissembling would be a waste of time. Mitch closed the door and, placing his hands on the edge of the desk, leaned toward Derring. "Let's start with where you went Monday night after you left Valerie."

Glaring at Mitch, Derring wrenched his necktie to one side as though he wished it were Mitch's neck, freed the top button of his white shirt, and bolted from his chair. Mitch braced himself, expecting Derring to come up punching. For a split second, Derring clearly wanted to, but instead he turned to the window and seemed to be peering through a crack in the half-closed blinds. He said nothing for several moments, and then he squared his shoulders and turned around.

"All right. I went to the Rheeves' house."

"At midnight?"

"I don't expect you to believe it, but it's the truth."

"I didn't say I don't believe it, but it'll be easy to check." Mitch reached for the phone. "What's the Rheeves' telephone number?"

"They'll be at the memorial service this afternoon. But they couldn't tell you anything if they were home. Nobody knew I was there."

Mitch replaced the receiver and rocked back on his heels. "Except Jeeter," he said softly. "Unfortunately, I won't be able to question Jeeter. As an alibi, Derring, this stinks."

Derring sucked in his breath and his nostrils flared. "I don't need an alibi, Bushyhead. I didn't see Jeeter. I didn't see anyone."

"Why did you go there?"

Derring seemed to cast about for something—anything. "I was worried about Jeeter. I thought he might leave after his parents were asleep. I parked and watched the house so I could stop him if he tried."

"Too bad you missed him," Mitch said sarcastically.

"I fell asleep. It was nearly dawn when I woke up, so I went home."

"Didn't bother to check if Jeeter was still there?"

He shrugged. "I was directly in front of the house, and the car windows were down. There's no traffic on that street at night. It was as silent as death. I assumed I would have heard him if he'd left. And I figured if he hadn't run by that time, he wasn't going to. Obviously, I didn't hear him, or he left before I got there."

Mitch laughed. "This alibi smells worse all the time."

"Look, Bushyhead, I'm a little tired. My God!" A croak of shock broke from Derring's throat. "You can't be trying to pin Jeeter's murder on me! What has your tiny brain decided was my motive?"

Mitch gazed at him with unruffled confidence, but he was alert for any sudden moves. "You thought Jeeter could identify the man who threw Joe Pigeon's ring into the lake."

Derring shook his head in disbelief. "You think I murdered Pigeon, too? Suppose you enlighten me as to why."

Derring's supreme confidence was beginning to get under Mitch's skin. The man thought he was untouchable. "Pigeon was humping your woman."

Derring jerked as though he'd been shot, and all the color left his face. "I ought to flatten you." His shoulders sagged. "Get out of my office, Bushyhead. Nobody's going to believe that." He shoved his chair around, sat down, and started leafing through some papers on his desk. His hands were unsteady.

"You believe it, Derring." He didn't look up, just kept shuffling papers. "I'll tell you something else, hotshot. You brought Kingfisher Pigeon into it somehow."

Derring looked up then. His tongue circled his lips before he asked, "Joe's brother? What the hell does he have to do with this?"

"You tell me."

"You're crazy."

"You sent Kingfisher to warn Joe to stay away from Valerie. I don't know how you did it yet—bribery or blackmail—but I'll find out." Mitch walked to the door and opened it.

"Bushyhead."

Mitch turned back, his hand still on the door. Derring dropped the papers and placed his palms down, fingers spread, on the polished walnut top of his desk, maybe to steady them. "Jeeter told me something," he said hesitantly and Mitch had the distinct impression Derring was making it up as he went along. "Mr. Rheeves and I put him to bed, after we took him from jail, and Rheeves left the room to call Dr. Sullivan. I asked Jeeter what he was so frightened of. He—he said he'd made a bad mistake and somebody was after him. He said he was as good as dead. It had to be the man he got his drugs from, his supplier. That's why I thought he'd try to run during the night."

"You seem to have forgotten that you sneered when I suggested Jeeter might have been killed because of a drug deal."

"I wanted to think about it longer before I said anything. For all I knew, they might decide to come after me if they knew Jeeter had talked to me."

"Sure, Derring. Nobody else heard all this, I suppose."

His eyes narrowed. "He told me they deliver the drugs to a place in the woods on Going Snake Mountain. Pushers from all over this part of the state go there to deal. You find that place, and you'll know I'm telling the truth."

"That ought to be real easy. I'll whip on out there and amble around a while. Can't be more than five square miles of woods to cover. I'll probably find it before sundown." Mitch closed the door on a blaze of hatred in Derring's eyes.

As Mitch passed through the outer office, he nodded at the pale, shaken secretary, who had undoubtedly heard the confrontation between Derring and Valerie and at least fragments of Mitch and Derring's conversation. Mitch had seen her in town, but he didn't know her name. He glanced at the nameplate on her desk and read FERN BRUBAKER.

"You haven't heard a peep from your boss's office all afternoon, have you, Fern?"

She swallowed and shook her head in emphatic denial. "No, sir."

BACK AT THE STATION, Helen was going through the mail. "Here's what you've been waiting for," she said, handing Mitch an envelope with the county medical examiner's return address. Surprised, he took it into his office. The medical examiner had done a rush job, for a change. Mitch scanned the report. Jeeter Rheeves had been shot with a .25 caliber slug from a distance of inches. Time of death, between 10:30 P.M. Monday and 2:30 A.M. Tuesday morning. The report contained no startling revelations, nothing else that was likely to help in the investigation.

Mitch unlocked the bottom drawer of his file cabinet and slipped the report into the case file. Then he reconstructed as accurately as he could the overheard conversation between Valerie and Derring and his own exchange with Derring that morning and added that report to the file.

For the rest of the afternoon he was occupied with investigating the burglary of a dentist's house. The dentist and his family had been away on vacation for three weeks. Upon returning that afternoon, they'd discovered a broken window at the back of the house. A coin collection and a few pieces of jewelry were missing. The theft could have occurred any time in the past three weeks, and the trail was cold. The dentist had already called his insurance agent to report the theft and, sensing the man didn't really want the missing items found, Mitch suspected he had overvalued the stuff when he took out the insurance policy.

He went back to the station and sent Duckworth out to question the dentist's neighbors, which turned up nothing helpful. After Virgil came on duty, Mitch called the three officers into his office and passed around the reports he'd added to the Rheeves case file that day.

"Hot damn," Duckworth said as he handed the reports to Roo. "Valerie Turnbull shacking up with Joe Pigeon, and accusing Derring of shacking up with somebody else. Peyton Place ain't got nothing on Buckskin."

"Derring has too much on his mind to be doing much shacking with anybody," Mitch said.

Duckworth digested this. "You mean you really believe he killed Jeeter? You weren't just fishing with Derring?"

"That's what I believe." Mitch hadn't shared his theory with anyone but Virgil and Lisa until now, and as Duckworth and Roo gaped at him, he wondered again if they would be able to keep it among the five of them and he cautioned them to keep their lips buttoned.

"Gawl-lee," Roo said. "You're gonna turn the whole county on its ear. How are you gonna prove Derring did it?"

"I don't know."

"Maybe," Virgil said, "we could get a warrant to search Derring's apartment and office for a .25 caliber gun."

"Not with what we have," Mitch said.

"He probably already got rid of it," Roo added.

"What was all that stuff about drug dealers being after Jeeter?" Duckworth asked.

"Diversionary tactics," Mitch muttered, "but at least it tells us what Derring will say on the stand if this thing ever gets to court. I took him by surprise when I told him I knew about Kingfisher Pigeon, and he didn't have enough time to weigh his words. He's probably kicking himself right now for tipping his hand."

Virgil looked doubtful. "Seems like he'd have thought about it plenty, in case he was ever questioned."

"The pompous ass figured he was too smart to get caught."

"But didn't you say Derring got hot under the collar when you suggested Jeeter was killed by drug dealers? It doesn't track. Looks like he'd have grabbed on to that right away."

Mitch grunted. "The only way I can figure it is that he was so sure he'd never be suspected, he didn't give a thought to laying any groundwork. He couldn't pass up the opportunity to make me look incompetent."

Worry clouded Virgil's black eyes. "Buddy, you better be ready for big trouble at tomorrow night's council meeting."

"Yeah," Mitch agreed, "Derring will be loaded for bear."

TWENTY

THURSDAY ARRIVED on schedule in the relentless manner of dreaded appointments. Fortunately, Mitch was too busy most of the day to worry about the council meeting. The station phone rarely stopped ringing, and several of the calls were from people who'd heard a rumor that Jeeter Rheeves had been a victim of a crime organization hit man. They all wanted to pass along the tip, and suggested Mitch should find out if there were any strangers in town the past few days. Some said they would attend the council meeting that night because they'd heard the handling of the murder investigation was on the agenda.

"Derring's rumor mill is grinding at top speed," Mitch told Duckworth. "He's making sure he has a big audience for his performance tonight. Guess we better cover our backs. You and Roo go take statements from motel and restaurant employees and people who work in downtown stores. Get a description of any stranger they've noticed in the last week or two."

"You know we won't get anything that'll help."

"I'd bet on it." Duckworth rolled his eyes in a put-upon expression and left.

After Virgil came to work, Mitch caught him up on the latest goings-on and ducked out the back door of the station. He had to get off by himself and plan his strategy for the council meeting.

Mitch went home, parked the squad car in the garage next to his Buick, and closed the garage door. Emily wasn't home yet, but she'd told him that morning she had pom-pom practice after school. He turned the ringers off on both phones and, leaving the drapes closed, stretched out on the living room couch.

Tonight Derring would repeat the story about what Jeeter had said to him when they were alone in Jeeter's bedroom. He would demand an accounting from the department. The council would want to know what steps Mitch was taking to follow up the lead, and Mitch would be able to say he'd had two of-

ficers on it all day. He'd check with Duckworth before the
meeting and get Virgil to follow up on any strangers reported
to have stayed at a motel or eaten at a restaurant in Buckskin
in recent days. Already anticipating Derring's next move, Mitch
would say the department planned to check surrounding towns
tomorrow.

Not for the first time, he wondered why Derring had felt
compelled to add that business about Going Snake Mountain
being a major delivery point for illicit drugs. To lend credence
to his alleged conversation with Jeeter? Maybe. It was possible that Derring did have knowledge of delivery points in the
area drug trade; he'd defended several people on drug-related
charges. Anything they told him would be privileged information, but he might have decided to put the information into
Jeeter's mouth, knowing details always give the ring of truth to
an alibi and reasoning that he hadn't violated any code as long
as he didn't reveal the true source. Could be Derring's way of
giving Mitch a diversion to keep him off his back.

The terrain of the Going Snake Mountain area—sparsely
populated, wooded, and remote—was certainly ideal for clan-
destine activity. As he thought about it, Mitch concluded it
might be the one bit of real information in Derring's story. He
would have to follow up on it when tonight's council meeting
was behind him, if he was still on the town payroll.

He added another embroidered throw pillow to the one his
head rested on and closed his eyes. If he could catch a nap, he'd
be in better form for the meeting.

But his mind wouldn't disengage. In a series of leaps and
starts, his thoughts roamed over every event of the past two
weeks related to the murder investigations and finally settled on
his meeting with Crying Wolf. There was something so se-
renely content about that old man, it was hard to treat him
lightly. He had succeeded in interesting Mitch in Cherokee
mythology, and Mitch wanted to learn more—when he had
time.

The *Uk'ten'* trailing fire across the sky and Thunder chasing
the monster away was a beautiful story. Mitch had often
thought about the origin of dreams and he wondered what had
sparked the medicine man's dream. The fire turning to rain was
easy to figure out, since it had started raining before Crying

Wolf awoke. The rain would have disturbed his sleep, forcing him slowly from his dreaming state. Perhaps he'd seen lightning and his still dreaming mind had transformed it into fire. Fire in the sky. Any kind of light could have been interpreted as fire by a dreamer.

Mitch's eyes flew open. Light in the sky. The lights of a low-flying airplane might appear to be streaks of fire at night.

He hadn't asked where Crying Wolf slept the night he had his dream. It hadn't seemed important. Now he wasn't so sure. He sat up, remembering the clearing in the woods, the battery-powered lamp. How far was the clearing from where Crying Wolf had slept before the rain woke him Sunday night?

He felt the tingling down his spine, the sudden burst of energy, that always came when the seemingly inconsequential and unconnected pieces of an investigation started to fit together. The feeling wasn't based on logic, at least not conscious logic, but it had alerted him to an overlooked aspect of an investigation too many times for him to ignore it. He couldn't wait until tomorrow to act.

AN HOUR LATER, after talking to Crying Wolf, Mitch left the old man's cabin on foot. Before leaving the house, he'd phoned the station to see if Virgil was free to accompany him. Virgil had been tied up with two elderly sisters who'd walked to the station, convinced somebody was going through their belongings every time they left their house. They insisted Virgil drive them home, examine their windows and doors, and tell them how the intruder was getting in.

Having dealt with the sisters before, Mitch was sure their intruder was imaginary. But their fears were real. He'd told Virgil to humor them and allay their anxieties, for the time being. Because of the council meeting that night, he hadn't had time to wait for Virgil. He was just going to look around, anyway. If a guard was posted today, he was prepared. This time he was armed with his .357 Magnum revolver, its chamber fully loaded with six shells, strapped on his hip.

He'd parked his car off the road in a covering thicket. This time he'd come ready for hiking through the woods. He had changed to a long-sleeved khaki uniform shirt and was wearing tough leather hunting boots that laced to midcalf.

Although it was less than a half mile from the cabin, it took Mitch thirty minutes to reach the area where Crying Wolf said he'd slept the previous Sunday night. Mitch had picked out the landmarks the medicine man had told him to look for on the way. There was the cottonwood tree under which Crying Wolf had slept. According to the old man, the *Uk'ten'* had appeared in the sky south of that spot.

A ripple of excitement raced down Mitch's spine. The mouth of Spider Creek, where George and Mitch has fished on Sunday, was farther south. The clearing where they'd been shot at was about a quarter mile east of the creek and directly south of where Mitch stood.

Ever since he'd left his house, a newspaper report he'd read about a year ago had been tugging at his mind. The article reported the arrest of members of a drug ring in eastern Arkansas. Small planes were flying Colombian drugs there from some intermediate transfer point. The same thing could be happening in Cherokee County. If so, his recent conversation with the Solomons at their ranch outside Tahlequah might be relevant—the Cessna 170 that landed and refueled at the ranch airstrip every couple of months, the pilot Gregory from Brownsville and his preference for sleeping in the sun-blasted metal hangar rather than accept the Solomons' hospitality. A man who was smuggling drugs and, therefore, had to be ready to make a fast getaway at the first sign of trouble would stay close to his plane. If he was a smuggler, Mitch would bet that Gregory wasn't his name, nor was Brownsville his headquarters. More likely, he used several aliases, a different one in each place he landed for refueling, and his flights originated south of the U.S. border.

Mitch pulled his handkerchief from a hip pocket and swiped his moist brow before starting for the clearing. The rough, wooded terrain was uphill and there was no discernible trail. It was like navigating virgin wilderness where no man had ever set foot before. By the time he reached the clearing, Mitch's uniform was thorn-snagged in numerous places, one sleeve was ripped, and he was damp with perspiration.

He paused near the edge of the trees outside the clearing to catch his breath and wished he'd had the foresight to bring a canteen of water. The sun had dropped below the trees to the west and dusk was approaching. Time was getting away from him.

He scanned the clearing and the surrounding trees for an indication that he wasn't alone. Finding none, he moved cautiously into the open space. Six battery-powered lamps identical to the one he'd seen there on his previous visit were evenly spaced in a big oval a few yards inside the outer perimeter of the clearing, adding strength to Mitch's fast-growing conviction that the clearing was the drop point for drugs delivered by planes flying over at night.

If his hunch was correct, the drugs were stashed somewhere in the area until they were distributed. If a drop had occurred recently, he might find the stash, if he could find the holding place. If Gregory was the smuggler, he'd made a drop last Sunday night; and Mitch, sitting on the porch with Charley and Nell, had watched, unsuspecting, as he took off Monday from the Solomons' ranch. Sunday morning somebody had been setting up lamps in the clearing in preparation for the drop; when Mitch had stumbled on the clearing, they fired a warning shot. What he was looking for now was a dry place, probably near the clearing, but hidden from sight.

He stepped back into the woods and made his way around the clearing in ever-widening circles, gripped by a feeling of heightened urgency. In less than an hour, he would have to hike back to the car and return to town for the seven P.M. council meeting.

The terrain rose steeply a few yards south of the clearing, slowing his progress further. On his fourth circle around the clearing, he noticed a thick growth of brush, higher than his head, which seemed to hug the side of the hill.

The brush had been parted in the center so many times that there was a permanent gap wide enough for a man to squeeze through. Dusk was darkening the woods quickly, and Mitch could see nothing beyond the gap. When he squeezed through, he found himself in almost total darkness. A line of thin, fading light from beyond the brush fell on what looked like solid rock. The place where he stood was noticeably cooler than the other side of the brush. There was a faintly musty odor overlaid with the stronger, sweetish smell of marijuana.

Hands outstretched, Mitch moved to his left and within a few steps he encountered an unyielding barrier. Running his hands over it, he realized that he stood, as he'd suspected, in a cave. It probably contained more lamps like the six in the clearing. He moved ahead, sliding his feet, until the toe of his boot hit something. He picked it up. It was a lantern; he could smell kerosene. Beside the lantern was a box of kitchen matches. He lit the lantern and raised it above his head.

The cave was about a hundred yards wide and roughly circular in shape. Bales of marijuana were stacked against the back wall and near the bales were more battery-powered lamps. Several boxes of small plastic bags sat on one of the bales with a scale and a pile of sealed bags, each containing a few ounces of marijuana.

Mitch stared at his find, feeling the tensions of the past two weeks gather his nerves into knots as he was torn between the necessity of leaving to make the council meeting in time and the desire to explore the area surrounding the cave more thoroughly. If he left now, the marijuana might be removed from the cave before he could return tomorrow, but he really had no choice. He stuffed a few bags in his pockets as evidence, in case the cave was empty when he got back. Before putting out the lantern, he looked around for any evidence that an intruder had found the cave. He didn't want the smugglers to be forewarned.

Suddenly there was a voice behind him. "Don't move, Bushyhead. Keep your hands away from that gun or you're dead meat." Mitch's hand froze inches from the wooden stock of his revolver. The words, bullet-hard and shrill-edged, came from a man who was scared and near panic. Mitch heard movement through the brush and his heart plummeted as he realized the speaker wasn't alone.

"That's right. You don't want to be dead, do you? Now set the lantern on the ground real slow, and put your hands on your head. My finger's itching to pull this trigger, so don't tempt me."

Mitch obeyed, turning slowly as one of the men flipped on a lamp. When he lifted the lamp above his head, his face was illuminated. Kingfisher Pigeon held a deer rifle in his other hand. The man in the middle with the new twenty-gauge autoloading shotgun—the one who had spoken—was a short but power-fully built Cherokee named Smith. The third man, a Cherokee who was unknown to Mitch, was unarmed. He was as tall as Kingfisher Pigeon but thin to the point of emaciation, and he had a dull, slack-mouthed look of mild retardation.

"Keep him covered," Kingfisher growled. He moved to-ward Mitch, his eyes fixed on the hands clasping the top of Mitch's head, and reached around to pull Mitch's revolver from its holster. Kingfisher emptied all six chambers and pushed the bullets into his jeans pocket. He holstered the revolver and backed off. "How'd you find this place, Bushyhead?"

Dry-mouthed, Mitch said, "You're under arrest, Pigeon. Your buddies, too."

Smith giggled shrilly, a startling sound coming from such a powerfully built man. "You ain't hardly in a position to be ar-resting nobody, Bushyhead."

"What're you doing?" the dense one said. "You ain't gonna *shoot* him, are you?"

"Shut up, Stick," Kingfisher barked. "I'm trying to think."

"He never told you how he found the cave," Stick said.

"Don't really matter. He's here now and we gotta figure out what to do with him." He leaned toward Smith and said some-thing too low for Mitch to hear.

"Yeah, yeah," Smith said, "you're right. One of us has to get hold of the boss."

"Tell Derring he'll get life for the two murders he's already committed," Mitch said, "but he'll get death if he kills a po-lice officer."

Kingfisher and Smith exchanged an odd look, then King-fisher stared hard at Mitch. "Get going, Smith."

Smith slipped back through the brush cover and disap-peared.

"Pull one of them bales over here, Stick," Kingfisher said, "so we can sit down."

"I don't wanta stay in here," Stick whined. "You know I don't like closed-up places. Makes me nervous. That's why I always do my work outside."

"Just do what I tell you," Kingfisher ordered.

Still whining, Stick obeyed. When the two men were seated, Kingfisher with his rifle aimed at Mitch's chest, Mitch asked, "Can I put my hands down now?"

After some consideration, Kingfisher said, "Go ahead, but keep 'em where I can see 'em."

Mitch sat down on a bale and spread his hands on his legs above the knees. "You're in big trouble, Pigeon."

"Up yours, Bushyhead. I'm the one with the loaded gun."

"You've had it, too, Stick. If you think this cave is closed up, wait'll you see the inside of a cell."

Stick clutched Kingfisher's arm. "What's he talking about?"

Kingfisher shook the hand off roughly. "He's trying to scare you, stupid. Ain't nobody going to jail. If you're gonna have one of your shaking fits, go on outside for a minute."

Stick didn't move. "I don't like this, Kingfisher."

"I ain't exactly thrilled myself. Somebody talked too much, and if I find out who it was, he'll be sorry."

"It wasn't me, Kingfisher. You told me never to say what we done here, not to nobody. I never did, neither. Not even to Mama."

"Well, I know it wasn't Smith or me."

"Must've been one of those card players in that fictitious game at Smith's Sunday night," Mitch observed.

"Think you're smart, don't you, Bushyhead?" Kingfisher muttered.

Not smart enough to arrange for a backup before blundering into this, Mitch thought grimly. "Too smart to make my relatives accessories to murder."

"Why does he keep talking about murder?" Stick asked.

"He's nuts. He thinks he can scare us."

"Your wife lied about where you were Sunday night," Mitch said. "That makes her an accessory."

"Maybelle don't know nothing about any of this. She told you what I told her. I wouldn't get her involved in anything illegal."

"Touching," Mitch said, "but she's involved, one way or another. At best, she'll have a tough time feeding four kids while you're in prison on a murder conviction."

"Shut up about murder!" Kingfisher barked. "We ain't done nothing but pick up the grass and package it."

"You'll get a chance to prove that," Mitch went on relentlessly, seeing that his words were making him increasingly uneasy. He had to try to rattle Kingfisher enough to make him careless before Smith returned with Derring and increased the odds against him. "I don't think a jury will buy it, though." Mitch didn't like breaking his word to Crying Wolf, but this was life or death. He thought Crying Wolf would understand. "You sent a medicine man to your brother's house to make medicine to separate Joe and his lover," Mitch said. "You've already admitted you went to Joe's house the night he was murdered. But you didn't talk to Joe about settling your differences. You told him to stay away from Valerie Turnbull."

Agitated, Kingfisher leaped to his feet, gripping the rifle. "Shut up, I said!"

Once Derring arrived, Mitch realized, they'd have to kill him. He preferred the present odds and pressed on. "What I don't know is whether you went back with Derring when he killed Joe. Not that it makes a lot of difference. You were implicated, and you'll pay."

From the corner of his eye, Mitch saw that Stick had risen, too, and was shaking like a palsied man. "I'm going outside, Kingfisher."

Kingfisher ignored him and Stick scuttled to the cave opening and pushed through the brush. Kingfisher stared at Mitch and leveled the rifle unwaveringly at the bridge of his nose. "You," he said, "stop that crazy talk right now." His voice was toneless, deliberate.

"Derring probably told you he could get you off."

"Shut up!"

"He can't, you know. He's going down, and you're going with him. It'll be a whole lot easier on you if you hand over that rifle right now. If you haven't actually killed anyone yet, you can cop a plea. You testify against Derring, and in return you face only the drug charges. That way you'll be out before your kids are grown."

Kingfisher took another menacing step forward, and Mitch saw the violent temper he'd heard about. Kingfisher's jaw was working but no words came from his mouth. He wanted desperately to pull the trigger and shut Mitch up, and he was fighting himself to keep from doing it.

It came to the point of now or never. Kingfisher's inner struggle required concentration and gave Mitch two seconds' advantage. He ducked under the rifle and lunged forward. There was a surprised grunt as Mitch's head plowed into Kingfisher's midsection and a loud clatter as the rifle skittered across rock. Both men sprawled on the rock floor. Kingfisher gasped as the breath returned to his lungs. Mitch's shoulder had received the impact of his fall; pain lanced through it as he shoved himself up on all fours, frantically searching for the rifle.

Flickering lantern light reflected off the rifle barrel. Mindful of Kingfisher's movements beside him, Mitch was on his feet and sprinting for the rifle, but Kingfisher's flying leap brought him to the weapon first. As Kingfisher gripped the rifle and whirled, Mitch hooked his fingers through the bale of the kerosene lantern and swung it round in an arc. The lantern hit the cave wall between Kingfisher and the marijuana bales with a crash and a shattering of glass. Mitch swerved and dodged, lost the cave opening in the darkness, and caught, in side vision, flames leaping up from the top bale of marijuana.

Abandoning his search for the exit, Mitch wheeled around. Kingfisher's attention was momentarily diverted by the fire. Mitch dove for the gun, jerking his knee up to crash into Kingfisher's groin. He howled in pain and his grip loosened. Mitch jerked the rifle from his hands.

"Move out!" Mitch shouted. Flames leaped higher, reflecting in eerie patterns on the cave walls. Doubled over, Kingfisher groaned and clutched his crotch. Mitch thrust the end of the rifle barrel against his back. "Walk!" He pushed the barrel hard against muscle.

"Oh, God, you neutered me—you son of—"

"Walk or I'll shoot you and leave you here to burn!" Mitch's tone got through Kingfisher's pain, and he darted a terrified look behind him at the flaming marijuana bale. Still half bent over and groaning, he crept to the cave opening. Keeping the gun at Kingfisher's back, Mitch followed him from the cave.

Mitch gulped in the night air and looked around for Stick. It was nearly seven o'clock and the surrounding woods were deep in blackness. The night was rapidly chilling with the snap of early autumn. He finally saw Stick hovering uncertainly beside a dark tree trunk a few feet away. "Come over here and stand beside Kingfisher, Stick."

"I ain't done nothin'," Stick whined. "I wanta go home."

"I'll shoot you if you try to run," Mitch promised. "Think about how much your mama would miss you."

Stick started blubbering, but came forward.

"Hands on top of your heads, both of you. We're going to the road where it ends at the creek." Mitch picked up one of the lamps in the clearing and turned it on. "Move out very slowly. If I even suspect either of you is thinking of trying something funny, I'll shoot first and ask questions later." Once they reached the squad car, he could radio for help and put them in the backseat with the dome light on, where he could keep an eye on them until Virgil arrived.

"Stop bawling," Kingfisher said to Stick. "That ain't gonna help."

The three men moved slowly through the woods. Before they reached the road, Mitch heard a movement behind him. He twisted around, dropping the lamp without thinking, but not soon enough. Pain exploded behind his right ear.

When Mitch was next aware of anything, he heard men talking—Kingfisher Pigeon, Smith, and a third man whose voice was all too familiar. For long moments, Mitch believed he was dreaming. But the pain behind his ear finally convinced him that he wasn't. He stirred and opened his eyes. A flashlight beam threw light on his face.

"Get up," George Turnbull said. Mitch tried to sit up and groaned. "Now!"

With the pain in his head threatening to send him to oblivion again, Mitch managed to get his feet under him. He rose slowly, weaving like a man maneuvering in a minefield. The light wavered away from his face and made a circle on the ground. It was a powerful beam and Mitch could see that Kingfisher had the deer rifle now. Smith still held the shotgun. They stood with Stick a few feet behind George Turnbull, who was pointing a .25-caliber revolver at Mitch.

Mitch moved his head back and forth slowly in an effort to clear it. He'd been so sure it was Derring, so sure Derring had lied about his activities the night Jeeter was murdered.

"Bad mistake, George. You should have ditched that gun after you used it to kill Jeeter."

Turnbull's wintery smile didn't warm his eyes behind the scholarly spectacles. "I knew you wouldn't leave this alone, Mitch, but, believe me, I never wanted it to come to this."

"Killing gets easier with repetition, George. The third time around it'll be a snap. Difference is, this time you won't get away with it."

"Walk," said Turnbull.

Mitch stumbled ahead, each step releasing a hammer to pound against his skull; but his faintness was ebbing. He forced his mind to focus on his future, which looked at the moment alarmingly short, and finding a way out of this with his life. The only thing he could think of was to keep Turnbull talking.

"If you're going to kill me, George, you might as well tell me how you got involved in drug smuggling and murder."

There was a long silence and then, behind him, Turnbull cleared his throat. "I didn't expect things to go so far."

"Naturally. Only a little smuggling, with the Indians doing the dirty work so you could keep your hands clean, right? You must have needed money badly. I guess the bank isn't doing as well as I thought."

"The bank's fine," Turnbull said evenly. "But I let my personal expenses get out of hand. Opal's hospitalization, Valerie's college expenses..."

"The Mercedes."

"That was in return for her promise to break off with Joe Pigeon." Mitch could hear the desperation in his voice. "She stopped before she came home from the university, but in July I found out she was sneaking off to be with him again. She denied it, but I followed her one night and saw her meet him."

"I don't see what her seeing Joe has to do with the smuggling," Mitch said.

"It's all so complicated." Turnbull sounded weary with the weight of his tangled descent into crime. "I'd used bank funds to keep up with my debts, and when I realized I'd borrowed over forty thousand dollars, I knew I had to return it before the auditors came again." He sighed heavily. "I can see how stupid it was now, but I took another forty thousand of bank funds to Vegas. All I had to do was double it—"

"You lost it instead."

"Yes. I've always gambled a little, but I knew when to stop. I'd never needed to win before, and I didn't know what else to do. I gambled until I lost it all. They were watching me—the mob—I realize that now." His voice was hoarse, shaken. "I went to the bar to get drunk, and one of them followed me. He seemed like any other businessman in Vegas for a few days. We talked and I drank—he was buying. Before the evening was over, I'd told him everything. The next morning he came to my room and offered me a way out."

"I see."

"They wanted to move their operations out of eastern Arkansas. There had been several arrests, and the police were putting on the pressure. He was familiar with this part of Oklahoma. He said it was perfect for their purposes, that all I'd have to do was set up the network, and with my cut of the profits I could return the eighty thousand to the bank before the auditors came in three months."

Ahead of Mitch, Kingfisher Pigeon and Smith halted. He followed them out of the trees to the road. With three guns on him, his chances of getting away now were nil. He faced Turnbull. Now that they were clear of the trees, moonlight flooded the scene eerily. "They never meant to let you get out in three months."

Turnbull nodded, his face slack with his accumulated mistakes, his naïve faith in the word of a mobster. "Jack overheard a conversation between the three of us"—he indicated Smith and Pigeon—"in my office. We were talking about where to have the drugs dropped. Jack started asking questions. I was able to satisfy him for a while, but it was only a matter of time until he put it together. Even then, I knew he wouldn't say anything, once he was married to Valerie."

"Ah, but Valerie had other ideas."

"She was irrational. She was going to break her engagement. She said Joe Pigeon would divorce his wife and marry her." In the moonlight, Mitch saw Turnbull's upper lip curl with revulsion at the thought of Valerie married to Joe Pigeon. "I begged her not to act hastily, to take plenty of time to think it over. She said there was no time—"

Mitch finished for him. "She was pregnant with Joe's baby."

Turnbull's eyelids flickered. "You know that, too. You've been busy, Mitch."

"You sent Kingfisher to tell Joe to stay away from Valerie. When he failed to convince Joe, you took matters into your own hands. What did you hit him with, George?"

Turnbull gazed at Mitch, his face now grimly composed. "It all happened before I could think. He laughed in my face. He said Kingfisher had told him enough for him to figure out that his brother was involved with me in smuggling drugs. He said he'd expose me if I tried to keep Valerie and him apart. When he turned his back, I grabbed the deer antlers off the wall. I hit him with the board so hard the whole thing flew out of my hand. He fell on the antlers."

"Derring must've told you that Jeeter Rheeves could identify the man who threw Joe's ring into the lake."

"He didn't know he was signing Jeeter's death warrant. He still hasn't figured things out."

"You threatened Jeeter. You knew he was afraid of you, but you couldn't trust somebody like Jeeter to control his tongue when he was stoned. So you killed him, too. How long before you have to kill Kingfisher or Smith or somebody else? Where does it end, George?"

Both Kingfisher and Smith stiffened, and Turnbull said sharply, "Get moving. I left the car down the road around the bend."

As they walked toward the bend, the lights of a car came around the corner, sweeping the trees. The car rushed toward them. "Get in the woods, quick!" Turnbull shouted and pushed Mitch from behind.

They stood in the woods at the side of the road as a Mercedes sports car approached too fast for a narrow, country lane. It screeched to a halt near their hiding place. The driver's door flew open and Valerie jumped out. "Daddy! I know you're here somewhere. I saw your car. Daddy, where are you!" Valerie stood in the shadows beside the car, out of reach of the headlights.

"What in hell is she doing here!" Turnbull hissed. "Keep him covered. I'll get rid of her." As he stepped into the road, Turnbull slipped the revolver into the pocket of his suit jacket. "Valerie, what's wrong? What are you doing here?"

Mitch spoke in a low, urgent voice. "You guys going to keep following orders until you land on death row?"

"We're behind in our mortgage payments to the bank," Smith said. "He said if we went to work for him, we'd be able to pay off the notes in a year or two. All we had to do was pick up the grass when it was dropped, move it to the cave, and package it. We never saw any of the people who picked it up. He took care of that. He said if we refused to go to work for him, he'd deny he ever talked to us about smuggling drugs and throw us off our farms."

"We didn't know he'd killed anybody," Kingfisher added shakily.

"Can I go home now?" Stick whined. He sucked in a pained breath when Kingfisher elbowed his stomach.

Out in the road, Valerie said, "Don't come any closer, Daddy." She stepped in front of the car. The two of them, father and daughter, stood frozen in the glare of the headlights, like actors in a melodrama. Turnbull's face was rigid with shock. Valerie held a shotgun. Mitch recognized it, an old single-shot twelve-gauge. For as long as Mitch had known the Turnbulls', it had hung on the wall of George's study at home. George told him once that his father bought the gun for him when he was twelve years old. He'd hunted a few times, but found he didn't have a taste for it. Mitch's mouth twisted at the irony of Turnbull's distaste for killing animals. Now he'd killed two men. How desperation changed people. As far as Mitch knew, the shotgun had been taken down only for cleaning, but it hadn't been fired in more than thirty years.

"Valerie, you're overwrought." Turnbull stepped forward.

The shotgun jerked up. "It's loaded, Daddy. I said don't come any closer."

"Sweetheart, what's come over you?"

"I found Joe's ring, Daddy, the one I gave him with our names engraved inside it, the one he wore on his little finger next to his wedding ring."

"I don't know what you're talking about, sweetheart."

"Yes, you do! I found it in your desk with the letters I wrote Joe. They were in the bottom drawer, the one you keep locked. I had to knock a hole in the drawer with a hammer."

"Valerie—"

"Jack came to see me this afternoon. He wanted to know whether I'd been having an affair with Joe before Joe was killed. I told him it was true. I said I was going to have Joe's baby—and I would have if you hadn't talked me into having an abortion! I gave Jack back his engagement ring."

"He'll still marry you, honey. All you have to do is go to him and say you're sorry."

She blinked at him. "I expected him to rant and rave, and then forgive me and beg me to reconsider. But he just put the ring in his pocket. Then he asked me if you knew about Joe and the baby. I asked why he wanted to know that, and he said he was afraid you'd done something bad. He said I should talk to you about it, and he left."

"You little fool! Jack didn't know anything until you told him!"

"After he left, I thought about what he said, Daddy. Especially about the bad thing Jack said you'd done. I started to wonder if you had killed Joe to keep me from marrying him. I remembered Joe's fingers being cut off. That never made any sense to me before tonight." Valerie's voice was edging toward hysteria. "I searched the house, and I finally found the ring I gave Joe—in your desk. You should have thrown it away like the other one. I guess you were afraid it'd be found with my initials in it. You killed the only man I ever loved, Daddy!"

"Everything I did, I did for your mother and you."

"You talked me into getting rid of Joe's baby!" She was screaming now, and sobbing. "You said it was the only thing to do, get rid of the baby and marry Jack, and in a little while I'd forget about Joe and I'd be glad I didn't ruin my life for him. I was hurting so bad, Daddy, and I listened to you!"

Beside Mitch, Kingfisher muttered, "This is where I get off, Smith. I been smuggling drugs, but I ain't gonna help a murderer get away with it."

"What're you gonna do?" Smith asked.

"Go out there and take that gun away from her and turn myself and Turnbull over to Bushyhead."

After a second's hesitation, Smith said, "Me, too." He looked at Mitch. "Stick didn't know he was doing anything wrong. He just wanted to please us. He wasn't there when they passed out the brains."

"How many others are involved in this?" Mitch asked.

Kingfisher and Smith glanced at each other. "Five," Kingfisher said.

"Are all of them in hock to Turnbull's bank?"

Kingfisher nodded.

"I want the names, or we can't make a deal."

Again, Kingfisher nodded and Smith said, "We'll give you the names. Can Stick go home?"

"Yeah, go on, Stick. Not by the road. Go back through the woods."

Stick bobbed his head. "Thanks." He turned and hurried deeper into the woods. They heard a thud and a yelp as he ran into a tree in the dark. Stick cursed and went on his stumbling way home.

"Come on," Mitch said.

The three men walked into the road as Valerie screamed, "You killed Joe and you killed my baby! I hate you!" Before Mitch could reach her or even call out, the shotgun went off with a deafening roar. The recoil knocked Valerie to the ground.

IT WAS AFTER TEN when Mitch finally went home. Emily had left him a note taped to the bathroom mirror. She was spending the night with Temple again. Mitch didn't blame her. It wasn't much fun sitting around the house alone. He would have to do something about that. He wondered what a housekeeper would cost him. It would be nice to have somebody there when he couldn't be.

He stripped and stood in the shower. Whew, what a night. When he left the station at nine, Derring was still there with Valerie. He planned to spend the night at the station, since he wouldn't be able to arrange bail until the next day. Mitch still didn't know if Valerie had meant to pull the trigger. She'd been too hysterical to answer questions when they got back to town, and then he and Virgil had been busy writing up the charges on her and the men. Once they'd finished that, Valerie had recovered enough to ask for Derring.

When Derring arrived, he wouldn't let her say another word to the police. Mitch pointed out to him that if he'd gone to the police instead of Valerie with his suspicions, she wouldn't be facing murder charges. Derring insisted that he hadn't been sure about anything, that he'd only wanted Valerie to throw a scare into her father. He certainly hadn't expected her to conclude her father was a murderer and take justice into her own hands. Mitch delivered a few well-chosen expletives, but his heart wasn't in it. There were too many thoughts going round in his head.

George had died instantly, of course. No other outcome was possible when you were hit with hundreds of twelve-gauge pellets fired from a distance of six feet. The body the ambulance took to the hospital no longer resembled George Turnbull, or much of anything else that was human.

After leaving the station, Mitch had dropped in on the council meeting, arriving as it was breaking up. The citizens who had been there earlier had given up and gone home before Mitch arrived.

The councilmen gaped at him in shock as he delivered a brief summary of the night's events. For once Devay had been speechless. Mitch had left them to rehash what he'd said.

He stepped out of the shower. He should be dead on his feet, but he was too stimulated to go to bed. He dressed in jeans and a sweatshirt and walked through the house, noticing that the colors looked brighter, as though before tonight he'd been looking at things through fogged glasses. He remembered how he'd felt when he stepped out of the station and walked along deserted Sequoyah Street to City Hall. Smells had assailed him, a subtle mingling of rain in the offing and the unpleasant odor of the tire factory outside town. Familiar smells, but they seemed stronger tonight. Then he had looked up at the few stars not yet hidden by clouds, and they seemed brighter than before. He realized that it wasn't his surroundings, but his heightened senses, and he'd thought how good it was to be alive, and how much he was going to enjoy telling Crying Wolf that his interpretation of his dream had been correct. No Nighthawk had murdered anyone. In that short walk from the station to City Hall, he had relinquished grief and kept only the good memories, tucked them away.

He went to the telephone and without the slightest hesitation dialed Lisa Macpherson's number. When she answered, he said, "I hope I didn't wake you."

"No. Mitch?"

"I've missed you."

"Oh . . ." She sighed. "Mitch."

"I want to come over."

"Now?"

"It's not too late, is it?"

"It isn't that. Oh, Mitch, I'm not sure it's such a good idea."

"You said you didn't want to see me again until I knew I was free."

"Yes . . ."

"Now I know."

"Mitch, are you sure? It's only been a few days."

"You won't believe all that happened since I saw you. Everything's changed. I want to tell you about it. I hope I can make you understand."

"Well." He could hear the tentative smile in her voice, and a shiver ran down his spine. He wanted to touch her. He wanted her in bed. "Maybe," she murmured, "you'd better come over here and try."

He laughed, and his heart lifted—no, it soared. "I'll be right there."

"Hurry."

He hung up and raced upstairs for his car keys.

UNDUE INFLUENCE
Miriam Borgenicht

GUILTY UNTIL PROVEN INNOCENT

Though reluctant to defend a man accused of rape and murder, criminal attorney Lydia Ness knew it was her shot at the big time. Moreover, she believed Jerry Eldstrom was innocent. Young, earnest and sincere, with an airtight alibi, he seemed like a dream defendant. Yet there was still a grisly murder to account for: a young woman in a corner of a parking lot with her face smashed, her body violated.

As the sensational trial proceeds, Lydia is caught between the Eldstroms' unshakable conviction of their son's innocence—and the victim's outraged family. . . who want vengeance at all costs. Racing against time to piece together a puzzle of twisted secrets and ruthless manipulation, Lydia discovers that even truth has its price . . . and she may pay the biggest one of all.

"The inventiveness and wit make Borgenicht a favorite of mystery fans."

—*Publishers Weekly*

UI-R

DELL SHANNON

Exploit of Death

A LUIS MENDOZA MYSTERY

September is the worst month for heat in Southern California...

And LAPD Lieutenant Luis Mendoza is feeling the burn as the sweltering temperatures raise tempers and violence. Heading the list is the bizarre murder of a young French girl—a search that eventually leads Mendoza to Paris. An old man smothered in the hospital bed...a polite holdup artist nicknamed Baby Face...a Hollywood matron who disappears while visiting a sick friend...the grisly murder of a family who has just moved from Wisconsin—keep the skillful Mendoza and his force pounding the scorching pavements in a crime wave that, like the heat, offers no relief in sight.

"A Luis Mendoza novel means superlative suspense."
—*Los Angeles Times*

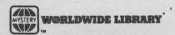
WORLDWIDE LIBRARY

ED-R

ATTRACTIVE, SPACE SAVING BOOK RACK

Display your most prized novels on this handsome and sturdy book rack. The hand-rubbed walnut finish will blend into your library decor with quiet elegance, providing a practical organizer for your favorite hard- or soft-covered books.

Only $9.95

Approximately 16" x 8" when assembled

Assembles in seconds!

To order, rush your name, address and zip code, along with a check or money order for $10.70* ($9.95 plus 75¢ delivery) payable to *The Mystery Library Reader Service*:

Mystery Library Reader Service
Book Rack Offer
3010 Walden Avenue
P.O. Box 1396
Buffalo, NY 14269-1396

Offer not available in Canada.

BKR-MLR

*New York residents add appropriate sales tax.

"A writer with a poetic and moving touch remarkable in this genre."
                                                              —Publishers Weekly

M.R.D. Meek
Order these spine-tingling Lennox Kemp mysteries ....

THE SPLIT SECOND $3.50   ☐
Lawyer Lennox follows the nuptial trail of a newlywed couple to
Scotland, investigating their disappearance. When Fiona, the wealthy
bride, is found drowned in a loch, the guilty finger points to Fergus,
the groom. He is a cunning and easy liar, but is he a murderer, as well?
Not available in Canada.

IN REMEMBRANCE OF ROSE $3.50   ☐
An elderly woman is found dead, victim of an apparent robbery
attempt. But Lennox Kemp is suspicious and discovers that facts are
scarce and bizarre, leading him to believe that there is something
sinister at play.
Not available in Canada.

HANG THE CONSEQUENCES $3.50   ☐
Private investigator Kemp gets more than he bargained for when he is
hired to locate a client's missing husband. He soon finds himself
involved in blackmail, adultery ... and murder!
Not available in Canada.

Total Amount	$ _____
Plus 75¢ Postage	.75
Payment Enclosed	$ _____

To order please send your name, address and zip code with a check or money order payable
to Worldwide Library Mysteries to:

> In the U.S.
> Worldwide Library Mysteries
> 901 Fuhrmann Blvd.
> Box 1325
> Buffalo, NY   14269-1325

Please specify book title with your order.   MYS-13

 **WORLDWIDE LIBRARY®**

Order now the spine-tingling mysteries you missed in stores.